Hawk

By Marie Powell

To Ben -

Dymuniadau gorau!
(Best wishes)

Marie Powell

Five Rivers Publishing
www.fiveriverspublishing.com

Published by Five Rivers Publishing,

704 Queen Street, P.O. Box 293, Neustadt, ON N0G 2M0, Canada.

www.fiveriverspublishing.com

Edited by Dr. Robert Runté.

Interior Design by Lorina Stephens.

Text set in Minion Pro, designed for Adobe by Robert Slimbach.

Titles set in ITC Benguiat, designed by Ed Benguiat for the International Typeface Corporation in 1977.

Published in Canada

Library and Archives Canada Cataloguing in Publication

Powell, Marie, 1958-, author

Hawk / by Marie Powell.

Issued in print and electronic formats.

ISBN 978-1-927400-93-7 (paperback).—ISBN 978-1-927400-94-4

(epub)

I. Title.

PS8631.O8374H39 2015 C813'.6 C2015-903790-5 C2015-903791-3

Dedicated to Leanne and Ben,

who were with me when the story began.

Contents

Hawk: Character Guide and Pronunciation Key

Hyw and Cat's family:

Hywel (huh--wel) or Hyw (huh-oo), a Welsh warrior-in-training and Cat's older brother

Catrin (kat-rrin) or Cat, Hyw's younger sister

Bran (brran), Hwy and Cat's father and Llywelyn's steward

Adara (uhd-ehrr-uh), Hwy and Cat's mother

Gawain, Hwy and Cat's uncle (Adara's brother) and a Cistercian monk

The Welsh royal family

Llywelyn (thluh-weh-lihn) ap Gruffydd, the Prince of Wales

(Elinor de Montfort, Llywelyn's wife, died in childbirth six months earlier)

Gwenllian (gwen-thlee-an), Llywelyn's infant daughter

Dafydd (dahv-ith) ap Gruffydd, Llywelyn's brother

Elizabeth, Dafydd's wife

Llyw (thluh-oo), short for Llywelyn, Dafydd & Elizabeth's son

Owain (oh-wayn), Dafydd & Elizabeth's son

Gwladys (gla-duhs), Dafydd & Elizabeth's daughter

Margred (mehrr-grred), one of Dafydd's illegitimate daughters

Rhiannon (rhee-an-on), one of Dafydd's illegitimate daughters

Other Welsh characters

Aeneus (eh-nee-aas), Master-At-Arms and part of Llywelyn's personal bodyguard

Berwyn (berr-win), the stable boy

Bronwen (brrahn-win), a childhood friend of Cat and Hyw

Cynfrig ap Madog (kun-vrig), warrior in charge of Castell-y-Bere

Dai ap Rhys (die ap hrrees), a warrior who joins Bran and his group on the trail

Elise, the wet nurse

Emrys (em-rris), a Welsh warrior and Hyw's childhood friend

Gwilym ap Einion (g-wihl-ihm ap eye-nee-on), a noteworthy bard

Ifan (ee-van), one of Llywelyn's personal bodyguards

Maelgwyn (myle-gwin), Welsh priest and traitor

Rhys ap Cadwgan (hrrees ap cad-oo-gan), lord of Meirionnydd (may-rree-on- ith) and Cat's fiancé

Various warriors serving with Bran

Aeron (eh-rrahn) and Vox, war stallions

Cadarn, Bran's gelding for everyday riding

The English

Edward I (Longshanks), King of England

Alan Acton, soldier who befriends Hyw

Edmund Mortimer, heir to Roger

Roger Mortimer, First Baron Mortimer of Wigmore, deceased

Gerald, soldier who befriends Hyw

Gilbert Le Clare (de Clare), Norman lord from the Marches (between England and Wales)

James, Shrewsbury's son and Hyw's friend (half-Welsh)

Lord Shrewsbury, Hyw's foster father, a Marcher lord

Robert, son of Shrewsbury's cousin, training to be a knight

Roger Lestrange, a commander of Edward's army

Stephen de Francton, a knight from Shrewsbury

William de Valence, Norman lord from the Marches (between England and Wales)

N
W
E
S
Gwynedd
Irish Sea
England
Ynys Mon
Aberconwy
Rhuddlan Castle
Garth Celyn
Rhaedr Fawr
Gwynedd
Dolbadarn Castle
Dolwyddelan Castle
Criccieth Castle
Llyn
Meirionnydd
Castell-y-Bere
Shrewsbury
Irish Sea
Abbey Cwmhir
Cilmeri
Builth Wells

Chapter One: Hyw

December 1282, Gwynedd, Cymru (North Wales)

He raised his arms, feeling bone and feather flatten against the wind, and knew himself tethered to air currents that smelled of salt and fish, somewhere off the horizon.

He ran below the bird, yet his mind and the hawk's mind moved as one. He could feel the dry December grasses beneath his bare feet, but he saw as the hawk saw: a flash of grey fur in the stubble, the swaying pattern of a tree branch.

He tried to turn the hawk's mind – his mind – to his will, and for a moment he succeeded. In the distance he could see the stone watchtower of his home at Garth Celyn, seat of the royal court of Wales. But the hawk's need was powerful, turning him back to scan the ground they circled. If he squinted – just so – at the yellow and russet clumps, he could make out the leaves of each tree. A shadow flitted from branch to branch.

Prey!

His talons ached for the soft flesh and his beak thrust forward –

No, not his. It was the hawk's beak that longed to rip the flesh from bone and feather. Hyw grasped the bird's thoughts again, and turned its head toward Prince Llywelyn's tower. There! A streak of movement across the grass. Was it some grotesque beast from the past? He urged the hawk to circle until he could see it more clearly. A single horse and rider galloped toward Garth Celyn.

A messenger! Fast horses in wartime never bring good news. Had the ceasefire broken again? He gasped, and his connection to the bird faltered.

The hawk gave a piercing shriek. Hyw felt himself fall, as if he'd dropped from its talons rather than its mind. His feet—the same feet that had seemed to barely skim the ground a moment ago—thudded against the earth. He stumbled and the momentum of his running threw him, over and over, until he landed hands down on the mountainside.

His body shook with the impact. Dry grass speared his knees and palms. He bit back a cry as his fingers buckled under his weight. *Tears have no place in a warrior's world*, his father had told him when Hyw had sprained his ankle five years ago. He flexed his fingers. Each one moved, painfully. Nothing was broken.

He pushed himself up and scarcely felt the grass prickle his bare feet. When he shared the mind of an animal or bird, he often lost the sense of his physical body. He was getting used to the consequences when he came back to himself. This time, though, he'd taken it a step farther. He'd done it! He had made the hawk turn, to see what he wanted to see through its eyes, if only for a moment. It was easier with horses, because they loved him and he them—but they couldn't see any farther than the men riding them. Hawks and other birds would be more useful in a battle. Now he had proven it.

But would his father listen? His father, Bran, was a trusted warrior of the prince's bodyguard. Every Welsh boy in training at Garth Celyn received a red sash on his fourteenth birthday, to mark his warrior status. Hyw had turned fourteen last winter at the English court of Lord Shrewsbury, where his father had sent him to foster and learn their enemy's ways and customs. Hyw had been a page in Shrewsbury's court for the past three years, and he would have become a squire had he remained. He had returned home from fosterage over a week ago. Surely now he would become a warrior, following the Welsh way instead. All last week he'd waited, but his father had not brought him a sash. Hadn't even mentioned it.

Did he think Hyw was still a child?

On his first evening home, his mother Adara had seemed glad that Hyw's ability had manifested while he was away. It was his inheritance from her family, similar to her brother's, she'd said. She'd even called it a "gift" that could help them. Bran had nodded but shushed her, glancing around at the priests and other wagging tongues in the Welsh royal court. He had not called on Hyw to serve as a warrior at Garth Celyn.

And what word did this messenger bring? If this meant war, Hyw would be needed. Wouldn't he? At the same time, Hyw felt a nagging doubt. *What of James*? His best friend, and Shrewsbury's son. But James was one of the *Saeson*—English. The enemy.

Fie on it! If his father rode with the prince, Hyw must be by his side. He would work harder to master his gift and to prove its value. He could prove himself—he would—if he could make his father listen. He would win his red sash. His cheeks burned as he sprinted for Garth Celyn.

As Hyw passed through the gates, he heard an anxious neighing. He sprinted across the courtyard toward the barns in time to see Berwyn, the young groom, holding the reins of a lathered horse. The sunlight caught a gleam of metal and Hyw saw a heavy English saddle, rather than the darker leather gear of the Welsh. The messenger's horse! The man who'd been riding it must already be inside the longhouse.

Berwyn crooned softly to the horse, but it blustered, jerking its head down. "*Hogyn da*," he repeated, but the horse reacted as if he were cursing it instead of saying "Good boy." Hyw caught sight of its wild eyes as its head reared up again, and its hooves skittered on the packed courtyard. Could it be reacting to the language itself? Hyw felt the wrath beneath the horse's bay coat like a fist in his own gut. Warhorses were bred to be fighters too. How often had he dealt with their tempers in Shrewsbury's barns? He took a deep breath, and held out his hand.

"Would you like me to try?" he asked in Welsh, and the groom passed over the reins.

"Why not? He's one of the *Saeson* too, after all."

Hyw took the reins and ignored the slur. It was mild compared to some he'd overheard since his return. After so many years away, he was like a stranger to his own people. He'd had to prove himself to the English in Shrewsbury's court, but it was hard to have to prove himself again here at home.

He took a deep breath and turned his attention to the horse, reaching out with his mind to make contact with the animal. He relaxed, probing the horse's mind to find the link that would bond them. He gasped as he felt his head lengthen. His back stretched. His nostrils filled with the smell of sweat and dust. Sunlight filtered across his blinkered eyes. He was all but overcome with a wild urge to kick out and pull away. He bared his teeth and snarled.

At the sound, he opened his eyes. The transformation always felt real, but he knew it had occurred inside his mind and not in his body. He was able to join with the animal's mind, to see and think as it did. Yet from the look on the groom's face, Hyw knew he saw nothing more than another boy calming a horse. Hyw stared into the dark intelligence reflected in the horse's eyes. Its skin shivered, but it stared back at Hyw with pride and defiance. As if he were an enemy, Hyw realized. Because he was Welsh? Hyw reached out once more, crooning in English as he had to the horses in Shrewsbury's barns. Gradually it calmed.

"I'll take care of him," Hyw told Berwyn quietly in Welsh, and the horse tossed its head again. The groom held his hands up in a gesture that clearly said he was leaving Hyw to his fate, and backed away to attend other duties.

As Hyw turned, he spied his father's lean frame by the doors of the longhouse at the other side of the courtyard. Bran was standing with Prince Llywelyn, easy to recognize in his black mourning clothes. The prince had no doubt been training with his men when the messenger arrived. Bran must have gone to let him know he was needed. Even now, they would be on their way to hear the messenger's words.

The two men appeared to be watching him. For a moment Hyw felt a faint hope that his father had seen him use his gift. Then he realized the groom standing right beside him had not known what Hyw was doing, so how could his father from that distance? Before Hyw could wave, they turned and made their way inside the longhouse.

Chapter Two: Cat

Deep breath," Cat's mam whispered, standing with her back to the heavy embroidered draperies that kept the cookhouse separate from the rest of the longhouse. She held a thin bread platter with their best ale and an assortment of meats. Cat stood facing her mam, balancing her platter of cheeses and honeyed sweetbreads. Then her mam backed through the heavy curtain, holding it open for Cat to go ahead of her into the large open room.

Their guest sat cross-legged on the floor. Cat knew he was one of the *Saeson*—English—but she wasn't prepared for how awkward he looked at their low table, waiting for his refreshments. She tried to give him a welcoming smile. After all, Cat and her mam had been hosts of Garth Celyn since Princess Elinor's passing that summer. Messengers came and went often at Garth Celyn these days, but most were friendly and courteous. And hadn't the English Archbishop even stayed with them a fortnight ago? The English priests had looked much the same as the Welsh, and English messengers were used to travel and adapted quickly. This tall, silent man in his riding coat and boots looked more like a knight than a messenger.

Cat placed the platter on his left. Her mam set her platter to the right, and handed the man a mug of ale and a thick flatbread trencher for his meal. Cat knew her mam was proud of the way they could adapt their Welsh fare to suit English tastes, but the man grunted. He downed the ale and gestured with his head towards the door. "Where is the prince?"

"He will attend you shortly," Mam responded, smiling. "My husband has gone to let him know of your coming."

At that moment the longhouse door opened for Prince Llywelyn, with Cat's da, Bran, close behind him. The prince cast a deep shadow as the door slowly shut behind them. His black mourning clothes made him stand out against the colourful tapestries that adorned the walls.

Cat stared up at the prince's face, and noticed for the first time the lines on his forehead and around his mouth and eyes. He had always seemed ageless, but her mam said he had been the country's leader for thirty years.

The prince smiled briefly at her as they passed, and Da laid a hand on her head in blessing. Cat touched the black band around her sleeve, a sign that she and her family shared in mourning for the Princess Elinor, who had died giving birth to the Prince's first child, Baby Gwen. Cat still missed the princess and her ladies, who had brought so much colour and laughter to the longhouse. Cat ducked her head and said a silent prayer for her soul.

Her prayer was cut short when the bowing messenger began to speak, in English. "My lord Llewellyn —"

"Prince Llywelyn," Da corrected, pronouncing the prince's name in the Welsh way.

"Erhm — I bring greetings from Baron Edmund Mortimer, lord of the March, the newly returned heir of Wigmore Castle."

"Yes, I knew his father and still miss his friendship and counsel," said the prince, his deep baritone echoing in the hall. "I trust the Baron is well?"

The messenger faltered for a moment, his mouth gaping like a fish pulled out of the lake. Cat realized he must have forgotten his memorized message. What manner of messenger was he? Frowning slightly, the prince gestured for the man to continue.

As he began again, Mam leaned down and whispered in Cat's ear. "Go and see to Gwenllian for me, if you please."

Cat started to remind her mam that she'd already checked on Baby Gwen when the messenger first arrived. What could change in an hour? Besides, she wanted to stay and hear what the Englishman had to say.

"Please, Catrin," Mam repeated firmly. Cat knew better than to argue when her mam used her full name. She moved toward the kitchen, but as she passed the draperies separating it from the main room, she lost herself in their heavy folds and stood very still. She often hid there to listen to the kitchen gossip, but today she was more interested in the strange Englishman.

"Attack!" she heard the Englishman say. She knew that word well enough. Those *Saeson*! They should have learned their lesson by now. Hadn't Da and the prince turned them back, time and again, but now they were coming once more? Why couldn't they just go back to their *Saeson* hovels and leave Cymru alone? Maybe Hyw would know. He'd spent years and years with them.

Then she heard the word "alliance." Did that mean friendship? She remembered the old Baron Roger. They'd had a feast when he visited last year, and she'd tasted her first pigeon pie that night. Cat frowned. She remembered another messenger a few weeks ago, bringing news of the old baron's death. That made the prince very sad, all over again. They must have been friends. Maybe his son Edmund, the new baron, would be the prince's friend now. Maybe he'd visit, and they could have another feast.

"...this letter," the Englishman was saying. Cat peeked from between the curtains in time to see him step forward to hand a parchment to the prince. Da took the parchment instead, and opened it. He scanned it, then handed it to the prince.

"Tell Baron Edmund that Wales accepts his offer of friendship," the prince said, in a commanding tone. "We greet him warmly as the heir to Wigmore Castle. He will be as welcome here at Garth Celyn as were his father and brother before him."

"My lord –" the messenger began.

"Your Royal Highness," Da corrected again.

"Yes, er, your highness, my master beseeches you to attend him at Builth," the man said, bowing formally.

Llywelyn stood with his arms folded. Her da turned to him, and they exchanged a few words too low for Cat to hear. She was listening so hard, she didn't notice her mam returning to the kitchen with the ale jug in her hand. Mam opened the curtains and Cat almost fell through them into the other room. Mam reached forward quickly, frowning. She took Cat by one arm and pulled her through the kitchens to the outside door. The serious look on her mam's face warned Cat not to argue.

"Gwenllian," she whispered loudly, and pushed Cat towards the hut next door, where Enid nursed the baby.

As Cat stepped into the hut she found Enid twisting wool threads into yarn on her spindle as she crooned a wordless lullaby. "Lullay, lully..." The wet nurse had lost her own baby a few days before Gwenllian was born, and she'd travelled all the way from her farm near *Rhaeadr Fawr* to nurse Baby Gwen instead.

Cat sidled up to the baby's crib and stared down at her pinched little face. Baby Gwen's eyes were tight shut, and she held one fist up to her closed mouth. Cat felt a sharp pang of sympathy for Gwenllian, who had no mam to boss her around, and for Enid, who had no daughter of her own to boss.

On her deathbed, Princess Elinor had made her mam promise she would keep Baby Gwenllian safe. Hadn't Cat even heard it, when she'd carried more water and blankets to her mam and the other ladies? They had shushed her from the room, but she had waited in the hall. She could hear the princess groan and plead and finally scream until Cat had ran outside of the longhouse and wept in the gardens. The next time she saw Elinor, she was laid out for burial, her body shrunken and her face pale and still.

Baby Gwen was the princess now. Cat's thoughts took another turn. If Enid's baby could die, what about Baby Gwen? *No!* There had been too much death lately, and it would not touch this baby. Didn't she have Cat and her mam to protect her? And Enid, too. Between them, surely they could protect one tiny baby. Cat moved the baby's coverlet gently around her, and sat nearby to listen to Enid's sad contralto.

Chapter Three: Hyw

Hyw was brushing the bay's hide to a mahogany shine when the kitchen boy found him.

"Lord Bran says to fetch ye," the boy panted in Welsh. Hyw wondered if his father had news of his placement at last. He told the boy he would come as soon as he stabled the big horse, and the boy ran back to the kitchens without another word.

At Shrewsbury, Hyw would have been expected to call another groom to look after the horse and immediately attend his lord's summons. But at Garth Celyn their lives were so dependent on the livestock—especially the horses—that he would be expected to finish with the horse before he reported to the longhouse. Besides, Hyw knew this horse would not respond to the Welsh groom. He let the big stallion loose in an empty pen near the geldings to avoid friction between this aggressive visitor and the Garth Celyn stallions.

Then he quickened his pace to the longhouse, where he found Bran sorting his gear.

“There you are, Hyw,” his father greeted him. “We must ride hard, and we need a squire who can manage the mounts. Are you up for another journey?”

Hyw was confused by the word “squire” and he shifted uncomfortably. He had still been a page when he left Shrewsbury. The Saints knew he would have had a spot as squire soon enough had he stayed, but he'd rather be a warrior and serve the prince and his father. This trip might be the way to show them what he was capable of, and so finally win his sash!

“Yes,” he said.

Bran turned to him. “Your prompt response makes me proud, Hyw,” he said. “But you have my leave to reconsider. I know you've just returned, and you might want time with your mother and sister before – ”

“No – that is, I will say farewell to them if I may, Father. I know there is risk in any journey, with the English on the march, but I would go with you.” He knew he was the best choice for this job, whatever the circumstances, but he wasn't sure how to say it. “Besides, none other has my gift—with horses.”

His father scanned the room, even as the corners of his mouth turned up briefly in a smile. “Yes,” he replied, “if your mam speaks truly, yours is a gift we will find most useful on this journey.” Before Hyw could ask more questions, Bran returned to his sorting and dismissed him with a parting comment. “Best get your gear and say your goodbyes tonight. We leave at first light.”

Hyw's first thought was to find his mother. Adara had set the spinning near the window to catch the sunshine. When she saw him, she stood and moved to him for a hug. As she released him, her smile was genuine.

“How have you settled in, Hyw?” she asked as she drew him to the window seat, holding his hands in hers.

“Well enough, Mother,” he said, loathe to tell her that he felt like a stranger again. During the years of his fosterage, just thinking of her round, smiling face had brightened his heart. Shrewsbury's older lady had taken little interest in him, save the one time she referred to him as "yon Welsh cur." She spat those few words like a bad taste in her mouth, and the others of her court had taken her cue. He wondered what his mam knew of what had befallen him in Shrewsbury.

He blushed again, and tried to turn his head away. Adara dropped his hands quickly. "I forget how near a man you are already. Forgive me, Hyw."

"Do not fear it, Mam," he said, wishing he could reach for her hands again. She reached up then and brushed the hair from his eyes.

"That's what I was hoping for," she said. He looked at her in surprise, and she laughed. "For you to call me Mam again, instead of mo-ther." She emphasized the English pronunciation and he smiled, realizing he had been using the English words. Maybe he'd been acting like a stranger.

"Ah, what brings that flush to your cheeks, then?" she continued. "Mayhap an English maid, left behind?"

"Nay, Mam," he answered quickly. "No English girl would have me." He spoke in Welsh, using "geneth" for girl with a smile, but at her look of concern he wished he had kept silent. The English girls had found little to their liking in his small, wiry frame. His copper hair earned its share of jeering from them, but he knew it came, like his own gift, from his mother.

"Well," she brightened, "there will be time for a' that, now that you are home again. And glad I am of it." She laughed again, patting his folded hands.

He made a pained face. "Now is not the time," he told her. "I must take my leave shortly, with my father and the prince."

"So soon? But I had thought—" Adara broke off, realization dawning in her eyes. "Well, that is good news, is it not? Your da asked for you at last?"

Hyw nodded, on the verge of telling his mother that he was neither a squire nor a warrior yet, but she continued with a look of delight.

"I prayed he would call you to the prince's service, and now I will not need to prompt him," she said. "I am not pleased to see you ride to war, Hyw, but I believe this mission may help prevent one. If your da and the prince can bring the new Baron of Wigmore to their side, it may give the English king a reason to hold his advance at Rhuddlan. And I am well pleased to see you serve the prince."

"It is only one mission, Mam. I am not yet *teulu*," he joked, referring to the prince's special bodyguard.

"And why should you not join your da there too?" she asked. He dared not admit he hoped to prove himself worthy, but she gave him a look as if she had read his mind. "Ach, we have tomorrow for goodbyes. Today we will make you ready. I have a fresh tunic for you."

"Not red, Mam," he admonished her, referring to the red tunics worn by Prince Llywelyn's *teulu*.

"Not yet," she answered, meaningfully. "And how does your surcoat?"

"Well enough, Mam," he mumbled as she looked his clothes over for tears to mend. As a page, he had learned to mend his own clothing in emergencies. But Adara's attentions also showed how much she cared for him, and for a moment he longed to throw his arms around her again. She often said she could call her gift when she needed it, and he wondered if he should ask her advice on using his to help him win his warrior's sash.

Before he could find the words, Enid entered, carrying Baby Gwen. Adara held out her arms for the child, and began to hum softly. His sister Cat came in behind Enid, and sidled closer to him. He reached out and pulled a strand of hair that had come loose from her not-so-careful bun before she could push him away. He had been surprised at how much she'd grown in his three-year absence. She would soon be thirteen. He wondered if arrangements had been made for her wedding, or if the war would delay that as well.

"Cat, your brother has news," Adara said. "And he needs his new tunic. Would you take him to fetch it?"

Chapter Four: Cat

Cat drew her brother toward their mam's bag of sewing projects, while Enid and Adara took the baby to be admired by the other women. As she rummaged through it, he told her he would be going to serve the prince as squire.

"You will be a warrior now, surely," she said, half listening. "Your gift can only help you get there." Hyw was lucky to have gained such control over his gift already. Her own gift had yet to appear. What would it be like to connect with animals like Hyw, or charm bees like their mam? Of course, some of Mam's family had no gift at all. Cat put that thought aside as her hand found the cloth. "Aha!" She fished out the plain tunic, shook it, and looked at him over it. "Don't fret. It will be red soon enough."

"It's fine," he said, taking it from her and unconsciously wringing the fabric with his hands.

"Then why aren't you smiling?"

He grimaced then, as if he was trying to smile. She made a face at him, and finally coaxed him into a grin. Then he shook his head.

"Your words reminded me of something," he said.

As his voice trailed off, Cat realized what he must be thinking. "James!" she said.

Hyw nodded, looking miserable. It was not the first time since his return. He often seemed stuck between the *Saeson* world and his own. She touched his shoulder.

"I cannot imagine it, Hyw. What it must be like to know you might meet a friend in battle."

"It's more than that," Hyw said, staring at the tunic in his hands. "James helped me forge my gift."

"He knows?"

"He guessed, one day when I worked with a nervous filly in Shrewsbury's barn. And instead of turning away or raising the alarm, he urged me to try with other animals. He helped me build something like a wall in my mind, to protect me from connecting with animals by accident. He kept my secret. It was—like a bond between us."

Cat wasn't sure what to say. Their mam had long warned them never to tell anyone outside the family about their special abilities. Did Hyw think of this *Saeson* boy as a brother, then? She almost felt jealous of him. Then she brightened, and put her hands over Hyw's.

"I heard the messenger when he told the prince. You do not ride to war, Hyw. You ride to make an al- ally- " She paused to think of the right word in English. "Alliance."

"What did you hear?" Hyw asked, and Cat told him everything, even her thoughts about the strangeness of the man's dress and bearing, and his poor skills at delivering the message. "I could have done it better," she declared.

"Where is he?" Hyw craned his neck to look around the room.

"He is gone already," she told him. "Fret not, brother. The man was so anxious to leave he saddled his own horse for the journey." They both grinned at that.

"Still, it seems strange that he would not break bread with us before he left."

"*Saeson*," Cat said with a dismissive shrug. She reached for his hand again. "Here, I made this for you," she said, taking a colourful finger bracelet from the bag and knotting it onto his wrist. "I made it for your birthday last year, thinking you would be here with us. Look, I braided in a few strands of my hair. The princess said everyone does it in France. For remembrance." She looked up to see him watching her, a look of concern in his eyes.

"Do you miss her very much?" he asked.

She raised her hand to her black armband again. Adara had called Cat to the princess and her ladies when they first came to court, to sing them children's songs and poems that might help them learn Welsh. The princess had welcomed her. Later Cat learned the complex meters of the bards so she could sing proper Welsh to the princess. At the princess's insistence, Cat travelled with their itinerant court as the prince visited his remaining castles. And Princess Elinor introduced Cat to Rhys, the boy she was promised to marry when she became the Lady of Meirionnydd. She could not find the words to say how much she had missed her princess, over the past six months, so she said nothing.

"I wish I had something for you in return," Hyw said. His face looked so serious.

"What of a deed instead?" she suggested. "Come and see *Rhaeadr Fawr* once more, before you go." Would he recall their old childhood races to the waterfalls? Before he could reply, she tagged him and ran off toward the path.

"No, you don't!" she heard him cry behind her as he followed, laughing.

The night's grey clouds had parted, allowing the wakening sun to slant off Tŷ Hir, the longhouse at the heart of Garth Celyn. Cat shielded her eyes as she looked up, and shivered to see armed warriors pacing on the tower.

Sturdy wood and stone buildings fanned out from Tŷ Hir, creating a small town that made up the royal *llys*. Already people filtered into the courtyard to bid farewell to Llywelyn's *teulu*, the trusted warriors who made up the royal bodyguard. Cat stood with her mam, counting the warriors who stood ready this morning. At first she was surprised not to see more of them: only eighteen, counting her da, wearing his gold torque and red sash, and her brother holding the reins of the prince's horses. Of course, it took fewer warriors to make friends than to fight off enemies. She felt a small swell of pride that her brother and father were included in this select company, although it was almost immediately overshadowed by a grey-like dread. No, she almost said aloud. She turned from it to see her da embrace her mam before he bent down to her. She snuggled into the warmth of his heavy fur cloak and put her arms around his waist.

"Tada," she whispered, using the phrase she had not used since she was a small child. He hugged her closer for a moment before releasing her and ruffling her hair.

"Worry not, little Cat," he told her. "We will be back before you know we're gone."

Hyw moved to hold Aeron, their da's brown warhorse, as Bran mounted, and then held the prince's huge black stallion steady for him. As she watched, Cat wished the messenger had remained to guide them. She suddenly thought of Father Maelgwyn. What had he said at Mass? Something about being rewarded by the "fruit of his mouth" while a transgressor would only "eat violence." She shivered.

"Are you cold, sister?" Hyw asked, draping his soft cloak around her shoulders.

"No, Hyw," she said, trying to give it back to him. "You will need this."

"I have another." He held it on her shoulders a moment longer, and pinned it in front with the gold clasp from her woolen surcoat. "This cloak was a gift to me," he said as he did up the clasp. "It is much too fine for where we are going."

She guessed that the cloak had been a gift from James. She felt the soft fabric, dyed a rich blue and lined with blue-grey squirrel fur. It was a mark of wealth.

Her earlier feeling of greyness returned and threatened to overwhelm her. To escape her thoughts, she flung her arms around Hyw in a final hug.

"Fare ye well, Hyw. May God protect you and Da," she whispered, "and may you keep the prince from harm."

"We will," he told her, kissing her cheek. "And you look after our infant princess, and our mam."

She hugged him fiercely another moment before he turned to mount his horse.

Chapter Five: Hyw

Through the morning they rode hard when the land allowed, dismounting to lead their horses through denser brush. As he rode his father's gelding, Cadarn, Hyw clicked his tongue and the horse's ears flicked forward in response. He had taken special care to groom Cadarn the previous evening, and knew the horse remembered and trusted him. In his free hand, Hyw held the reins of Llywelyn's fresh mount, ready in case of ambush. Vox was a stallion, powerful and used to action. Hyw connected with him often to keep him calm and quiet. He found himself glad that, since this was to be a short trip with no hunting, Llywelyn had left the dogs behind—which meant fewer animals for him to marshal.

At first, it was just a matter of keeping the horses abreast and not letting the stallion take the lead. The ground in several places was already covered with snow, making the narrow trail increasingly dangerous for the horses. As the path twisted, Hyw had to make Vox fall in behind Cadarn.

Vox pushed against the lead, snorting. Hyw didn't need his gift to know the stallion was not pleased to follow the gelding, but both horses were well trained. Hyw created an image in his mind of the bushes and thickets around them, projecting his sense of urgency to Vox in a strong command: *Enemies. Be watchful.* Vox's head veered from side to side once, as if he was scanning the terrain. After that, he followed, ears forward.

The men spoke little, and the prince even less. No one sang, as they would have on most journeys. Often the prince had surprised his enemies with the swiftness of his response to battle. His warrior *teulu* – the men he often called his true family – had it down to a discipline.

Hyw scanned for birds in the trees, especially the hawks with which he felt special connection. His gift would help the men avoid danger if it came. But with Bran riding behind Llywelyn, and several warriors between them, how could he give the alarm without explaining his gift? How receptive would his father be, with the prince and his warriors so near?

They stopped to water the horses, which most of the men accomplished without dismounting. He'd almost forgotten what the *teulu* were like, and what it meant to ride hard through the mountains. At one of these stops, he made his way to his father.

"Da, I am able to see farther than most," Hyw began, holding Vox's reins as the horses drank their fill. At his father's raised eyebrow, Hyw pointed upward at a hawk circling nearby. "I can see what he sees. But how can I let you know if we see—*Saeson*?"

Bran looked around at the wooded stream, patting Aeron's broad neck. "Once, when you were young, you and I disturbed a nest of red-tailed hawks near Aber Falls. Do you recall the sound they made?"

Hyw nodded. The chicks had made a shrill near-whistling sound with a slight warble in its centre. He felt sure he could reproduce it. "If you hear that sound today, Da, it will mean trouble," he promised.

Bran nodded as he turned Aeron's head back to the path.

The day waned into the next morning as they pressed on. Years of training under Aeneas served Hyw well. He set his mind not to feel the cold or the hunger that gnawed at him. They needed speed and stealth. There would be no stopping to hunt or make a fire. Adara had slipped him bread with dried meat strips from her pocket. He ate these from the pack he'd tied to Cadarn's saddle as he saw the other men do, and he knew to make them last as long as he could.

Several times he had to jump down to wade beside the horses as they crossed treacherous fords with fast currents. Hyw had to shake himself more than once, as he began to slide from the saddle in sheer weariness. Then in panic he connected with the hawks again, making certain no enemy was near.

They were forced to a halt at the River Wye, black and swollen to the level of its banks. Impassable.

The remnants of a bridge still clung to the near bank.

"*Saeson*," one of the warriors grunted, and spat on the ground.

Llywelyn motioned for Bran and a younger warrior named Goronwy to walk aside with him. They stood contemplating the river. Hyw could see the younger man gesturing down the bank and across the river.

Hyw dropped from the saddle and led the horses to the water to drink. As the waning sun glinted off the surface, he stared down at his reflection. With one hand he fingered the threads of the bracelet his sister had woven around his wrist.

Chapter Six: Cat

At first, all she saw was water.

She was in the chapel with her mam and some of the other women, listening to Father Maelgwyn's baritone as he sang the prayers. She had worn the cloak Hyw gave her, and she stroked the rich material with one hand.

"Let us pray," Father Maelgwyn sang. Cat closed her eyes —

— and suddenly she could see the wide, dark expanse of water.

Was she dreaming?

She tried to open her eyes, but the picture became clearer. It was a river. Black water rumbled, swollen and churning against the banks. This wasn't her familiar Aber. What river was it? Where was it?

She turned as if to ask someone, and saw her brother standing on the bank, staring into the water.

"Hyw!" She called his name, but he didn't look up. Couldn't he hear

her? Then things began to move around her. It was as if the scene broke apart and came together again. She was standing in a meadow. The stench of blood and death filled her nostrils. She heard a high-pitched whistle – no a scream! Someone screaming. She raised her hands to cover her ears —

— and found herself back in the church, kneeling.

She could feel the wooden balustrade in front of her, and hear the chant rising and falling around her.

"*Dominus vobiscum*," the priest sang in Latin.

The Lord be with you, Cat thought automatically, the familiar words anchoring her in the ritual.

"Et cum spiritu tuo…" she sang back. *And with thy spirit.*

Cat looked up and found her mam's eyes, which slipped from smiling to alarm. Without dropping a word of the prayer, Adara touched Cat's forehead and then drew her into her side for support.

"*Sanctus, Sanctus, Sanctus*," Adara's clear soprano rang out. Holy, holy, holy. This was always the part of the *Te Deum* that Cat liked best, and she joined in, harmonizing automatically.

"*…Pleni sunt caeli et terra maiestatis gloriae tuae*."

Heaven and Earth are full of thy glory. Had she just seen some of it? Or was it a dream? She felt a chill like the spray from the waterfall on a wintery day. Father Maelgwyn warned of darker forces. Was that what caused her vision? Was her gift evil? But how then could it come to her in church? She turned to her mam, but Adara touched one finger to her lips briefly and encircled her shoulders with her free arm.

When the service was finally over, Adara drew Cat aside to walk with her toward the waterfall. They had often walked together after church when Cat was younger, but they had been too busy of late. When they had gone far enough to be out of earshot, she told her mam what had happened in the church and what she'd seen.

"Was it some kind of dream?"

"I don't believe so," said Adara slowly. "It's an old gift, Cat. One I haven't seen for a long time."

"Gift?"

"Yes, Cat. Like the connection your brother has to animals. My own brother—your uncle Gawain—has such a gift as well. As did our grandfather."

"And you as well." Cat thought about the way her mam could take honey from beehives without ever being bitten, and the way no gnats or insects ever bothered their banquets and campfires. "You're a bee charmer."

"Bee charmer," Adara replied, smiling. "Yes, I suppose I am. I like that, Cat."

"But I have no gift," Cat responded. "Or at least, I thought I didn't. Why did this happen now?"

"Maybe because we need it now," Adara said. "I've watched for your gift too, but there has been no sign. It comes to men and women in our family, but it does not come to all. I thought you might be like my youngest sister, your Aunt Cadi. It seems she has no gift. One or two of each generation have been passed over, and sometimes the gift will skip generations and pass to the children or grandchildren. My mam used to say it was to balance the scales. But perhaps that can change, if the need is great."

"What—what is it?" Cat asked. "My gift, I mean. What did I see?"

"My grandfather used the term 'seeing beyond the veil.' There are different ways that comes to us. My great-aunt —rest her soul—could see the future. Our grandfather called it the Second Sight."

"Is that what I have?" Cat hesitated, unsure she wanted such a gift.

"I know not, Cat. At least, it seems you can see what is happening to others at a distance."

"You think I really saw Hyw?"

Adara thought for a moment, and then nodded. "It seems clear to me that you saw him. And possibly more. The meadow in your vision marks a change. If it is yet to come, if it is the future, then you must have seen it for a reason." Adara put her arm around Cat and turned them both back toward Garth Celyn. "Perhaps it is a warning. If your gift is the Second Sight, we must not ignore it. Let me think on this. Mayhap there is a way we can send a warning to your da and brother."

Chapter Seven: Hyw

What can you see?” Bran asked.

“There are two armies.” Hyw stood staring at the sky, seeing through the eyes of a hawk as it spied on groups of men milling about a field. Some cleaned weapons, while others put armour on each other and their horses.

“Can you see the sigils?”

Hyw drove the bird closer and described what he saw on the banners of the enemy. Bran quizzed him carefully, and then nodded.

“Giffard the Saxon,” Bran said. “And Roger LeStrange. We must tell the prince.”

Hyw watched anxiously as his da spoke with Llywelyn, just out of earshot. He had learned about the allies and enemies of his prince’s house almost from the cradle. Giffard was Llywelyn’s cousin by marriage. Hyw wondered how it must feel to have the man turn against him yet again. The prince seemed to ask many questions, and then abruptly turned toward the others. Bran nodded and smiled at Hyw as the prince rallied his men.

Llywelyn's response was decisive. "The English king is upon us. We must send word to our allies."

Hyw felt relieved that the prince had believed them, although he knew Bran would not name him or his gift as the source of the information. Llywelyn was known as a modern Welshman, with tolerance but no fondness for the old ways. The prince acted quickly, sending a man back to Garth Celyn for his army, and others to muster his allies in Gwynedd and Powys Fadog.

"We will meet here in no less than three days. All haste is necessary."

After the messengers rode out, Llywelyn turned to the men remaining. "You must stay here and hold this position until my return. When your brothers come back, bid them keep their tidings for me, and together we will plan our attack. Meantime, I will meet with the Mortimers, and rally them in their father's name for our cause."

He turned with a gesture to Bran and the horses. Hyw's heart was pounding as he brought Vox forward. He must go, to help protect his prince. But how could he convince his father?

Then he heard his da's low voice. "We must bring him."

Prince Llywelyn stopped for a moment, and looked back at Hyw. The expression in his eyes was unreadable. Then he nodded.

The next morning they arrived at Abbey Cwmhir. The imposing building sprawled across the field in front of them. At Llywelyn's gesture, Goronwy remained on the path with the horses in readiness for their departure. Hyw followed Llywelyn and Bran down the long stone nave, the main aisle of the church. The vaulted ceiling rose high above them, and Hyw counted fourteen bays.

"Impressive," Bran said softly, crossing himself and bending one knee as they came in sight of the altar.

"Yes," Llywelyn responded, kneeling also. He bowed his head for a moment, and rose to continue down the aisle. "After this skirmish, mayhap I can return safely and finish it." As Hyw knelt, he realized this abbey reminded him of the abbey at Aber, near Garth Celyn. His time in Shrewsbury had taught him there were many kinds of monks, something he had not realized in Wales. The familiar look and style of this nave meant these were the White Monks, Cistercians, who believed in the simplicity of prayer and work.

The abbot saw them, and came forward with two other monks in their characteristic white robes. Llywelyn turned the abbot aside, and they spoke in a low voice for a few moments. As Hyw politely turned to look again at the church, one of the monks clasped Bran by the arm, warrior style. The two embraced briefly, and then the monk turned to Hyw.

"He has certainly grown," the monk said, using his hand to mark a space by his waist, and then by the top of Hyw's head.

"Gawain," Hyw said, recognizing his mother's brother and throwing his arms around him in a bear-hug.

"We are grateful to have this chance to see you again," Bran added.

"And lucky, for I am traveling to Aberconwy this week," Gawain said. "Now I shall have an excuse to stop in on my lady sister."

"That would please her, I am sure," Bran said.

"Enough of this family reunion," Llywelyn said, clapping Bran on the shoulder. "The abbot has given me a blessing for our actions, and given us a brother to ensure our success."

"You have missed the morning service, I am afraid," said the old abbot with a kind look. That meant they would not have a regular service until noon. "I must remain, but mayhap Brother Gawain will attend you, to aid your mission."

Llywelyn offered Vox to Gawain, since the horse was already saddled and their need to get back on the road was pressing. Hyw helped him check the cinches on Vox's gear before they mounted.

"Shrewsbury treated you well?" Gawain asked quietly, placing his spare robe into the soft leather bag attached to the horse's saddle.

"He did, uncle, but—" Hyw broke off, unsure how to tell his uncle. "It seems I am like you."

"Oh? In what manner?"

"Mam says you and I have a similar—gift."

Understanding dawned in Gawain's eyes. "Then I may be able to advise you, Hyw. Perhaps I will journey to Garth Celyn for Twelfth Night, and we can spend some time together. Meanwhile, we must get the prince into Builth Castle to meet his allies."

Gawain tousled Hyw's hair. He had not realized he was holding his breath until he felt it expel in relief. He knew his uncle would make good his promise as soon as their mission was complete. Other questions crowded into his mind, and he blurted out the first one almost without thinking. "Is that why you packed a second robe, uncle?"

"You have sharp eyes, I see." Gawain looked into the distance, his expression almost sad. "I forget you children were born in war, and weaned on watchfulness." Then he smiled a little as he continued checking Vox's saddle and gear. "Mayhap this second robe will come in handy. With a castle shut as tight as Builth, a simple monk may gain entry with less notice than a rival prince."

Hyw nodded, beginning to understand his uncle's role in helping Llywelyn. Gawain turned his attention to Vox. It was strange to watch his uncle use their shared gift to make contact with the skittish stallion. Hyw wondered if he looked as intense when he used his gift, and if that's how James always knew. He wondered if others could tell, or if he could school his expression to hide it.

When Vox quieted, Gawain mounted. Bran motioned for Gawain to join him farther ahead in the line of men, and there was no more time for talk.

Later that day they neared Builth and stopped to make camp.

Llywelyn and Gawain moved aside to speak together. Bran and the other men began to tend their horses, and Hyw took Vox and Cadarn to the stream.

He dunked his own head in the cool water as the horses drank. Then he removed their saddles and took his brushes from Cadarn's saddlebag to groom them.

He finished Vox first, and then turned to Cadarn. His father's gelding nickered softly as Hyw came closer, and nuzzled at his side to take the small apple he kept hidden there. Hyw smiled, stepping easily to Cadarn's side as he had so many times before. He had been grooming Cadarn since he was a boy, before he went away to England. Sometimes it seemed the horse remembered him better than his old friends or his family.

As he finished brushing Cadarn's shaggy winter coat to a shine, he thought he heard the clashing of armour in the distance. Could the men be practicing, with the English army so near? Cadarn nickered uneasily, swinging his head around and twitching his ears. Hyw put away the brushes and looked up, choosing a rook from a flock hovering overhead to be his eyes. The bird could hear the faint sounds of clanging armour as well, and he willed it to look closer. Its vision caused his stomach to fist: men fighting and bleeding in a clearing.

He released the bird, left the horses grazing on the bank, and sprinted toward the clearing.

He arrived panting, more with alarm than exertion. The reek of blood and sweat surrounded him. He crouched, looking around him for soldiers, but nothing stirred. Spotting one familiar figure lying on the ground, he ran to it. He turned the body without thinking. It was not his da's face. He felt a moment's gladness before he recognized the man was one of the prince's *teulu* from Garth Celyn. The warrior's eyes were open and unseeing, and his skull above shorn off. Hyw crossed himself and reached forward to close the man's eyes with a blessing. Then he turned and retched into the grass.

"Help," someone cried behind him. Hyw turned to spy another warrior lying a short distance away. "Help the prince."

The man pointed over the hillock and Hyw ran, leaving the fallen warrior to bleed into the hillside. His neck prickled with panic. He ran heedlessly over the hill and almost into the arms of an armoured man. The man grabbed Hyw instinctively and swung him around with the momentum of his body.

"Here now," an English voice said. "What's this?" Hyw found himself dangling in the air. He stared at a group of armed soldiers, who seemed to be merely standing on the hillside together.

Then he paled: Llywelyn was there, kneeling on the ground. A spear pierced his body from front to back. Yet the prince supported one end of the stake aloft, or perhaps it held him upright. The prince was not in armour, and Hyw realized he must have been surprised by the English soldiers.

Where was his da? And his uncle Gawain?

"He's just a lad, Mortimer," said another voice to his right, this one strained and thick. "Leave him be. Has there not been enough killing this day?"

Hyw dropped roughly to the ground as the soldier laughed. "This from the man who struck down the Prince of Wales? Have you a woman's will, de Francton? Bah. Take him then. Enough of this. It ends here, prince or no."

Before the men could stop him, Hyw leapt up and ran to the prince. His knees hit the ground in front of the dying man.

"Get me a priest," rasped Llywelyn, in English. Then his black eyes focused on Hyw, and he seemed to recognize him. In Welsh, Llywelyn said, "Protect my daughter. She is the hope of Wales now."

Hyw met the prince's gaze. Llywelyn's dark eyes never wavered. As Hyw stared into them, his felt his mind expanding. Hyw felt he was floating on a dark river, and his consciousness opened to the prince. He saw himself kneeling in the field, and knew he saw through the prince's eyes, as if he and the prince were one.

The prince cried out, "God have mercy on our souls!" And finally the dark eyes broke contact, even as the prince's head was cleft from his body.

Hyw saw as if through a veil as the English knight held the prince's head high in the air, roaring with triumph. Somehow he knew it was Edmund Mortimer, and he did not question how he knew it. Blood gushed from the prince's headless body, still kneeling in the field, impaled by the spear. And blood dripped from Mortimer's sword onto the grass.

Something like mist spread over Hyw's mind. Clouds appeared from nowhere to dim the sun. The world turned ashen, and then as red as blood. He saw the stars fall toward him and birds plummet from the sky like rain as the ground thundered and rose up in its place.

As if from far away, he heard someone screaming and did not know it was himself until he felt a blow on the side of his head. Then he heard and saw—nothing.

He floated in a sea of cool water and soft cloth. He thought of Elinor, her scent and the softness of her skin. But when he opened his eyes, he saw her not. Instead, he saw a blue-eyed man in a monk's cowl.

"Hyw, glad I am to see you waken," said the monk.

"Who is Hyw?" he asked. His voice croaked, and the monk sponged his lips with a wet cloth, dripping some of the water into his mouth. He swallowed.

He recognized the monk's voice. Or did the boy recognize the voice? He shook his head and almost swooned from pain. How could it be that he, Llywelyn, could see at all? Was he not dead at the hands of the traitorous Mortimer?

Was he in hell then? He almost laughed. Had he not already been there? Any place was hell, without his wife. Again he felt the anguish of her loss, and the monk laid a cool cloth upon his brow. "Rest, Hyw."

"Nay," he rasped. "I am not Hyw."

"He is bemused," the monk turned to an armoured soldier at his side. "But he is strong. He will rally."

Llywelyn recognized the mounted soldier who had struck him down. Somewhere inside his mind he heard the echo of a name: de Francton.

"Murderer." He tried to rise, but his head felt thick. "I am not Hyw."

The monk looked at him deeply then, into his eyes. Llywelyn read a mix of shock and horror in his face.

"Can this be?" the monk half-whispered. Then his expression became thoughtful. He moved closer and spoke the next words into Llywelyn's ear. "Fear not, my liege. All will be well."

Llywelyn's eyes began to close. He heard a voice singing, and thought of Elinor. He whispered her name as he sank beneath consciousness again. It was like floating underwater.

As he sank, he saw a lad swim past him, pulling hard for the surface. Why, it is Bran's son, he thought, and slept again.

Chapter Eight: Cat

Cat knew before the kitchen boy came to get her.

She had tied some colourful ribbons on a spinner, and was kneeling in front of Baby Gwen's cradleboard, blowing them gently. Baby Gwen reached out her chubby fists to the ribbons—which Cat held just out of reach—and giggled. Cat sang a short rhyme of the colours as she pulled the ribbons away. Enid smiled at them.

Cat took a drink to clear her throat and leaned forward to set the goblet down, adjusting her new cloak to a more comfortable position. Her eyes caught the glint of the swishing liquid as her fingers brushed the fabric—

— and she found herself in a meadow, kneeling in front of Prince Llywelyn instead of his infant daughter. The prince's face was contorted in pain. Then she saw her brother's face instead. And a head held high in the air by a mailed gauntlet. Was it her brother?

She heard an echoing laughter, the deep unpleasant laugh of a man, and it sent a shiver down her back—

—and she was kneeling in front of Baby Gwen again.

"Hyw!" she cried out. "Where are you, brother?"

But the vision was gone.

Startled, Enid set down her mending and stood. "What is wrong, child?" Before Cat could answer, the boy appeared at the door.

"Your mam sent me," he said. "Ye must come—right now!"

Berwyn, the stable boy, looked decidedly uncomfortable in the hall, a small figure turning his cap over and over in his hands as he answered Adara's barrage of questions. Aeneus was there as well, his arms crossed over his chest and his face a grim mask. Adara paced in front of them. Cat had never seen her Mam so anxious.

"We must go at once," Adara began as soon as she saw Cat.

"Hyw is hurt," Cat said.

"As you have guessed," Adara said, casting her a warning glance. Cat, flustered, turned to Berwyn. He told them he had called on the abbey and heard of the battle and the death of the prince. Hyw was in a sickbed there, but he had not tarried to discover what wound he suffered.

"No word of your da," Adara said, a worried frown creasing her brow. Cat flew to her mam and they hugged, making Berwyn turn away in embarrassment.

"Lady, the *Saeson* will come to claim Garth Celyn," said Aeneus. "We will fight them." He turned to Berwyn. "Did your abbot tell you how many troops Edward brings with him?"

"Th-th-thousands," stammered Berwyn.

"How's that?" Aeneus stepped back and swung his arms expressively. "Tell me truly, boy. How many?"

"Th-the monk said, begging your pardon, sir," Berwyn stammered. "He said to tell ye they mean to– to– "

"Monk?" Adara broke in. "Was it my brother?"

"It was, Lady," Berwyn stammered. "He was with the prince in the field, he said. They let him go because he was in his robes, and because he demanded to look after Hyw."

"My son yet lives," she whispered. "God be praised."

"He said Mortimer comes in force, and to tell my lord Aeneus that your only hope is to flee Garth Celyn."

"We must secure the princess. Tell Enid to get the baby ready for travel," Adara said decisively to the kitchen boy. She turned to Berwyn and Aeneus. "Aeneus, you know my brother. He would never interfere if he was not certain. See to the men."

"I will see you to safety first, Lady," the warrior answered. "Whither thou goest."

Adara frowned and then nodded. "I know you will." She put one hand to her brow and thought for a moment. "We will take Gwenllian to Criccieth Castle. Word came yesterday that Dafydd has sent Elizabeth there, with the children." Dafydd was the prince's brother and heir, and Cat realized he would now be the Prince of Wales.

"Aye." Aeneus nodded. "Criccieth is more fortified than our *llys*, and the garrison is loyal. With its twin towers between us and the English, the princess will be safe."

"Dafydd will protect her as he does his own children. Send to Anglesey for more defenders to make a stand here, lest the *Saeson* get through to burn our winter stores as they tried to do five years ago."

Aeneus nodded. "I will see to it."

"Once Gwen is safe, I must go to Builth." Adara turned to Cat, her unspoken concern for Bran and Hyw bright in her eyes. Cat thought she was about to ask her something, but Aeneus took a step toward them.

"Nay, you must stay with the babe," he said. He raised his hands before she could protest. "I will go to Builth and fetch your son to you. And I will find his da, or bring his body home to you. On that, I give you my word."

Chapter Nine: Hyw

Hyw rose to consciousness only to sink again into a place he could not remember on waking. He sensed himself rising and falling, like the tides surrounding Garth Celyn. Yet he knew he was not near his home at all; he was in a monk's cell, stark and cold, at the crossroads near Builth.

Whenever he woke, his uncle Gawain was there, sponging his brow or holding his hand.

"My da? I did not see him. Was he—?"

"Shh. There's no news, Hyw. I will tell you as soon as I hear. Try to sleep."

Hyw glimpsed a soldier standing behind Gawain. "Who—?"

"Hello, boy," the soldier said, smiling at him. "Glad I am to see you waken."

"This is Stephen de Francton, Hyw. He brought you to us."

He knew the man's name, but it was lost inside him for a moment. Yes, this man had spoken for him against Edmund Mortimer on the hill near Builth.

At the same time he felt this recognition, he also felt rage against the soldier that seemed to burst out from inside and outside of him at the same time. He remembered someone hitting him on the head. And something else—a spear, blood.

Gawain saw his agitation and shooed de Francton from the room. Hyw closed his eyes and slept.

He could not tell whether hours or days flashed by this way. Finally he surfaced in a cavern pool. He was able to float gently on its surface, and was surprised when the water did not splash with his movements. It was blue, and thick, and as warm as the goose-feather quilt they used at Garth Celyn in winter. He looked about to see reflections of light on the stone walls. Was he somewhere deep under the mountains of his home?

At the edge of the pool, he saw his uncle Gawain standing with his head bowed. His lips were moving, but Hyw couldn't hear what he was saying.

You, lad, he heard a deep voice rumble to his left. At the same time, he felt his own breath vibrate with the words. *You are Hyw.*

He turned to find the prince sitting on a rock at the pool's edge, staring at him. Hyw frowned. It couldn't be the prince, he thought. For a moment he couldn't remember why he knew that. Then his mind flooded with the sights and sounds of the hillside again. He saw Edmund Mortimer, sword raised, with his other hand grasping the prince's head.

Hyw flailed in the water. Sputtering. Drowning. As he disappeared underneath the blue surface of his consciousness, he heard Gawain's voice, and clung to the sound.

Hyw heard singing. The voice was low, as if from far away, but he knew it was his uncle. Gawain sang of the mountain, and its sleeping spirits. His words were not the Latin of Cistercian monks, nor the Norman of English lords, but the soft words of old Cymraeg:

"*Cysgu mae ysbrydion o dan y mynydd...*"

"*Spirits sleep beneath the mountain…*" Gawain sang of the world that had been, and the world yet to come. He sang of the pool at the edge of the world, and he sang of Hyw and of the gift they shared.

When Hyw broke the surface of the thick blue water again, he saw Gawain still standing at the edge. His uncle raised his head, and Hyw watched as Gawain's eyelids fluttered and opened. For a long moment they stared at each other.

"Where are we?" Hyw wondered.

"A safe place," Gawain told him, as if he could hear his thoughts. Or perhaps Hyw spoke aloud; he could not tell. Goose down seemed to fill his mouth. He concentrated, and tried again.

"How came we hither?"

"The old songs," Gawain said, smiling. Hyw couldn't understand what he meant, and thought he must be dreaming. Then he remembered the other dream, of Mortimer and the prince. He began to shudder. Gawain reached out to him with one hand.

"The prince yet lives, Hyw. He lives in you, if you will it."

"How can it be, Uncle?"

Gawain shook his head. "'Tis true."

Hyw reached out, and felt himself pulled from the pool, although he did not touch Gawain's hand. Then he realized he was not wet. What appeared to be a pool was not one at all. Hyw stood on the rocks at the cave edge as Gawain continued.

"It would seem that in the moment of his death, your minds joined. Whether you are kin, or kindred spirits, or whether it was mere accident, the true-born Prince of Wales is here with us. With you. When his spirit left his body, it entered yours."

What magic is this? The prince's low rumble came again, and Hyw turned quickly. He opened his eyes – eyes he thought were already open – and found himself in bed still, in the bare monk's cell.

His uncle stood motionless, with his cowl hiding his face. Gawain had his head bowed and he was reaching forward, one index finger touching the middle of Hyw's forehead. Inside his mind, Hyw heard his uncle's voice, calling to him as if from far away: "Close your eyes, Hyw."

Hyw did as he was told, and saw Llywelyn seated on a rock in front of him. Gawain appeared to be standing with them again, at the edge of the same pool-that-was-not.

"If I close my eyes, I can see you here."

Gawain nodded. "This is where the prince lives. Inside your mind."

Will you sell me to the Tylwyth Teg next? Llywelyn spat the old words for what the English would call "fairies" with contempt rather than fear. His voice echoed as if it were drawn from deep within the earth. *Is this some demented OtherWorld?*

"Nay, my lord," Gawain replied, his voice low and even. "It is but the gift with which our family has served yours all these years. As we serve you still."

The prince stood. *I told your great-grandfather I had no wish for your gift. I freed you—all of you—from those old bonds of fealty. I want freedom for all of our people. An end to these superstitions that cripple us.*

Gawain waited in silence. The prince moved restlessly and spoke again.

Was I wrong then? Am I being punished? Must all of Wales suffer, because of my mistakes? Because I chose to follow God, and not the old ways? Is that why—why my Lady Princess had to die?

"Nay my lord, I cannot think it. I also choose to follow God in this life, and to put my gift to His service. Our gifts are strong, but they are natural. Part of nature."

Then why did you not prevent her death? Llywelyn's voice thundered on the cave rocks, but Gawain did not shift his position.

"You know our family, my lord. You know our hearts are true. We believe human beings can be evil, but the gift has no power over the one who wields it. We bear no ill towards your Lady or any other. She was a pure and good woman, and as a woman our Maker called her home."

Gawain fell silent as Llywelyn's shoulders shook. The prince wiped his hand across his face. Hyw drew in a deep breath. He was not sure it was his place to speak, and yet he felt he must.

"My mam says—" He faltered.

Go on, lad. The Lady Adara was Elinor's truest friend in life. What says she of my lady wife's demise?

"She has told me childbirth is the most natural of events, and just as natural for a woman to give her life to save her child's. Mam would have acted to prevent it, if she had known."

For a moment Llywelyn did not speak. He turned from them, and they heard him groan. When he turned back again, his face was drawn and his dark eyes glittered. *You, lad, you have the power to keep me here. Is that true?*

Gawain nodded. "If he agrees, you may share this time with Hyw. At least, until Nos Galan Gaeaf this autumn, when we must lay all restless spirits, for their sake and our own."

Then I will have ten months. The prince shook his head. *Mortimer did not act alone. It bears the mark of my old enemy, Gruffydd ap Gwenwynwyn --*

"My lord," Gawain said. "I must caution you. If you stay for vengeance you will corrupt your immortal soul, and this boy along with it."

Llywelyn stared at Hyw for a moment, and slammed his fist into his hand. *To know, and not wreak vengeance! How can you ask me that? How can I not act?*

"You must not, my lord."

And who will stop me? This boy?

Gawain stepped closer. "In peril of your soul, and Hyw's, you must act only in justice while you remain among us."

The prince's face was red, and he snarled like his namesake, the lion. *Cannot vengeance for a wrong be a kind of justice?* His will was as powerful in death as his body had been in life. His need to reunite Wales at all costs had made him take actions that cost him the allegiance of some, and yet he had prevailed. Hyw could see another side of that will now, and he had the sense to fear it. Had he somehow damned them both?

"You are no longer part of this world, to decide this world's justice," Gawain was saying. "How can you be sure what is God's will, and what is your own?"

Llywelyn struggled to bring himself under control. *Release me from this torment. I demand it.*

"I—I cannot, my lord," Gawain replied, faltering.

"Can I do it?" Hyw asked. "Can I release him?"

Gawain shook his head. "I cannot tell. In truth, much of this lore has died with those who knew it, in these past years of war. I have not seen it done since I was a child, myself, and then only on Nos Galan Gaeaf. All I can do is guide you to abide together until then, as best I know how, if you will accept my guidance."

"What will happen to us, if we do not?" Hyw asked.

Gawain shrugged. "Madness, mayhap. Or worse. It is a thing of legends. All I know is to follow the way as I was told it. There may be those who know better, but I know them not."

Then, from the centre of his fear, Hyw felt his gift begin to stir inside him like the pure bell tone of the harp. He began to see what had happened in the final moments of his prince's life in a new light.

From the beginning, Hyw had followed his gift. He let his instinct guide him. It stood to reason that what had happened on the hillside had been his gift again. But it was also his choice, and he had chosen to act. Wales needed her prince now more than ever. And Hyw had chosen to save the prince in the only way he knew. His family had always served Llywelyn's. And without thinking, he had chosen fealty. He, Hyw ap Bran ap Rhys ap Maredudd ap Eineon, chose to stand with his prince. And his gift, his fealty, his will, all that he was, he would pit against his prince's rage. He concentrated again, and managed to make his thoughts known to the prince.

"You must let me act for you, my liege. Just as I saved your spirit that day, so will I act to save your soul."

Llywelyn contemplated Hyw for a moment before he spoke. *Some would call the Prince of Wales the soul of the country. Verily, may you save all Wales, master Hyw.*

Hyw nodded, crossing himself. "And my own soul as well."

Hyw had been raised Catholic and had taken the Church for granted. He understood the Latin, but he had never really stopped to think deeply about what the priests said. He hesitated now, unsure if he could remember the words properly, and heard Llywelyn's voice again, first in Latin, and then in Welsh. *For what does it benefit a man, if he gain the whole world, and loseth his soul*?

Hyw turned to Gawain. He noticed his uncle frowning still.

"Uncle, with your help the prince and I will make peace between us until Nos Galan Gaeaf. But what will happen then?"

"We will lay the prince's soul to rest, God willing," Gawain said, keeping his eyes averted.

"Will it be difficult?"

Gawain glanced at him. "If God is with us, we will prevail."

Then God be with us. Llywelyn bowed his head a moment, and when he raised it to look at Hyw, his eyes were determined. *Until then, let us work for peace.*

Chapter Ten: Cat

When they heard the clamour at the gates, Cat was kneeling in front of her trunk, choosing what to take. She dropped her things and fled to her mam's chamber.

"Quickly," Adara said, and they ran to the main hall where they found Enid. She had just finished feeding Baby Gwen and wrapped her soundly for sleep. Aeneus rushed into the hall, followed by a group of warriors.

"Lady, we are sore pressed at the gates," Aeneus said. "We must make you safe."

Adara hesitated a moment, and then gestured for them to follow her toward the kitchens. Cat was no stranger to war, or to secret escapes from Garth Celyn. She took Enid's arm, careful not to jostle Baby Gwen, and their small group made their way to the centre of the longhouse.

Opening the trap doors to the cellar, Aeneus helped Cat drop down into it. She lifted the wooden ladder into place for the others. Adara held Gwen as Enid stepped down it, and then handed the baby down to them before she descended. Three of their warriors came after, making little sound. Before Aeneus dropped through the trap door, he clasped the final warrior's arm in salute. Aeneus descended and nodded grimly up at him. The warrior's face showed no emotion as he dropped the trap door into place. They heard a scraping overhead, and then light footfalls as he ran from the room. Cat realized he would rejoin the other men at the gate, holding the *Saeson* off as long as he could to cover their escape.

Baby Gwen stirred with a small cry, but Enid placed her little finger in the baby's mouth to suckle, soothing her. Aeneus replaced the ladder on the ground as an extra precaution. Adara and Cat each lit a candle from a package stored against the cellar wall.

Adara pressed her hand on the wall, and a section of rock scraped aside to reveal a dark opening. Cat knew the release could not be found easily. It had confounded would-be attackers in years past, and she was not sure she could locate it again.

Adara nodded to her and Cat led their way into the darkness, with Enid and the baby close behind. She paused for a moment as Adara pressed another hidden catch on the dark side of the opening, and the rock swung to behind them, scraping a little louder than the table along the floor earlier.

With the candles, they lit one of the rushes waiting in readiness and moved noiselessly along the dim passage. There was a familiarity to their movement - almost a ritual, a disappearing act they had mastered through long years of strife with English siege-masters. Their leather walking shoes barely rustled the pebbles on the worn stone floor.

The long dark tunnel seemed to stretch ahead of them forever. Cat's mind raced. How many times as a child had she fled in the night, to hide with her mam at dawn? This time, there was no prince to rescue them, and her brother was injured. Would he live? And what of Da—where was he?

In one section the walls had crumbled to rubble, creating a small opening barely large enough for some of the men to go through. Cat was the only one who would not have to go on hands and knees. Enid placed her triangular nursing shawl across Cat's shoulders, tucking both ends around Baby Gwen in the traditional style. Cat bent as low as she could, with Gwen cradled snugly to her chest in the shawl, and felt her way forward with her toes to keep her balance. Finally the tunnel opened wider again. Enid took Gwen, who sighed and turned a little in her swaddling. Cat had barely felt the baby's weight, in spite of the awkward position.

When they came to the threshold, Adara touched Cat's shoulder and the group halted behind them. Cat knew this passage ended at the top of the hill outside the castle walls. Always before Hyw had checked to be sure the English soldiers had not discovered it, using his gift to protect them. Cat's heart thumped in her chest as she realized her mam wished her to take Hyw's place this time.

But my gift is not the same.

Cat reached up to pull at a length of leather twine hanging near the top of the low wall. Her hands pushed up against twigs and brambles. A smattering of old sealing wax flaked into her face as the curtain of thatch covering the entrance gave way. She marvelled again at her mam's ingenuity in hiding the tunnel entrance from prying eyes. Cat pushed the thatch aside, to be replaced later. Cat snuffed her candle as she stepped through, stopping just outside the opening beneath an overhang of shale.

Late afternoon had turned to night while they made their escape. A sudden fork of lightning split the sky, and she crouched, drawing her cloak around her. All she could hear was her own hushed breathing and the light patter of raindrops. She looked down, and saw the reflection of the half-moon in a shallow puddle of water at her feet—

—and found herself in a thicket of trees. In front of her, she saw a small mound, and realized it was a man sleeping on the ground. She looked around her, and saw a group of sleeping English soldiers, with their horses tethered near. One man sat awake, his back against a tree, keeping watch.

They must be scouts, she thought, or perhaps a small group sent to capture the women.

She spotted Aeneus crouched in the underbrush, leading their small party through the forest and along the Aber River, straight toward the group of men. The soldier on watch spotted them as well. He stood, waking one of the others with his boot and motioning toward their small party. The group of sleeping soldiers was suddenly awake. The first soldier drew a knife from his belt with a grim smile. Cat tried to cry out a warning—

—and she was back at the mouth of the tunnel.

It was another vision, she realized, but not about Hyw this time. Armed *Saeson* soldiers set to prevent their escape. Surely they had to take another road. She frowned. Something else from her vision played at the edges of her mind: the soldiers had horses. Horses could hasten their journey and help them get Baby Gwen to the safety of Criccieth.

Was this vision sent to her for a reason? Was it to give her knowledge of their fate, or could she influence the outcome? As the others hovered near the tunnel entrance, she gestured to her mam. Quickly she whispered what she had seen. Adara's eyes opened wide in alarm.

"We must not take the path," she began.

"But we have no time," Cat said, and quickly explained about the horses. "These visions, Mam, are they a certain fate? Or can they be changed?"

Her mam's brows knit together and Cat knew she was trying to recall what her grandfather had said, and what she knew from her own childhood. "Mayhap we must find out." Then she nodded to Cat and took Aeneus's arm to draw him into their circle.

"When Cat first stood here, she spotted a band of men ahead on the path," Adara whispered to him. "They have horses tethered, and only one guard watching. What think you?"

He looked at Cat strangely, and then his eyes became thoughtful, roaming past her toward the dark mountain path ahead of them. "How many men —and how close?" he asked, his voice lower than a whisper. "Can you point to where you saw them?"

Cat tried to recall her vision as clearly as possible. "There were eight, I think. I cannot be certain now," she admitted.

"How is it that you came to see this?"

"I—" Cat faltered, unable to explain.

"The moon revealed it to her," Adara told him, and they exchanged glances. Aeneus nodded grimly, and Adara continued, "Let Cat lead us, and she will know the place."

"Fear not, Lady," he said. "I will see to the rest."

Cat nodded and willed herself not to think about the implications of what she was about to do.

"This way, Mam," she whispered, and the others followed her, bending low to hide their passage as best they could. When they neared the spot she had seen, she turned back and caught Aeneus's eye.

He took out his knife, placed it between his teeth, and without a word gestured to two of the men to follow him. He waved the other, a younger warrior Cat knew as Ifan, back toward the women.

Cat, Enid, and Adara sank to the ground to catch their breath. Baby Gwen stirred again, and Enid spread her cloak over the baby to feed her. Cat knew without needing her gift again that they would reach Criccieth the next day, on the backs of English horses.

Chapter Eleven: Hyw

The ringing of the bells woke Hyw the next morning. Bells marked the daily routine of prayers in the Abbey: *vigils* in the early hours and *lauds* at daybreak. After each, he was soothed back to dreaming by the faint voices of the monks chanting prayers in the nearby chapel. Gawain came to Hyw's room shortly after *terce*, the third prayer of the morning.

"We buried the fallen on the hill," Gawain told him, "but rest easy, Hyw, for your da was not among them."

"Is there no word from him?"

"Nay, but take hope," Gawain put his hand on Hyw's arm. "A villager brought in a wagon of supplies to trade. He told us he saw wounded warriors in the forest on the other side of the River Wye."

Hyw's next thoughts were for the horses, Vox and Cadarn, but Gawain shook his head. Hyw felt some relief that his da's body hadn't been found on the hillside, but he worried for Bran's safety, and for the fate of his sister and mother at Garth Celyn. "What news of home?" he asked.

Gawain had heard nothing, but tried to reassure him by reporting news from the handful of villagers who had taken refuge inside the monastery. Before long, Gawain bade him rise. "We must begin," he said, placing two fingers on the centre of Hyw's forehead. "Close your eyes, and call yourself to the cave where we saw the prince."

Hyw's initial attempts failed. The cave he imagined was a pale image, lacking the depth it had during his meeting with Llywelyn. Gawain showed him how to slow his breathing and focus his mind. After one more try, he was able to feel the cave around him and see the prince again.

They fell into routine quickly, helped by the disciplined life of the monastery. Gawain often reminded them Hyw could not leave this room until he and Llywelyn found a way to co-exist. The first day was difficult. At first, Hyw would move about the room as he moved about in the cave in his mind. He bruised his knees on the bed, and once even banged his body into the wall.

By the second afternoon, Hyw had nearly mastered the trance-like state and could call the cave into his mind's eye as soon as he closed his eyes. Gawain worked with Hyw until the bells rang *sext* at noon, then return until *none* at mid-afternoon, and again until *vespers* at sunset. Hyw rested in his room then, echoing what he could hear of the brothers' prayers. Gawain seemed to have more energy when he returned from the chapel.

"It's the prayers, Hyw. Each hour has its own colour and feeling. Singing the hours with my brothers, even in this time of trouble, restores my strength."

Gawain had also been released from manual labour to work in the infirmary while Hyw was there. The Cistercians, a new order, were devoted to working the land, and Hyw soon realized Gawain missed this part of his daily routine. Yet his uncle did not complain, and Hyw took that as his example.

He also had Llywelyn to consider. After their sessions, the prince was often angry. Hyw thought he had seemed aloof or preoccupied before, and now he seemed to resent his dependence. There was something else as well. Llywelyn had bound himself to Elinor when she was young, although they had never met. The prince had lived a life of strict discipline, especially after the English king had captured Elinor and held her in house arrest for three years before finally allowing them to marry. Llywelyn was almost fifty years old then, and she was twenty-six. She was the first person he had allowed himself to trust. Now that she was dead, Hyw could sense a deep loneliness in him.

Hyw said nothing, mindful of his family's obligation, and tried to be patient. He was surprised the prince did not expect him to bow or humble himself.

A warrior is expected to fight and die for Cymru and should be treated with deference by all, said Llywelyn, *and with gratitude by his liege. You are a warrior's son, and I am asking more of you than ever I have of your father.*

Hyw worked to separate his thoughts and actions in the trance-world he shared with Llywelyn from the real world of his physical body. The more he concentrated, the more his mind's landscape seemed to come into focus. When they moved in the cave, his body remained still. Gawain reported that Hyw's lips no longer moved in the physical world when he spoke to Llywelyn in his mind.

At that point, Llywelyn began training him. The prince trained every day, his weapon appearing in his hand as it might in a dream: a sword one day, a bow and quiver of arrows the next. Hyw stood alongside him, matching his movements and trying to learn what Llywelyn knew of fighting. When they took a break for a drink, they needed to wipe the sweat from their eyes and faces. Yet in the physical world, Hyw's face was barely flushed.

"How can this be?" Hyw asked Gawain.

"It must be as the legends describe: the OtherWorld seems as real as our physical life, but exists inside our minds." Gawain shook his head. "I believe few could call up that plane in the way you are doing, Hyw."

Hyw marvelled that he could be one of those few. He wondered how much of it he would recall when he was able to train in the yard again.

Llywelyn would often ask Hyw questions about his life. Hyw told him about fostering in Shrewsbury, about the horses he tended, and about the way he first learned of his gift. He even told the prince about his friendship with James, Shrewsbury's son and heir.

Hyw longed to ask the prince about himself, especially whether the whispers of Shrewsbury's court were true: had he really hugged his cousin with one hand and driven a knife into his body with the other? And how could he imprison his own eldest brother? Yet Hyw dared not ask. Llywelyn offered nothing; only advice on how to place his feet, or how hard to pull the bowstring.

Chapter Twelve: Cat

Criccieth Castle rose white and majestic against the morning sky. One of the men pointed out its twin towers on top of the rocky headland.

"No worries, Lady Cat," Aeneus told her. "The wee princess will be safe inside those stone walls."

The path to the gate wound around the mountainside. They dismounted. Ifan and another warrior had been leading the remaining horses to prevent them from returning to the English. The two now took the leads of all their mounts, to leave Aeneus and the others free to defend them. Cat offered to take Ifan's horses, but he shook his head.

"The way is treacherous for the horses, lady," Ifan said. "Best that I lead them."

Two Welsh guards appeared, dressed in armour. Aeneus called out the opening of a Welsh bardic poem. They spoke for a moment, until one clasped forearms with Aeneus in a warrior's greeting. Then the guards stepped back and waved them on.

Enid tucked Baby Gwen into her cradleboard and let one of the warriors sling it onto his back for the walk along the rocky path to the gatehouse. Cat made the climb nimbly enough, helping Enid and Adara as they needed.

When they gained entry into the courtyard, they were taken to Princess Elizabeth, wife of Dafydd, who had rightfully claimed the title Prince of Wales after Llywelyn's death. The new princess received them in her private solar, still in her dressing gown. She embraced each of the women, including Enid and Baby Gwen.

"You have done well to come," she said. "Dafydd left for Dolwyddelan yesterday. You might have passed him on the road?"

"Nay, we passed no one," Adara shook her head. "Has there been any news of my husband Bran, your highness?"

Elizabeth frowned and turned slightly away, rocking the baby. "How strange it is to think of myself as Princess of Wales now. Please, among ourselves, please continue to call me by my name."

Adara took a step toward her. "If I may be so bold, Elizabeth, to put my heart at rest. Will you tell me what you have heard?"

Elizabeth spoke quietly. "Our messenger said—Adara, I am truly sorry. He said all perished with Llywelyn."

Adara went white, and turned her eyes to Cat. Cat moved to support her. For the first time, Cat noticed how frail and thin her mam had become in the past few weeks; or perhaps it was that she herself had grown.

"I am most sorry, Adara," Elizabeth said. "You are weak from your journey." She called to her servant. "Make room for Cat with the girls. Lady Adara and the baby will stay here in my rooms. The men will be welcome in the guardhouse." Turning back to Cat and Adara, she added, "I will have food and drink brought to you. Come, Enid, let us see to Baby Gwen."

Elizabeth herded her servant from the room, along with Enid and the baby. For a moment, Cat and her mam found themselves alone.

Adara sat on a stuffed chair in front of the fireplace, and gestured to Cat to come closer.

"He is not dead. I would know. Or you would, surely. Cat, tell me again what you saw."

Cat recounted her vision again, but she had seen nothing of Bran or his fate. Finally she stroked her mam's hand, curling up beside her on the arm of the chair as they comforted each other.

Chapter Thirteen: Hyw

Gawain worked every day to help Hyw and Llywelyn develop the ability to communicate in a way no one could detect, a way that would not change Hyw's appearance or actions in physical reality. Gawain also cautioned Hyw against bonding with the minds of birds or animals while he held Llywelyn's spirit.

"You may be able to put yourself between the prince and the beasts in time, but for now focus on maintaining the space between you. Let your skills grow as they must."

During one training session, Hyw opened his eyes to find Gawain asleep on the small bed in spite of the bright sunlight streaming in the window. Hyw hadn't realized how exhausting the work must be for his uncle. He resolved to let Gawain sleep, and worked on his own with Llywelyn for the rest of the day.

When Gawain woke again, it was late afternoon. Gawain looked guilty, but Hyw explained what he had been doing. He couldn't help but smile when his uncle clapped him on the shoulder.

Gradually, Hyw moved more easily in the physical world while keeping his mind open to the prince. Hyw could always sense Llywelyn and hear his voice, but unless he closed his eyes he was unable to see the prince.

He also discovered they were not restricted to the cave beneath the mountains. In the trance, he "took" them to an open field like the one outside Garth Celyn, and once into a wooded meadow. Llywelyn could also suggest new landscapes for their training, as long as the areas were familiar to Hyw. The prince had only to think of a place, and Hyw could see it in his mind and create it almost as if he was transporting them there.

Once, when Hyw closed his eyes, he found himself on a flat field of green and red squares. It was familiar, but not a natural field. He saw what looked like stone statues surrounding the prince, some upright and others on the ground, broken in pieces.

Hyw blinked: it was the chess set brought back by Llywelyn's grandfather from the Holy Crusades. Llywelyn had kept it in the study where he met with his councilors and nobles. Hyw had often served his father in that study when he was younger, and again since he'd come home. The pieces were carved in stone, each forming a different human figure that might live in a castle. His father had explained the figures and their placement to him, and had begun playing the game with him in the evenings.

Now he and Llywelyn were the size of pieces on the board. Hyw turned to the prince. "This is how you see the world?"

Llywelyn stood with his arms folded across his chest, and nodded. Hyw knew showing him this board was a gesture of trust, and one not given easily. He stared at the figures carefully. Llywelyn stood in the king's position. Hyw remembered his father talk of a secret move called castling that could only be done if the king-piece had not moved.

Then another piece caught his eye. It had fallen away from the prince and broken into two pieces. Hyw felt himself connect with Llywelyn's memories, as if the prince had opened a door for him, and he recognized the grizzled face: it was Simon de Montfort, Elinor's father and Llywelyn's best friend. Hyw could even hear the knight's laugh booming off the walls at Garth Celyn. De Montfort had died a decade earlier at Edward's hand, before Edward became king of England.

Like you, I fostered with the English, Hyw, and came to appreciate their ways. De Montfort was more a brother to me than any of my own.

Hyw looked up, and saw an empty space behind and to Llywelyn's left. It almost seemed to glow. He sensed that this area held great importance for Llywelyn, and knew it was the Queen's position. Elinor had been Llywelyn's wife for three short years, yet she had changed the game entirely for him. He could not present her fallen or broken, as he had her father. So the space was empty but luminous.

Llywelyn was dressed in black. The stone figures near him shone ebony against the colourful landscape of the chessboard. That meant the prince was not the first to move, but rather the defender of the board. It was easy to guess that the board was Wales.

Few pieces remained around Llywelyn. The castles still stood in their spots at either end of the board: Garth Celyn, and a large, imposing stone castle.

Castell-y-Bere, Llywelyn said.

One piece in the robes of the councilor or bishop had moved into a protective position a little ahead of Llywelyn. The piece seemed to change shape in front of Hyw's eyes. Once it looked like Gawain, his uncle; then it changed to a likeness of Bran; and once he glimpsed his mother's face as well. He realized the piece represented his family, and felt a flush of pride that Llywelyn saw them in this way.

Slowly, Hyw swiveled to face the enemy. As expected, the white king stared back at him with the face of Edward, King of England. Beside him a white knight was poised in his advance, sword raised: the grinning face of Edmund Mortimer.

Hyw was shocked to see other familiar faces in the white army: the face of Dafydd, Llywelyn's brother, crouching as a pawn in front. Several Welsh courtiers crouched with him, identifiable by their coloured emblems and coats of arms.

Their in-fighting serves the English king. Llywelyn's voice held more sorrow than anger.

"It seems they do not know a pawn cannot be crowned king," Hyw quipped, and heard what might have been a snort of laughter behind him. Hyw realized there were no black pawns on the board; in fact, no other black pieces at all.

Now you see the game for what it is. What part will you play, Hyw?

He turned back to Llywelyn. "I will not be a pawn. Even for you, my lord."

The prince studied him and nodded slightly. He unfolded his hands and gestured at the board. *Choose your piece.*

Hyw looked around him again. Then he crouched beside the fallen de Montfort, and took the hilt of the knight's sword. With a *zing* he pulled it from the stone and held it high. Instantly he found himself dressed in black like his prince, and under his legs was Aeron, his father's warhorse. Hyw raised his sword, as Aeron rose with hoofs drawn, and found himself and the horse frozen in attack formation. Behind him, he heard the welcome sound of Llywelyn's gruff laugh.

"Have at us," Hyw yelled.

Chapter Fourteen: Cat

Two of Elizabeth's three children were with them at Criccieth. Gwladys was a cheerful toddler and Cat enjoyed playing games with her. Owain was a serious boy of about seven, but Cat soon discovered he knew a wealth of information about this part of Wales. He told Cat his older brother Llyw had joined the garrison at Castell-Y-Bere.

A group of six girls in varying ages and sizes shared the nursery with them. Adara quietly explained that these were Dafydd's children by other mothers, and Elizabeth showed great charity in taking them in to protect them during the past few months. Cat noted that Elizabeth was not unkind to the girls, but she did not pay them the same attention as Owain and Gwladys. Owain called them all sisters.

The day after their arrival, Cat rose early while the other girls still slept. She crept downstairs and met Owain with a few of the other boys. He should have sat at the "high table," set crosswise to the rest for Elizabeth and her family in the English style they preferred. It had seemed strange to Cat after the more relaxed dining in family units at Garth Celyn. Today she was glad to see Owain sat with his friends instead.

"How fare you?" he asked as he grabbed more flatbread and cheeses.

"Well enough," she answered, "but I look forward to working out the kinks this morning."

He raised his eyebrows as if he wasn't sure what she meant, so she continued, "I will join you for the early exercises today."

"But you are a girl," he said.

"Yes, of course," she said. He laughed then, as did the other boys, and she looked at him quizzically. Aeneus had always included the girls in the exercises and defence training at Garth Celyn. "Surely your sisters will join us?" At that the boys began to laugh in earnest.

Before Cat could take them to task, Aeneus walked through the doors. He had already been in the yard, tending his horse and preparing for the morning's training sessions. He smiled at Cat, and turned to the others.

"Share the joke?" he said to them.

"They seem to be laughing at me," Cat told him.

"She thinks she will be training with us today," Owain said.

"Aye, so she will," Aeneus said. "You boys should always be ready to protect your families, and any woman who comes within your company. But we must also help our women prepare for anything they may face in the days ahead. May it help them against the heathen English," he added with a grim look that sobered the boys.

Cat filed out to the yard behind Aeneus and the other boys, but Owain disappeared. As Aeneus began a series of daily exercises to improve their agility and toughen the muscles of feet and legs, she saw Owain return with his two older sisters. They grinned at her as they joined in the drill, and she smiled shyly at them. That night they joked with each other, flexing their sore muscles as they climbed into their shared bed.

"Sleep here," said Margred, indicating a spot between herself and her sister. She was the eldest of the two, and close to Cat's age. "That way when Rhiannon pulls the covers, you'll still be warm."

The other girls settled quickly, but Cat had a restless night in spite of the down-filled quilt. When she closed her eyes, she dreamed of people running and screaming through the halls. Were these prophetic dreams? She wanted to ask her mam, but Adara was impatient for anything but news of Hyw and Bran. Of them, Cat had seen nothing more.

What good was this gift if she could not control it?

Aeneus left the next day to search for Bran and Hyw as he had promised. Criccieth's man would not let them join in weapons training, as Aeneus had, so they spent their afternoons inside with Elizabeth, Adara, and the other women.

One afternoon while Cat played with Gwladys and Princess Elizabeth tended Baby Gwen, another messenger came. He told of troops that took every Welshman prisoner on the road. With a glance toward the children, he whispered something in Princess Elizabeth's ear that made her face go white. Cat felt fear for her da and brother then, and for Aeneus in his search for them.

Chapter Fifteen: Hyw

By Christmas Day, Gawain pronounced Hyw fit to make an appearance for the Feast of Saint Stephen the following evening. The abbot had taken in many people displaced by the fighting, and this feast honoured the saint known for his service to the poor. Llywelyn was pleased by the chance to see his people and discover how they fared. Gawain thought it would be a good test for their alliance, since many people would attend and they could pass unnoticed in the crowd. Still, he hesitated.

"My lord, you will hear of our continued defeat at the hands of the English," he warned. "You must be careful to give nothing away."

The monastery was full of people as Hyw descended the stairs from the infirmary to the common eating area. He felt Llywelyn's anguish at the austerity of the room. Cat had written to him the previous year of the festivities at Garth Celyn. The newly pregnant Princess Elinor had decorated the halls and corners of the longhouse with traditional holly and ivy, along with bits of ribbon and bells, until the whole world seemed alive with the promise of the Christ child. Hyw was glad to concentrate on the stairs so he could not close his eyes to see the prince's face.

Supper was quiet and spare: roots, flatbread, and mutton stew with few spices, as befits the frugal Cistercian table. As Hyw ate, he looked more closely at the people around him. They were speckled with mud and their clothes were in tatters. Some had old blankets wrapped about their heads and bodies, and most were barefoot. He felt the prince's grief turn to anger. *Let me up, boy.*

Hyw stood and walked back to the stairs. He moved up a few steps to be visible to the crowd of peasants below. When he opened his mouth, Llywelyn's voice came from it.

> Open your ears to my words, and
> lift your head from your arms.
> Let the old poet lend me his voice.

It was an old song of the brave 300 who stood together against an army they could not hope to defeat, to protect their people. At the end of each verse, the poet named a fallen warrior, so they would not be forgotten over time. Hyw had heard the song enough to have memorized the words, but Llywelyn changed it just enough to praise each of the warriors who had fallen with him at Builth. He created a new verse for Bran and the others whose bodies had not been found, bringing hope to his listeners.

Hyw fingered the cord Cat had tied around his wrist and thought of his sister, and Christmases when they were children. He was surprised to hear his own voice harmonizing:

> Let the mountains hide their voices,
> Let forest and fountain keep them safe.
> For Cymru, let them bring us peace.

"The boy," someone whispered in the crowd. "Look to the boy."

Hyw did not know if they heard their prince's voice in harmony, or perhaps saw the prince's shape mix with his in the way he had seen figures shifting on the chessboard. But one by one other voices joined with his. Soon the cold stones of the Cistercian monastery rang with their voices.

Chapter Sixteen: Cat

Cat was still burdened by bad dreams, and threw herself into the festive preparations to take her mind off her fears. Princess Elizabeth was determined to give the children all the Christmas cheer that could be had, with their father and elder brother away. Cat decided to make something to cheer her mam. Elizabeth allowed her to look through her stock of woolens and fabrics, and Cat settled on making a scarf of bright Italian red. She embroidered a small tree in one end, with initials for each of them fanning out from the trunk like branches: Adara, Bran, Cat, and Hyw. It took several tries to finish, since her stitches were as loose and poorly formed as ever. She sighed and wrapped it in ribbons, hoping Mam would find it useful as well as comforting.

At the Feast of St. Stephen's, they sat at the high table with Elizabeth and her children. Cat reached forward to take some roast duckling from the platter, and as she placed it on her bowl of hard-crusted bread she glanced at her cup of light wine. The liquid seemed to be swirling—

—and she found herself at another table, in a room much more Spartan than Princess Elizabeth's domain. She looked up at the sound of a familiar voice, and on the stairs she saw Prince Llywelyn.

"For Cymru, let them bring us peace!" he sang. And then his face and voice seemed to melt into the face and voice of her brother Hyw as he sang the line again. Then Hyw seemed to look right at her and smile. She did not see his lips move, but she heard him as if he whispered in her ear.

"I live, Cat, and the prince lives within me." She turned toward him—

—and dropped her knife onto the table with a clatter.

Her mam turned to her, and Cat smiled and took her hands. She could hardly wait to finish so she could take her mam to a quiet corner and tell her the vision. Now she had a proper gift to give her this Christmas!

Chapter Seventeen: Hyw

Shortly after Christmas, the abbot again broke into his stores for the Feast of the Holy Innocents. That night a band of weathered soldiers banged on the abbey door, and demanded tribute to feed Edward's army.

Hyw was in the hall with the others when the soldiers clanged in and sat, expecting service from the hardworking Cistercians. In the spirit of the season, the abbot had welcomed them at the door. His concern showed on his face as he re-entered with them, and Hyw wondered if the English soldiers returned a full measure of seasonal goodwill. Hyw wondered if he should try to fight, so as not to shame his lord. Then he felt or heard Llywelyn's voice, as if whispering in his ear. *Live to fight another day, lad. Yet tarry, that I may listen to their prattle.*

Gawain gestured toward their rooms, but Hyw shook his head and remained seated with the others. Gawain and another monk brought in the trenchers and served the soldiers.

"Ugh," complained one soldier, who looked to be the captain of the rest, as he sopped up the stew with flatbread. "Sodden tasteless mess. I thought you Welsh crusading went. Brought you nothing back to spice this gruel?"

The abbot shrugged. "We are but simple brothers here."

"Simple indeed," another soldier guffawed. "Simpletons."

"Leave them be," another said. At the man's voice, Hyw could sense Llywelyn bristle. Hyw glanced over to recognize his champion on the hill. From his dress, the man appeared to be a minor English lord. Hyw remembered his name as Stephen de Francton. Hyw closed his eyes to find the prince in full war armour. Hyw placed himself in front of Llywelyn to hold him back.

"Why do you hate this man so?"

He it was who ran me through with his spear. Lucky chance for him, but not so lucky now.

"Yet it was not he who finished you," Hyw pointed out. He remembered the look of remorse on de Francton's face as Llywelyn knelt on the hillside. "He saved me on that day—and you with me."

Llywelyn shook with rage, but made no further move. Hyw opened his eyes again. De Francton was speaking with the abbot. The captain was still sloshing back the abbot's ale.

"Ah," the captain said, banging his cup down on the wooden table. He wiped his mouth on the back of his hand. De Francton cringed a little, but said nothing. "Well, good man, have you Welshmen here?"

The question caught the abbot by surprise. "We are all brothers here," he began.

"Aye, but have you Welsh brothers, Father?" The other soldiers guffawed with him at this poor joke. "For you know, do you not, that every Welshman's head will fetch a shilling at Rhuddlan?"

Hyw felt Llywelyn stiffen. *So the fool lets slip the whereabouts of his king. Let's see what else we may glean from his manly ignorance.*

Hyw understood, and slipped to the kitchens to bring more ale for the soldiers. The night wore on, and the men were fully in their cups before they uttered the words the prince had been waiting to hear.

"So we took the silver seal from that devil's own pocket, before we sent the body to his cousin's wife," a soldier offered. "It seems he will receive a Christian burial after all. What's left of him."

"Aye, and the seal awaits its companion at Rhuddlan," the captain added. "We hear the babe has one too, and as soon as Garth Celyn falls, we will have it."

Garth Celyn still stands! Hyw was impatient to hear more of his family home, but he dared not speak. Instead he poured more ale, and listened to what poured forth.

"Of what use is this silver to the king?" the abbot asked.

"Of no use, I would say." The captain laughed loudly, and burped. "Save never to give these Welsh devils an excuse to rise against their betters again. He will march against them within the fortnight."

The talk went on a little longer, before the captain's face fell snoring against his arm. His men left him half sitting at the table and bunked down on the floor by the fire. The abbot showed de Francton to a guest room.

We must learn more of their plans, Llywelyn said in Hyw's inner ear. *Make haste to Rhuddlan. Afterward, if we can get word to Dafydd, we may yet stop this war.*

Hyw continued cleaning tables until he heard the other soldiers snoring too, then made his way to Gawain. "I must go to Rhuddlan."

"I heard them," his uncle whispered back. "We can leave at dawn."

"Nay, Uncle." Hyw laid a hand on his arm. "Not with a shilling on every Welshman's head. I must go. They will not notice me."

"Hyw, I cannot – "

Llywelyn again whispered to Hyw, and the boy reached out to touch his uncle's arm, concentrating. "*Then consider it an order from your liege*," said a low, deep voice from somewhere inside him. It felt odd to have Llywelyn speak through him in that way, although he had allowed it. He added in his own voice, "It will be fine, you will see. Even Edward cannot countenance killing children. And we—the prince and I—have a plan."

"What will you do?"

"Nay, 'tis best you not know, Uncle. Take my thanks, and I will take your love to my mother when I see her next."

"Tell her she has but to send word, and I will take her and the babes to the Sisters of Light for sanctuary."

With that Hyw continued clearing food to the kitchen. In the process he gathered bread and cheese in a brown cloth wrapper that would travel in his tunic.

Before he left the abbey, Gawain handed him a cloak. It was frayed but warm, with thick, serviceable lining. "I am due another soon." Hyw thanked him, wondering how long that would take, given the scarce supplies of the monastery. He drew the cloak around his shoulders. They hugged and moved separately toward the doors: Hyw to the kitchen, and Gawain to his plain monk's cell.

Dawn found Hyw slipping through the hedges to the old Roman roads that led to Rhuddlan Castle, as his mind wandered beyond it to Garth Celyn.

Chapter Eighteen: Cat

On the first day of the new year, as they sat working together in Princess Elizabeth's solar, Cat heard her mam begin humming a familiar tune under her breath. Cat looked up from her attempts at embroidery. It was Y Calan, the traditional song of New Year's celebrations. Cat and her family—and the entire court of Prince Llywelyn—had been celebrating the Christmas feasts with Princess Elinor and her French ladies for the last four years. But she knew the traditional Welsh holidays were still being celebrated in the countryside. Her mam shot her a rare grin and touched the scarf around her neck, before she changed the tune and began to hum a more traditional hymn. Cat ducked her head, pleased and embarrassed that her mam had chosen to wear her present.

At dusk, Cat heard the song echoing again at the castle gate, in a chorus of men's voices loud enough to reach them inside the castle.

> We beg your permission,
> We beg your permission,
> We beg your permission,

To sing…

The sonorous three-part harmony gave Cat a thrill of recognition and a sense of safety, as if their rituals and traditions would continue no matter what threats the Welsh faced. She couldn't help running for the castle door, along with Owain, his older sisters, and the servants. Adara stood to follow, but Cat noticed Elizabeth sniff and take up her embroidery again.

"Will you not come to see the *Mari Lwyd*?" Adara asked, using the Welsh term for the Grey Mare.

"Nay, not I," said Elizabeth. "But it's important to the servants."

"And the children, apparently," said Adara. "I will go and make sure they stay out of trouble."

Adara smiled and touched Cat's shoulder as they went through the doors. Perhaps Elizabeth's English background made her reluctant to take part in the more bawdy Welsh traditions, Cat thought. But at least the princess wouldn't stop the mare, or the luck she would bring the castle once she was allowed inside. The other children ran for the gates as the singers began the third verse, and Cat couldn't contain herself any longer.

She got to the gate just in time to hear the last of the ribald insults that accompanied this ritual.

"What's that? Didst thou say thou art a pathetic, pigeon-livered, pribbling pignut?" called a lusty voice from behind the gate. "A mewling, milk-livered, maggot-born miscreant?" A chorus of neighing followed his words. "What's that, my lady? Ah, the mare says she would not have credited thee to speak such truths!"

She saw the castle bard draw himself up and turn red in the face, barely able to control his rage. The man's ample girth and jiggling belly made Cat worry if his rage would do him more harm than it could ever do the mare and her merry men. Up to that point, she had heard him recite the family's genealogy and a few children's rhymes in the nursery. She leaned forward intently to hear how he would fare in their verbal sparring.

"Woudst thou try to match wits with me, thou bear-biting, beef-witted churl," the bard began, but the booming voice from the mare's entourage cut him off.

"Nay, not beef, but mare, thou clod-brained cockerel. If brains were beef, thou wouldst not have enough to feed the porcine strumpet who shares thy bed."

The bard balled his fists and hoisted himself toward the gate.

"Grab him!" called the captain of Criccieth's guards. Two warriors took the bard by both arms, dragging him back toward the castle courtyard. "Give him another flagon of ale for his trouble," the captain called. Musicians launched into another traditional tune, and singers on both sides joined their voices in the traditional welcome songs.

The final notes turned from a hoot to a laugh as Criccieth's warriors opened the gate wider for the Grey Mare and her entourage. One of the players led the mare by a long halter, and the pipers piled through the gates behind them.

Although Cat knew what to expect, she gasped at the sight. The "mare" was over seven feet tall. Its bone-white skeleton head and long neck led to a white cloth body. Like a macabre legend, it walked on a man's legs. Harness bells jangled as the head shook its mane of bright-coloured, fluttering ribbons. Its long snout clacked at the children as it came through the gate. Owain screamed along with his sisters. Cat ran around the mare with the children and singers, their laughter ringing the stones.

The musicians played and danced once around the courtyard and into the castle hall where servants rolled out barrels of ale. Criccieth's warriors mingled with the four Garth Celyn warriors as well as Dafydd and Elizabeth's guard. Other women and children—the warrior's families, Cat guessed—streamed in behind the players as if called by the procession. One of their warriors tried to offer Cat a flagon of ale, but Adara frowned and bade her drink the less potent wine-and-water mix instead.

The Grey Mare cavorted around the ladies until one consented to dance a few steps. Cat laughed as the bells strung through its ribbon mane jangled in time with the music to bless them all with luck and good cheer.

"Who is it?" whispered the girls, trying to guess the mare's true identity beneath the bone mask. "Who can it be?"

"Why, it's Drem, isn't it?" Margred breathed to Cat, pointing to the soft leather shoes on the mare's feet. "He's the butcher's son from town. Already he runs his father's business, they say." Although that meant little to Cat, her new friend's excited eyes told her Margred thought very well of Drem.

A niggling doubt made Cat uneasy. She knew Margred was likely betrothed to another lord's son to form an alliance for her father, Dafydd. Cat thought briefly of Rhys, the boy her da had arranged for her to marry. She had met Rhys several times while she traveled with Princess Elinor and the Welsh court, and thought herself lucky in the match. But being betrothed didn't need to stop them from enjoying themselves on New Year's eve, did it? They weren't doing anything improper.

"She's been eating mistletoe," called the woman leading the mare, and the warriors whistled. Cat saw sprigs of mistletoe sticking out of the skeleton mouth. The "mare" held out its bony muzzle for a kiss, and the older girls screamed and ran away. The mare lowered its head and shook its mane in mock despair. It tried to lay its skeleton head on Cat's shoulder until Margred coaxed it away to dance. When it turned to dance with another girl, Margred grabbed a flagon of ale from a passing servant.

Finally the mare removed its bony head for a moment to reveal the man beneath. Margred held up the flagon, and Cat knew it must be Drem. He grinned at Margred as he took the flagon and tipped it back for a long drink.

The battle of wits that had begun outside the gate continued with riddles and stories as the celebration got underway.

"Can you say the days of the week?" sang one of the players to the children. As one of the girls began to recite them, he shook his finger at her. "Can you say the days of the week—but without naming them?"

The children stared at him and at each other, perplexed. Then the player turned to the adults and asked again, "Can anyone say the days of the week without naming them?"

The cook grinned. "That's a very good riddle, very good indeed. But I have guessed your riddle, if you please." The musicians stopped and the player turned toward her expectantly. The cook continued, "Why, it's the day before yesterday, yesterday, today, tomorrow, and the day after that, isn't it?"

The player bowed to her, and the crowd clapped.

"Your turn, Cookie," called out a woman's voice from the crowd.

"Oh, aye, verra well for you, isn't it? Let me think. Ah! I have in my kitchen a pot the whole sea cannot fill. Can you guess what it is?"

"Your stew pot when you make our supper, I hope," laughed a warrior.

"Nay, 'tis not, as you well know. Guess again. I have a pot the whole sea cannot fill. What is it?" She turned to the musicians and players, since it was their turn first. If they could not guess, the crowd would have a chance.

After a few unsuccessful tries, one of the musicians called out. "That's a very good riddle, very good indeed. But I have guessed your riddle, if you please. It's a sieve, is it not?"

The cook clapped her hands and the musician took his turn. So it went until one of the musicians struck up a bawdy song. Then both groups joined in the singing.

Suddenly the castle doors opened, and a guard entered, followed by another group of people.

"Father Maelgwyn," cried Adara. Their priest from Garth Celyn and a bedraggled group of women, children, and older men entered. Cat ran to the priest and gave him a hug, and hugged as many of the others as she could reach.

One of the castle warriors stepped forward and greeted them formally, welcoming them to the castle.

"Call the Princess Elizabeth," Adara said to a nearby servant, who dashed up the long stairs.

"Time to fetch a proper supper for them, isn't it," the cook said quietly, motioning to her kitchen boys and heading for the castle kitchens.

Chapter Nineteen: Hyw

Rain and the noises of the forest slowed Hyw's progress. He dared not use his gift to find out more this time, after Gawain's warning. Twice he followed sounds he thought were Welsh voices, hoping to find some sign of his da. None of the sounds led to camps or soldiers. The hairs crept up on his neck as he peered at the dark thickets, but he persevered along the path at the prince's urging.

This way. Follow this stream and it will lead you to Rhuddlan.

When Hyw closed his eyes he could see Llywelyn dressed in his fur traveling cloak, and without thinking drew Gawain's quilted one tighter around himself.

We must make haste.

Once his stores ran out, Hyw picked frozen roots and berries he knew to be edible, wrapping them in the cloth held next to his body to warm them. The stream was frozen, but he melted snow in a skin pouch the same way. A steady drizzle of cold wet snow wrapped him in mud and grime from the road. More than once he consoled himself by remembering he would soon be closer to Garth Celyn. He might at last reunite with his mother and sister.

At dawn on the fourth day of his journey, Hyw saw the spires of Rhuddlan. Sounds of clanking metal traveled across the still valley. He recognized the clank of swords against armour, reminding him the English occupied the castle. He circled around to the rear of the castle, where Llywelyn told him the doors to the kitchen were located. As he tried to dash through the back entryway, someone grabbed him by the scruff of the neck and lifted him up so his feet dangled off the ground.

"What do you think, Thomas? Worth a shilling?"

Hyw heard a short bark of laughter behind him as he dangled in the air.

"Nay, brother," said another voice. "Probably some village brat. You know the king won't pay for women and children."

"Just need to dip the heads in their own gore," came a third. "I hear they ain't looking too closely. These Welsh women with their short-cropped hair look like men anyways. Good for a tup and a shilling, eh? Boys the same."

"Oh please, sir." Hyw mimicked the accent of the boys he'd fostered with as best he could, and held up the roots remaining from his lunch. "Cook sent me for som'at to spice the stew. These Welsh devils never use anything, and the king is plenty sick of bland."

"Ah let him go. He'll be in the kitchens when we need him."

Hyw's legs hit the ground and he managed to scramble upright. One of the soldiers landed a kick on his behind that shoved him through the entranceway, and he ran without looking back.

He'd been worried what Llywelyn might think of his outburst, but he was reassured by the prince's laughter in his inner ear. *Quick thinking, boy. Now follow through and we might get out of this with our skins.*

Hyw slipped into the kitchen. He wiped the road dust from his face and hands with the traveling cloak. In case he needed it again, he folded it and stashed it in a corner by the door.

Two cook's helpers were already starting to prepare the evening meal while a third was setting up a tray of loaves and fish for the breakfast tables. Hyw knew the English cooks would have used peasant boys from the castle and villages, especially on feast days. Likely they hadn't looked too closely, and he could pass for a willing kitchen worker.

As he thought, the harried cook called out to him. "You, boy. Take this plate of eels to the high table."

Hyw picked up the dishes pointed out by the cook and followed the other helper into the great hall. Hyw glanced toward the centre of the high table and spotted a figure in purple silks that must be the English king. Edward lounged in his seat, fingers steepled in front of him, staring out over the tables of soldiers. Hyw closed his eyes and noted Llywelyn glaring in the king's direction. Hyw thought it was a good thing Llywelyn didn't have a sword in his hand, and opened his eyes again.

At the tables, people laughed and talked as they cut portions from the main dishes and set them on the thick bread trenchers that served as edible bowls. Hyw breathed a small prayer of relief that this meal was being served English-style with much ceremony, and several courses carried by many servants. He would never have escaped notice at Garth Celyn, with the simpler fare and more intimate groupings around a traditional Welsh meal.

Then he spotted a face that gladdened his heart: James, seated at a long table with a group of knights and squires. What luck! If he could get a sign to his friend, he might have an ally to help him discover the fate of Garth Celyn, and perhaps his father. Yet he knew he must tread carefully so as not to give himself away and startle James into revealing his identity.

Hyw stepped up onto the dais, and stopped near the end of the high table. He set the plate of eels between two lords wearing silk surcoats. He started when he heard one murmur thanks: it was Lord Shrewsbury himself.

Hyw ducked his head into his tunic, hoping his former lord would not recognize him in this setting. He knew lords and ladies rarely looked at servants, especially in another lord's home. Just as he hoped, Shrewsbury reached toward the plate without seeing him. The old knight had developed a lifelong habit of courtesy that had caused him to thank his host's servant, but he did not recognize that servant as his former ward.

Just then, James looked up toward the high table and his father. For a moment he merely chewed and watched. Then his mouth fell open and he stared right at Hyw. Hyw moved his hand to his lips in a shushing gesture. He had barely turned to leave the dais when someone thrust a bottle at him. "Boy, fetch my lord more wine. Be nimble."

The voice made Hyw's blood run cold. It was Robert, the boy who had beaten him on his last day at Shrewsbury's manor – and beaten James as well. As squire, Robert now stood behind Shrewsbury's chair.

Hyw bowed and backed away. Robert moved to help Shrewsbury get a choice morsel for his trencher. Hyw moved swiftly down the tables toward James again. Many times at Shrewsbury they had helped each other escape to play after mealtimes, unnoticed by the bigger boys with table duties. One would touch the other on the shoulder as a signal, and they would leave separately to meet outside or in the kitchens. Hyw touched his friend on the shoulder as he passed, hoping James would remember the game.

Glancing back, he saw Robert's eyes following him. Had he been recognized after all? Then Hyw remembered the wine, and knew he would need to be quick. Perhaps he could run the wine back to the table, and arrange to meet James afterwards.

He filled the decanter and started back toward the dining room. As he reached the door, James appeared. Hyw drew him aside into a darkened recess.

"You didn't write or send word," James whispered fiercely. "I thought—I didn't know what to think."

Hyw whispered back, “Much has happened. I don’t know how to begin. And I must return to Robert with this wine.”

James nodded. “We are housed in the wing across the courtyard, nearest the gates. The residences here were recently completed. My father fears the treacherous Welsh—oh, I’m sorry Hyw.” James broke off, realizing what he had said. Hyw raised his eyebrows.

“It is what both sides think of the other. Mayhap both are right.” He grinned and lightly punched his friend’s shoulder. “Yet now I must return this wine before Robert comes to find me.”

“Can you slip away after the meal?” James looked hopeful. “There are many sheltered spots along the walls where we might talk in peace.”

Hyw had come in through the back gate to the kitchens, and was not familiar with the layout of Rhuddlan castle. Would Llywelyn know? He only knew one way to communicate with Llywelyn. Dare he take the chance, with James so near? Would James understand? Hyw had to chance it. He took a breath and closed his eyes. He found Llywelyn staring at him, arms crossed across his chest.

Aye, said the prince. *I know this castle well. ’Tis one of Edward’s favourite holdings, and he has stolen it from me before. I was forced to submit to Edward here five years ago, after the invasion by sea. Never mind. We will find your friend this evening. Indeed, I would discover more about the new stronghold.*

Hyw opened his eyes again. Llywelyn planned to spy on the king, and his plan might compromise James. James, in turn, was staring at him. “What is it?” he asked. “Why did you stop in your tracks? You look like you’ve seen a ghost.”

“I will explain anon. Tonight. I will find you, never fear.” Before he could say more, Robert burst in upon them.

“I would not have known you, had I not seen James follow you here,” Robert hissed. “Have you used your witchcraft to hide your shape?”

“He is no warlock,” James said, standing up to the bigger boy.

“Let the priests decide.”

Robert meant to turn him over to the English priests. Hyw had seen their witch trials. Throw a man in the river bound with rocks: if he floats, he must be a witch and is put to death; if he sinks, he is no witch, but just as dead. He thought quickly. If he dropped the wine decanter would it create enough distraction that he could run? Then James stepped in front of him, glaring at Robert.

"And you will serve no master. My father will not have you as squire if you do this. And you will ne'er become a knight."

Robert stepped back from James in something like fear. Hyw felt a glimmer of hope. Then the bigger boy smiled. "But there is one thing they will believe more easily than witchcraft." He shoved James aside and grabbed Hyw by the ear, dragging him back into the hall.

"A spy!" Robert shouted, throwing Hyw in front of the long tables of soldiers. "A Welsh spy in our midst."

Chapter Twenty: Cat

Princess Elizabeth swept into the room, her golden hair down around her shoulders as if for bed. Cat thought she looked like an angel as she offered Father Maelgwyn and their people sanctuary. The cook brought in plates heaping with meats and cheese, and the guards broke out another keg of ale.

As the people were eating, Elizabeth beckoned to Father Maelgwyn before starting up the stairs to her solar.

"Come with us, please, Lady Adara," she said in a low voice. She motioned to one of the serving boys to bring the priest's plate and follow them. Adara held out her hand for Cat to come as well.

The servant set the priest's plate at the table with the women around him. The boy brought wine from a decanter on the sideboard. As the door closed behind him, Princess Elizabeth nodded at the priest to tell his tale.

"We were brought from the castle by Llywelyn's man, one of those I had thought was to accompany you, Lady Adara," he began. "He managed to get us through the gates behind the fighting. He bade us to meet you here at Criccieth, and so we made haste."

"Have you any word of the English troops?" Elizabeth asked.

"The force that attacked was small, and from what I saw, our men held their own. But I fear it was merely a scouting force, with the army to follow."

"Had you any word of my husband, Father?" Adara asked. Her voice and bearing seemed calm and composed but Cat saw her fingers clutched in her skirts. "Or did you meet Aeneus on the way?"

"Nay, we heard nothing of Lord Bran, although I heard your son Hyw was being tended in the Abby Cwmhir. A lad was later dispatched to Anglesey for more men, or so I heard. But we saw no one on the trail here, my lady. Neither Welsh nor English."

Adara nodded gravely and looked down.

"The whole of the north will be at war if the English take Garth Celyn." Father Maelgwyn shook his head.

Elizabeth took a sip of her wine, and they sat in silence a moment. The priest pushed his food around his plate. Cat thought of the warrior who had replaced the trap door for them, and presumably joined the fighting.

"What happened to the warrior who helped you?" she asked.

Father Maelgwyn bowed his head and made the sign of the cross. "He went back to rejoin the fighting, and said he would return if all was safe." He looked up at Cat, and she could see the sorrow in his eyes. "He did not return. We waited on the trail as he bade us, but no one followed. The following morning, we came here."

Cat said nothing. Adara put an arm around her, and she knew they were both thinking of her brother and Da. Would Aeneus find them? Would she ever see them again?

Chapter Twenty-one: Hyw

Hyw landed hard as Robert threw him down in front of the English knights. With the agility he had regained under Aeneus' training, he recovered to one knee in time to see James step forward.

"He's not!" cried James. "Father!"

At Robert's first cry of "spy," many of the knights drew swords, and a gallant few clustered around the king. Edward stood on the dais, much as Llywelyn had moments ago, arms folded and glaring down at him. Shrewsbury also stood with his fingertips on the tabletop, frowning intently at his son, his squire, and finally at Hyw.

"Where is the spy?" Edward demanded. His voice boomed in the great hall. Several soldiers flinched, while those guarding the king moved their swords menacingly.

Fear not, lad, he heard Llywelyn whisper in his ear. *Hope is not lost, where life remains. Show them respect but no fear.*

Robert gestured toward Hyw, who had remained on one knee and turned slightly in a proper greeting to Shrewsbury, his former lord.

"That child?" Edward's voice was incredulous. When no one moved, the king spoke again. "Are you Welsh, boy?" Hyw could only nod. Edward watched Hyw with narrowed eyes.

Hyw was unable to find his voice. Was he a spy? He had come to Rhuddlan to discover what he could about the English plans in order to help his people. Indeed, in serving one lord he had betrayed another. He was miserably aware of James, kneeling beside him, compromised.

"He serves my father, my lord," James said stoutly.

"And who is your father, boy?"

"Lord Shrewsbury, sir."

The king turned to Hyw again, more kindly this time. "Are you in service boy?"

In answer, Hyw held the decanter up. He looked toward Shrewsbury, still unable to find his tongue.

"My lord king, if I may," Shrewsbury said. "I believe he was bringing me wine."

The king looked astonished. "He is your squire?"

Shrewsbury gestured toward Robert. "I believe my squire asked him to."

"Squire," the king boomed, turning back to Robert. "Am I to understand that you asked a Welsh spy to serve us?"

Robert, who had been mirroring Edward's stance, unfolded his arms and took a step back. His face flushed. "Nay, my lord – " he spluttered.

Shrewsbury took that moment to pick up his glass, gesturing for Hyw to come forward with the wine. "I apologize for my squire, my lord," he said graciously. "His zeal against the Welsh leads him to be ever watchful. These boys have both been in my service four years."

"And you vouch for this one?"

"He has been loyal to me."

"Then may he be so to his liege as well."

"I – I will, my lord." Hyw found his voice. His liege was Llywelyn, after all, and he served as well as he could. He sent up a silent prayer, thankful he could speak the truth, although it might not be the truth Edward heard.

Edward resumed his seat. Hyw stood, keeping his eyes on Shrewsbury, and walked around the dais away from the king. He relied on his training to keep himself erect and pour the wine into the old lord's glass with a steady hand. The soldiers soon lost interest in him and went back to eating. An old soldier cuffed Robert on the ear and sent him sprawling.

"Do not bother your betters with your boyish rivalries, lad," the soldier growled.

On the dais, Hyw bowed low to Shrewsbury.

"So I find you in my service again, Hyw," the old lord said. "Come to me first thing tomorrow. I would have words with you."

"Aye, my lord." He stumbled from the dais. James had stood as well, and moved back toward his own place at the tables. Before they could speak again, another kitchen boy grabbed Hyw's arm roughly.

"Come, Welsh," he spat, "we have work for you anon."

Hyw saw the boy nod over his shoulder toward Robert, as he dragged Hyw from the room toward the kitchens. Robert had recovered himself and was staring at them, his face almost snarling. Hyw knew he would not soon forget the incident.

The kitchen boys kept Hyw busy cleaning grates and all the dirtiest places of the kitchen. All the while they cast insults and well-aimed kicks at him. He was able to dodge most, but his pride was wounded. Robert came to gloat once.

"Make sure he has too much to do to spy on anyone," he growled, handing a copper coin to one of the kitchen boys.

"Welsh devil," laughed the boy, excited to be noticed, lashing out at Hyw again with his bare foot. Hyw dodged easily and the boy fell on his behind as his foot connected with nothing but air. It did little to help him though, because Robert kicked him instead, and sent Hyw sprawling in turn.

One of the boys sent Hyw to gather the last of the plates from the tables as the soldiers bedded down on the floor of the great hall. James had not come to see him before the old lord and his family retired to their wing. Hyw was both glad and sorry. Glad because he knew James would try to defend him and they would both end up being beaten -- and sorry because they might have stood a chance together.

He closed his eyes, but Llywelyn was nowhere to be found either. Hyw wondered how the prince could hide himself. And whether he might be able to hide someday, if the need arose.

After the cook chased the other boys back to work, they more or less forgot about him. Hyw did the work they set him and said nothing. When the servants had taken themselves to bed, he curled into a warm corner of the kitchen. The cloak he had left there had disappeared, but he had little energy left to mourn its loss. He slept as soon as his eyes closed.

Chapter Twenty-two: Cat

After the Garth Celyn survivors arrived, Elizabeth sent her guards through the countryside to warn the people with an offer to help any who would fight the English. Cat had taken to walking the battlements in the early hours to dispel her dreams, and she saw the first group of men making their way to the castle gate with grim expressions. That day and the next, many more followed. Some brought small herds of cows with them.

She discovered that these farmers, like the people around Garth Celyn, had fought the English many times. The guards spent their days enlisting their help in fletching arrows and javelins, or curving long shafts of yew into longbows. Often they would train in the cool of the morning and spend afternoons fashioning weapons and armour. Women from the neighbouring towns came to tan and fashion leather into protective gear, or help feed the growing numbers as the people prepared for war.

In the evenings they gathered for stories and songs near the fire in the outer ward. Cat, Adara, Enid and Gwen, along with Elizabeth and her family, shared rooms in the inner ward. Many of Dafydd's special bodyguards had remained with Elizabeth, including a few loyal English guards who had come to Wales with her when she married Dafydd. They slept near the women's quarters, as did the Garth Celyn guards who had come with Adara and Cat. If Cat got up to use the latrines in the night, she often saw Sir Ifan patrolling the halls outside their rooms.

As January winds turned to heavy rains and sometimes snow, Cat was glad she and the girls had their fireplace, thick wall tapestries, and coverlets. The guards stayed in less fortified timber buildings of the outer ward. She knew horses and other animals shared one end of the timber buildings where some of the farmers and townsfolk slept. It was not surprising when sniffles and colds made their way around the courtyard.

The day after he arrived, Father Maelgwyn put a stop to the girls' training. He had already joined Criccieth's more amiable priest in the chapel, and was accompanying him on his rounds to fortify the guards and the people at their work. As they passed by the girls, who were warming up with stretches and exercise, Father Maelgwyn called to Cat.

"What is it you are doing here, Lady Cat?"

"We are training, Father," she replied.

"War is not the work for women," he told them. "Go about your business, ladies."

Cat tried to protest but he was adamant.

"I know you did thus at Garth Celyn, Lady Cat, but it was no more right there than it is here. And now you have no other guide but me, you must let yourself be guided." Cat wanted to say she still had her mam, but she knew the priest believed the male head of the household should guide them. Without intervention from her father or brother, she could not change his mind.

"Come on," Margred said to her, and the sisters ran toward the castle.

Cat shook her head, needing time to think things through. At one time, she might have found Hyw and enlisted his aid. Instinctively, she walked toward the horse pens where she had always been sure to find him. She leaned on the stone fence, watching the shaggy coated horses.

She had never disobeyed the priest, but she had a sudden flash of vision: Margred, her long black tresses streaming, being chased by an armoured horseman with sword raised. Cat could not let that happen! She was not really sure if it was a true vision, or her imagination run wild, but she had to do something. Surely training would make them fit and wary, better able to cope with what they may have to face.

She set out to find Owain then, and a plan hatched in her mind as she walked. By the time she found him lounging with the other boys, she had the details worked out. She drew him aside and explained what she meant to do. At first he tried to argue, but he could see how determined she was.

"If you don't help me, I will find a way to do it myself," she said.

Owain studied her a moment, and then nodded. "Come with me."

They strolled casually toward the armoury, and he told her a riddle he had heard at the fireside the night before. She laughed, and he said quietly, "That's better. You cannot carry out a devious plan while you look so serious, Lady Cat. Trust to me on that. I am the master of mischief in this castle."

She laughed again, glad he was helping her. At the armoury, he swept up a horse blanket from a bench and handed it to her. Then he began to inspect the children's wooden swords and blunted javelins, placing several on the blanket in her outstretched arms.

"What is it that you seek, Master Owain?" asked a voice. Cat turned to see Sir Ifan, the young warrior who had accompanied them from Garth Celyn, with his arms folded across his chest.

"Some of the boys mean to skirmish later, to please my Lady Cat and her friends," Owain replied smoothly, bowing slightly to him. "She is helping me choose the terms."

Ifan frowned for a moment, then nodded and moved toward the javelins. Owain turned to the light daggers then, choosing a few and hastily grabbing belts and sheaths for them. "Come," he said, and wrapped it all in the blanket as he took it from her. He grabbed a thick shank of rope and tied the package. They made their way out of the armoury and he turned a sharp right, taking her toward the wall. He threw the blanket over the wall, and turned to her.

"I will wait on the other side until you arrive. This field is sheltered from the town by the castle wall, and should suit your purposes. Now you must gather the girls."

"Thank you, Owain," she began, but he cut her off with a wink.

"If you can beg a round of cheese from Cookie, that will be my reward."

She found Margred and Rhiannon, as well as a few of the Garth Celyn girls she knew had participated. Owain stayed to help with their practice session, and found an old squirrel hole in a tree trunk to stash their gear. Although Cat could not manage one of the cook's prize cheese rounds, she did get a quarter piece by saying she was taking the new girls on a walk around the castle to orient them to their new surroundings, which was at least partially true. From the look on Owain's face when she presented him with it, he was pleased with their morning's work. He gallantly shared it with the girls, and took the time to walk with them to the path on the other side of the castle where they could survey the town in daylight.

Chapter Twenty-three: Hyw

Hyw jerked awake again before dawn. Rhuddlan was a Welsh castle, but there was no ritual shaving while the English held court. Hyw spotted a vat of cold wash water from the pots the night before, and washed some of the grime from his face and hands. He wasn't sure what direction to go to find Shrewsbury's rooms, or how to make his way around the huge stone castle. It was larger and very different from the welcoming wooden structures of Garth Celyn. The stone was cold to the touch and felt menacing. He closed his eyes in the dark. Llywelyn reappeared, and Hyw was glad to find company. He sent his thoughts to Llywelyn as a question.

"Last night I sought you. How came you to disappear?"

I did not think you wished a witness to your ordeal, lad. Llywelyn appeared to turn away. *Many times as page and squire in an English house, I suffered so.*

Hyw was a little touched by Llywelyn's consideration. He still wanted to know how it was done though. "It was a neat trick, to disappear."

The prince stared at him and then laughed. *You mean could you do the same if you tried? You know more of this process than I, boy.*

"Mayhap we both act on instinct then, my liege."

Llywelyn showed him the way to Shrewsbury's rooms, but in the near-dark Hyw almost stumbled into Shrewsbury's new page. The boy slept outside the door. Hyw didn't recognize him. He felt a pang to remember this was his own position a few short months ago. With a sigh he gave his name to the boy and asked him to tell Lord Shrewsbury he was waiting.

The boy disappeared through the doorway. When he returned he gestured for Hyw to follow, sneaking glances at him as they went. Hyw couldn't help wondering if the child was trying to see the pointed ears or tail of a "Welsh devil." Yet he said little, more concerned with how to answer the old lord's questions.

Shrewsbury was dressed and ready for him, and Hyw knelt before his former master as custom demanded. For a few moments Shrewsbury looked through some rolls of parchment without acknowledging him. The older man wore a familiar wool tunic over his other clothing. Hyw remembered the soft texture of it, but also the tightness of the weft in its weaving. He wondered if the new page had enough strength to stretch it wide over the man's broad chest, as Hyw had when he'd dressed the lord for training exercises in the yard. It seemed much longer than four months ago.

His knee began to ache with kneeling. When Shrewsbury finally looked up, he did not smile. "So, Hyw, it seems you have found your way into my service again. Or do I flatter myself?"

"My lord, I could do no better." Hyw meant what he said, but felt his face redden.

Shrewsbury finally gestured for Hyw to stand. "Robert is no fool, Hyw, as you and I both know. I wonder why you did not come to me plainly last night."

Hyw raised his eyes as far as the garnet clasp at Shrewsbury's neck, but could neither speak nor look into his eyes.

"I promised your father I would foster you, Hyw, and I will keep that promise. Yet if it is a spy's game you play here, you must know it cannot come to good. Many young men are tempted by gold or glory, but this king does not take treachery lightly. And Robert's are not the only eyes that watch you now."

"Lucky none but my lord can see my soul," Hyw said softly. He was thinking of Llywelyn, trapped inside him, and was tempted to tell the old lord everything. Shrewsbury folded his arms across his chest.

"Many a Norman lord would cuff you for speaking out so, Hyw. Lucky for you I know your ways from my own fosterage in Wales, where I met my first lady. Yet know this: only God can see your soul, and that is as it should be. Be faithful and do your duty well."

"Yes sir."

"If it is your intention to return to my service, know that I will not tolerate any action that stinks of spying. What is in your mind is between you and God, but your actions on this earth reflect on me. I cannot and I will not protect you, if you prove disloyal. Do you understand me Hyw?"

"Yes, m'lord."

"Then we will not speak of it again." Shrewsbury stared at him a moment longer, before unfolding his arms. "What news have you of your father?"

Hyw felt his chest cave, and kept his head down. He could not find his voice. Shrewsbury spoke more softly.

"We had news of Llywelyn's death before Christmastime. I thought your father could not have been far from his lord. Is he also—?"

"I know not, my lord. No trace of him has been found."

"I am sorry to hear it, yet I fear worse. Wars in the borderlands come and go, but this time Edward will stay until it is finished. When that happens the world may seem a topsy-turvy place for you, and for all with Welsh blood. Yet, for my son's sake, and the sake of his dear mother, you may have a place with our guards."

Shrewsbury reached out then, and clasped Hyw's shoulder. James' mother, the first Lady Shrewsbury, had been cousin to Hyw's father. They shared bonds of kinship as well as fosterage. She had died birthing James, and as eldest son he would someday be the lord of Shrewsbury. Hyw could think of no better fate than serving in his guard. Yet, that could lead to fighting against his own people in border skirmishes. Hyw's head whirled with divided loyalties.

Always I have liked this man, Marcher lord or no. He heard Llywelyn's voice in his ear again. *He has honour and kindness in him. I envy him that. You must stay with him, Hyw. He may be useful to us yet.*

At Llywelyn's last words, Hyw shrugged away, and out of Shrewsbury's grip as well. Then he knelt again at the old lord's feet.

"My lord," he said, "I could have no finer master than you, and will serve you in my heart long after I am a man. I know not what I might do, if this war ends as you say. I am Welsh and wish to please my father also. In good conscience, I cannot fight against my own people. But I pledge you this: if I become a knight hereafter, I will never take arms against your son James in battle. I love him like a brother, and will protect him as well as I am able, against all calamity."

The old man considered what Hyw had said. "Your honesty commends you, Hyw, and your bond with my son is well known to me. I appreciate your wish not to fight your own people, but your knowledge of Garth Celyn may compromise you." He paused, stroking his beard. "As soon as I am able, I would get James to Shrewsbury, away from this war. Mayhap you will come with us. Young Robert may win his spurs in the next battle. That will occupy him well, and he would be better served to forget your enmity in service to Edward. I would make you my squire, Hyw. You might then come to Shrewsbury again when this is done, and serve me without betraying your own."

"So I will, if you will have me, my lord, and thank you." Hyw was surprised at the old knight's offer, and grateful not to be parted from James again.

"See you do your duty well." The old lord's arm was still strong, and he cuffed Hyw on the shoulder. Hyw stood fast, anticipating the cuff he might receive upon knighthood would be much stronger.

That's right, Llywelyn spoke in his ear. *Do your duty, as you pledged you would.* Hyw wondered where his deeper duty lay: to his master Shrewsbury, who offered him a place and the chance to serve James after him, or to the dead prince he had pledged to help? *Your purpose here is to find out what you can and get word to your people,* Llywelyn reminded him.

Shrewsbury beckoned him to the door. "Come Hyw, let us find James, and try our skills in the yard, before we break our fast with the others."

"What did happen to you after you left us, Hyw?" James asked one night. "When you did not send word, I was sore afraid for you. When we saw the prince's head – "

"You saw?"

"Oh, 'twas horrible. And all I could think was that your father may have been nearby. And you—?"

Hyw nodded, but could not speak. He longed to confide in his friend about events on the hill, but he could not find words to explain. James patted his shoulder. "You do not need to say, Hyw. I can see in your face how it was with you. Know this: you can confide in me as you choose. I will not betray you. I would die first."

"Nay, never say it James. Have no fears for me, but protect yourself. For I am pledged to give my life for yours—and I am not ready to lie down yet!" Hyw grinned away his embarrassment. "Come, you fat slug, let me teach you how to dodge the quintain again."

At that they leapt up, glad for an excuse to run again.

Chapter Twenty-four: Cat

The girls quickly settled on a routine of training each day after chores, explaining it away as a walk or a chance to show the newcomers around. Few noticed them in the bustle of activity and people milling about the castle yard. As soon as they got outside the gate, they would meet in their field to begin.

Margred naturally led them in warm-up exercises, since she was the most agile and enjoyed the chance to show off a little as the others struggled to keep up. Cat, who had the benefit of Aeneus' tutoring at Garth Celyn, then led them in a series of exercises with the wooden weapons designed to help build their arm and upper body muscles. Although Aeneus had never let the girls participate in hand-to-hand combat training, he had encouraged them to throw javelin and lightweight knives at targets. The girls tied planks of wood together to fashion a target, and took turns throwing the javelins and knives Cat and Owain had purloined from Criccieth's armoury.

Owain's younger sisters often joined them, as did several older girls from the Garth Celyn group and a few of the farm women and servants from Criccieth. Cat made a point of swearing them to secrecy, lest the priests discover their activity. With all the extra souls in the castle she hoped Father Maelgwyn would be busy enough ministering to them to forget the girls—at least for a time. They often returned in smaller groups to begin their afternoon chores. For Margred, her sisters, and Cat, that meant joining Elizabeth at her embroidery.

One morning the fierce rains and wind of January howled around the castle. Cat sat in the hall at breakfast, chewing staunchly and waiting for Margred. Beside her, Owain groaned.

"You're lucky to be born a woman, Cat," he said. "At least you can stay inside this fine day." He laid his head along his arm on the tabletop.

Cat bristled, recalling Aeneus' words to the warriors of Garth Celyn on wintry days. She repeated them to Owain now. "Do you think the sun will always be shining when our enemies attack?"

"You sound like our captain of the guards," he told her.

She worked hard to recall that he was several years her junior, and calmed herself. "We do not choose the trials that form us." She was quoting her da this time. Owain peered up at her, and she could not resist poking his arm playfully. "Are you going to let mere women show you up?"

"You're not going out in this, surely," he said, more statement than question, raising his head. "You cannot. You will be blown away."

"We shall see."

"You will be alone. My sisters certainly will not join you. I cannot allow it."

Prince's son or no, there were times when his arrogance irked her. Cat said nothing more, pushing back from the table and marching up the stairs to the room she shared with the girls. Owain, his eyes snapping with laughter, trooped at her heels.

She burst into their room and shook Margred and Rhiannon awake. Owain leapt onto the bed beside them all.

"Awake, awake," he sang, composing an englyn on the spot:

> Awake, awake, my sisters here abed.
> Now end your dreams of bliss.
> Do not make the young Cat hiss.
> For her, your moaning dismiss.

"You have little grace and less harmony," laughed Rhiannon, hitting him with the feather pillows. He laughed and pulled her from the bed into a heap on the floor, where he tickled her mercilessly until the servants came in and chased him from the room. By then, the girls were awake and there was no going back under the warm quilts.

Yet for all Owain's teasing, only Margred went with her into the gale. After an hour lashed by wind and rain, the two girls had missed more targets than they hit and had fallen so many times their clothes looked and felt like a wall of slush and mud. But their energy kindled against the elements as they stowed their gear in its hidey-hole and raced each other back to the castle.

Margred burst through the doors a hair before Cat. Drenched and laughing, Cat almost didn't notice a man warming his hands by the fire in the inner hall. She thought perhaps he had just arrived. He turned toward them and bowed. The girls bowed in turn, but refrained from speaking to him until they could be introduced. Cat thought he looked very familiar to her, and then recognized him as a bard who had travelled with Llywelyn's court the previous year.

"Good day to you, Gwilym ap Einion," she said, curtsying to him. "Pardon our appearance, but we were caught in the weather."

"I am sorry to hear it, young Lady Catrin, but glad to see you here," he responded. He made a strangled sound she thought might have been laughter, but he deftly turned it into a cough.

"May I introduce you to Margred, daughter of Prince Dafydd," Cat said. She stopped abruptly, realizing she did not know Margred's mother's name, and hoped he would not notice as she quickly introduced him in turn. As they exchanged greetings, he gazed at

Margred longer than seemed polite. Margred made their excuses, grabbed Cat by the arm, and turned toward the stone staircase.

The two girls slogged up to their room to change from their wet things, and Cat all but forgot him as they combed their hair by the fire in their room. She showed Margred how to plait her long black hair the way Princess Elinor and her French ladies preferred. "You are so beautiful this way, Margred," Cat said.

"Mam says beauty is a curse for a poor woman," Margred said. Before Cat could ask her anything more, she grabbed the bone comb and began to brush Cat's unruly copper locks for her. Rhiannon and the younger girls demanded to learn the new braiding style. By the time they were finished all of them sported the new look, and Margred had mastered it also.

Afterward, Cat and Margred went to Elizabeth's solar, where Cat planned to resign herself to better her skills at embroidery. But the servant making Elizabeth's bed said the ladies had both had gone down to entertain "a gentleman" —although the quirk in her mouth told them the girl was not altogether certain he was a gentleman. Wandering bards had a poor reputation in the Welsh countryside, but a bard of Gwilym's stature and skill had always commanded respect at Llywelyn's court. Cat frowned a little, wondering what had happened to make the girl think poorly of him.

Margred grabbed her hand and they raced down the stairs again. Princess Elizabeth had joined Gwilym to sit near the fireplace, and they stood to greet the girls. Elizabeth frowned at them as Cat and Margred came to a clattering halt. Adara, holding Baby Gwen, stood then too, hiding a smile as she held her free hand out to Cat. The girls came closer.

"It is a pleasure to greet the daughters of the house," he said, bowing to them.

"My husband's daughter," Elizabeth said quietly, her face frozen in a polite smile.

Gwilym turned to her with an encouraging smile. "As we protect all of our children now, may they return to aid us in our nether years."

He smiled at Cat and she liked the twinkle she saw in his eye.

He certainly did not seem much like the disreputable wandering bards she had seen come through Garth Celyn, or on her travels with Princess Elinor in past years. As he turned to Margred, his expression changed again. Before he could say anything, Princess Elizabeth spoke.

"Gwilym brings us good news this day, Cat."

"Aye," he said, turning from Margred with what seemed like reluctance, before he smiled at the other women. "I had been across the borderlands these last few months, working out the details of a land settlement for Prince Llywelyn. When word came to us of his untimely murder, I travelled through Builth to learn as much of the truth as I could. I discovered two pieces of information that may interest you.

"First, Prince Dafydd survived the loss of Hawarden and is still at liberty. I have it on good authority that he is safe at Dolwyddelan Castle, and intends to prevent King Edward's troops from passing farther north.

"Second, I passed through Abbey Cwmhir, and spoke to a man who claims to be your brother, Lady Adara. He tells me that no trace of your husband was found after the fray. We may surmise that he leads the Welsh army against the remaining English."

"And my son? Was there news of him?"

"Aye, Lady. Your son Hyw has taken the northward road to Rhuddlan, and come under the protection of his former foster father, Lord Shrewsbury."

"He is with the English?"

"It cannot be." Cat spoke without thinking, and ignored her mam's signals. "He would not return to them."

Gwilym turned to her. "I have it on reliable authority," he said. "Yet have no fear. He is not a traitor to his country. Nay, rather, he plans to return with news that may help his people."

She frowned, scarcely listening to her mam's questions. Could the poet be right? Would Hyw betray his friend to save his country?

"—and you are welcome to share our hospitality, such as it is, for as long as you may need it," Princess Elizabeth was saying.

"Winter's bite can scarce be felt with two such early roses to brighten the room," Gwilym said, turning back to Margred and Cat. Gwilym's bow included them both in the compliment, but his eyes never left Margred's face.

Chapter Twenty-five: Hyw

War came upon them swiftly. One afternoon, Shrewsbury was called to Edward's chambers along with several of the other Marcher lords. When he returned, he had already issued the command to his soldiers to prepare to march the following morning.

At dawn a priest gave a hasty blessing, and they formed up in companies. The knights around them were keyed up. These were mainly personal guards, set to meet the bulk of their companies in camps outside the castle gates. Hyw noted many of the more seasoned were quiet or even surly, lacking the enthusiasm of the younger men.

Hyw's heart thumped to the rhythm of hooves pounding the cold ground as he rode out of the gates at James' side. He couldn't help but wonder whether the Welsh were nearby. Where was his da? Would he be with the warriors? Would he have to fight one of his own countrymen—or his own Da? If he did not, would harm come to James, or to Shrewsbury?

Llywelyn spoke in Hyw's ear. *Remember your duty.* Hyw nodded, keeping his thoughts to himself.

He needn't have worried. Shrewsbury sent them as far from the fray as he could. Hyw and James waited with two of Shrewsbury's soldiers on a hillside near the English camp. Around him, he could hear the clanking of arms and men's shouts. Llywelyn whispered again. *If only we had a bird's eye view of this field.*

At those words, Hyw looked up and saw the sky full of black rooks. Then, circling with outspread wings, a huge and beautiful hawk. *Boy, if you use your gift, can we become this bird?*

Careful that James and the other soldiers did not notice him, Hyw closed his eyes to make contact with Llywelyn. "My liege, I cannot take its corporeal form, but I can see through its eyes. Its world can be as real for me as mine own. Or as yours."

Then we must do so.

"There may be a way, but this is what Gawain warned us against. It poses danger for us both."

Llywelyn considered his words. *Always the paths fork ahead of us. The path of green fields and well-trodden ground may also hide a hole to snare the foot of an unwary horse. Its rider then lies face-down in the dust. The path beset by brambles and thorns will breed caution before ever we lay a foot upon it. Thus may a man bravely set out to conquer the way, and more safely reach the end of his journey.*

Hyw understood then why the Welsh lords had followed Llywelyn, even when they intended to fight him. He dismounted to gain better balance, checking his mount's saddle to cover his actions. Mindful of Gawain's cautions, he closed his eyes, placed himself in front of the prince, and threw his mind to the hawk in the sky. He made contact with greater ease than he expected, then felt the shock of wary fear in the bird. Looking down from the bird's mind, Hyw could see the valley of Clwd below, and knew it to be a battlefield.

Llywelyn, as if looking over Hyw's shoulder, pointed out one Welsh lord or another who had stood with him in battles over the past five years. They watched as the Welsh lords lined up in squares, arms moving to make the sign of the cross on their chests. Row upon row of men crowded together. Where Romans would have linked shields and swords, the Welsh warriors had leather jerkins and lances, and bright war paint on their faces.

No, you fools, Llywelyn cried. *The men don't know this form of fighting. Let them rush and retreat, as they always do.*

The hawk would not go nearer to see the faces of the men who urged the warriors into battle. Then with a roar, the Welsh ran down the hillside. Their lords rode at their sides, streaming proud Welsh colours down into the valley below. The English in their armour rode at them, clanking, from the other side.

As the English swords dove into their lines, the Welsh drove their lances upward. The larger warriors pulled men from their horses, killing armoured knights with their bare hands. Then those same warriors were cut down, sharp steel hacking them in two from behind. The battle began to shift. Armour and steel won out over sinew and bone.

The Welsh turned to flee to safety in the hills. Row upon row of their own countrymen stood in their path. The English rode in from the sides and forced them together. Like a wave turning upon itself, they fell to the sword and to their own fear. Llywelyn screamed useless commands. No one heard him but Hyw.

The proud hawk that shared his mind with Hyw was sickened at the smell of sweat and blood. It was held there by Hyw's will, but wanted only to be gone. Hyw tasted copper in his mouth and knew the hawk would not hunt for prey in this field for many months to come. He felt the bird's disgust at the carrion-eaters, black rooks that dove and plucked at eyes and faces.

The hawk shrieked once as it circled, slowly drawing closer at Hyw's urging. Scores of men lay dead and dying. A hundred—nay, two hundred Welsh warriors lay among them. A mere handful of armoured English knights had fallen. Riderless horses screamed and thrashed, or milled about with fear, banding together in clumps or running wildly across the hills.

Welsh colours trailed upon the ground. English knights on horseback drove Welsh lances into the bodies of the dying. Soldiers hacked at the bodies and flipped something up onto a wheeled cart. Hyw realized it was a cart full of heads, many still shining with the golden torques that marked a warrior's prowess and skill.

The world blazed red and Hyw felt himself fall into the sun, his wings melting like the stories of Icarus his tutors once told him. He plummeted downward, his mind full of the sights of war and the screams of his countrymen. Llywelyn's voice was silent.

Chapter Twenty-six: Cat

During the following day, Gwilym made no secret of his admiration for Margred. Princess Elizabeth met his hints with that same frozen smile, and Margred grumbled. "She means me to wed a man of more influence," she told Cat at night in their room.

"Would you rather have Gwilym?" Cat asked. "He is a notable poet and often argues disputes of law before Prince Llywelyn's court—I mean, he once did."

"But he's so old, Cat," Margred said, turning away. "Anyway, one old man is much the same as any other. Will you come with us to Market Day in the town tomorrow?"

Cat raised her eyebrows. Margred was skilled at conversation, and this change of subject was more abrupt and clumsy than she had managed previously. Then Cat wondered if it really was a change of subject.

"Will the butcher's son be there?" she asked, teasing. "What was his name again?"

Margred laughed but caught Cat's arm. "You must not mention him! Truly, you must not. Promise me." When Cat nodded, Margred laughed again, a little more light-heartedly, and handed her the bone comb. "Will you braid my hair again?"

On Market Day, it was raining before they left the castle. Adara had asked Cat to buy some ribbons and thread, pressing a few pennies into her hand. "That should leave a little something for you, and enough for breakfast for you and Margred," she said with a smile. Cat felt badly for a moment, wondering what Mam would think of Margred's butcher boy, but she took the money and kept her friend's secret.

Cat covered the beautiful cloak her brother had given her with her old rainproof one, and pulled the hood up over her careful braids, as did Margred. They kept well within sight of Sir Ifan, who accompanied them, but far enough ahead so they could still speak privately. Not that they spoke much on the journey to town. Even with the extra clothing, both girls were red-cheeked from the cold by the time they reached the market.

At first it seemed dreary and grey. Puddles dragged at their skirts and plastered their hoods onto their hair. Then the rain stopped for a moment, and the girls were able to throw back their hoods and loosen their fastenings. The market stirred around them. The quiet streets unnerved Cat. She had been looking forward to the voices calling out from stalls around the square, harmonizing to attract their attention and tempt their pocketbooks. But today the sellers showed few wares from their stalls and wagons, and those who were out in the street stepped with silent purpose through the puddles. Margred had to ask the silk-seller to show Cat her thread, but there were no ribbons to be had. Cat thought she heard the woman muttering under her breath about ribbons in war-time when they heard a deep voice chime from a nearby stall.

"Laverbread."

"Ah," Margred exclaimed softly as she turned toward the voice. "I told you we didn't need breakfast at the castle." Looking past

Margred, she saw the butcher's son beckoning to them with a smile. She wondered why the butcher's stall would serve laverbread, the tasty seaweed rolled with oats.

Margred held her hand out for a penny. He must have known this was her friend's favourite. Perhaps it had been pre-arranged between them? As Margred took the coin and headed for the stall, Cat lagged behind a little, hoping to give her friend a moment of privacy. The rain dripped from the makeshift stalls to fall in puddles near her feet. A droplet shimmered and coiled in the act of falling. It seemed to expand around her, until—

—she found herself standing at the castle battlements. Below her the stones seemed to smoulder with grey smoke. The wind filled her nostrils with the smell of burning flowers, burning flesh, burning torches and the clash and ring of steel on steel. Somewhere nearby she could hear the screams of children, and the frightened cries of men and women. She saw a dark-haired woman running and a man chasing her down, heard the raucous laughter and the screams of what came after.

She saw a man raise his sword and cut the head from a young boy with flaming red hair and then she was screaming his name. "Owain! Owain!" But the wind carried her voice away, up into the air, and she could see it as if the words were flying.

Then it wasn't her voice, at all. It was another sound. "Caw! Caw!" Flocks of jackdaws and ravens filled the air, circling and cawing. One of the jackdaws flew by her, and its yellow eyes bore deep into her soul, and it cawed one word: "Death!"—

—and she felt swallowed in its blackness.

"Cat!" Someone was calling her name, and shaking her. "Cat! What happened?"

It was Margred's voice. She struggled as she felt a woman's hand on her forehead.

"She's burning up, poor thing."

"We must get her back to the castle."

Cat frowned. She tried to tell Margred she would be all right. She didn't want to interrupt her friend's plans. Her mouth felt dry and she could not seem to form the words.

Wait – wait! She remembered her vision. She did need to go to the castle. She must find Mam. Cat struggled to open her eyes. But all she saw was the giant head of a raven, its yellow eye staring into hers, and then blackness again.

Chapter Twenty-seven: Hyw

"Hyw! Are you injured?"

He heard a voice as if from far away, and was surprised to find himself prone on the hillside. He stared up at the overcast sky.

"Wake up! Hyw, are you all right?"

The voice was closer now. He knew it was James, but his head felt too heavy to raise. He heard James leap down from his horse, and the swish of footsteps as his friend flopped down beside him.

"Did you—" James' voice grew quiet, so the soldiers wouldn't hear. "What did you see? Did you see the battle—"

"No." Hyw struggled to sit up then. James offered an arm. Hyw grabbed it and hung on even after he was sitting on the cold ground. "Your father is right, James. This is not a battle. It's a slaughter."

"Have you seen it, then? Tell me."

Hyw let go of James and plucked a fistful of frozen grass instead, letting the cold sting his fingers. He stared across the hilltop. James laid one hand on his. They sat together for a moment. Then James cleared his throat.

"Your silence tells me all."

Hyw put his other hand over James' hand, linking them like chainmail as James helped him to his feet. After a long silent moment, James added, "I'm sorry for your countrymen."

They heard a distant horn. "Come, Hyw," James said, mounting his horse again. "That horn recalls our troops. Ride with me to my father. Mayhap we will hear more of this."

On top of a large tent pitched in the encampment, Hyw recognized Shrewsbury's standard of three lion heads. As they made their way toward it, he saw a smattering of soldiers and knights, some in armour, some with bandages over wounds, and some polishing or repairing their equipment. He was relieved to see they'd managed to arrive before Robert and the other knights returned from the field.

Shrewsbury had spread out maps and other parchment upon a makeshift table in the large tent. The lord had removed his armoured leggings and mail for comfort. His dark velvet surcoat hung loosely over his shoulders. Three lion heads with roaring mouths were embroidered on it, in an intricate pattern of gold thread. Shrewsbury stood at his full height, one gloved hand under his chin, staring down at them. He was formidable, and Hyw understood then what it was to be a Norman lord.

"Father," James said, catching Hyw as he stumbled forward. "Is it over? Do we return to Rhuddlan?"

"A fair question, James." The old lord looked steadily at Hyw as he spoke. "Nay, we march on Dolwyddelan."

They remained camped in the field two days. The old lord had pitched his tents on a sheltered hillside, close enough to the battle to engage if needed and far enough to escape the worst of its sounds and smells. Shrewsbury set James and Hyw to fetch and carry for the squires as they cleaned the blood from blades and armour, and made ready for another front. As he worked, Hyw could hear Llywelyn's questions, pushing him to learn all he could of their plans. Hyw had his own reasons for wanting to know, and listened for scraps of news. He preferred to stay busy, for whenever he stopped, he was plagued by worries about his mother and sister. He wondered also if his da was still alive, and if he would be among the Welsh warriors fighting them on the way or at Dolwyddelan.

Knights and squires alike seemed weary and more than a little subdued by the carnage of the battle. Even Robert did not crow over his first kills, although it became known that he would be knighted by the king himself, along with several others who had seen battle on the hillside near Builth.

Learn from those who have survived the longest, the prince commanded. Since soldiers and mercenaries had no squires, Hyw helped one old soldier polish his armour. The man, Alan Acton, came from a border town so he was familiar with the ways of Welsh and English. "See the crests and coats of arms?" Alan said. "That be the only means of knowing friend from foe on the battlefield. Once these fellows have their armour on and helmets down, you cannot tell one man from his enemy."

"Whose are the gold lions on a red background?" Hyw asked.

"That's the king himself, Hyw. Three gold lions 'passant guardant.' That means they face you, there, waving their right forepaw, as you see. Anyone who carries those colours carries the king into battle, so to speak."

"Is that on everything the king owns?"

"Aye, that or the rose with gold petals and a green stalk. Those be the king's own, mind. Our Shrewsbury, he also sports lions, but with three heads instead. He has savvy, our lord. You can see by the grey in his hair and beard. Follow him into battle, young master, and like as not ye'll follow him out again."

Hyw also heard disturbing news as he listened and worked among the soldiers. Another group had already marched north to take Garth Celyn. At the same time, they would lay siege to several strategic Welsh castles leading through the Eryri mountains, including Dolwyddelan, to cut off any hope of retreat inland. Edward's superiority at sea would prevent the Welsh from sailing over the strait to find refuge in Ireland.

"Some bloody Welsh traitor and his son from Powys are fighting with us, I'm told," Alan told him.

Gruffydd ap Gwenwynwyn and his son Owain. Long have they been the bane of my life, Llywelyn growled inside Hyw. Hyw knew their names from the stories his father had told him. Before Hyw was born, they had tried to assassinate Llywelyn, and then gained sanctuary with the English.

The old soldier leaned closer. "Aye, and they draw point in this march." He grinned, and Hyw realized Gruffydd and Owain would face their countrymen first, before the English. The old soldier swore. "Mortimer and his men will no doubt follow, keeping their eyes on that Welshman. Devil take them all."

Llywelyn uttered a soft laugh, but Hyw tried to concentrate on what Alan was saying. After Moritimer's company, Alan expected the troops of Henry de Lacy, followed by the king. Gilbert le Clare would keep close watch as the king's rear guard. Hyw knew le Clare's name from the many discussions around the fire at Garth Celyn. He was the scourge of the south, keeping the king's peace with an iron fist.

Shrewsbury's knights would be glad enough to follow the king, Alan told him, grinning. It meant they were cushioned between le Clare's troops in front, and Richard Chester's troops behind to take the brunt of any action the Welsh might muster from the rear. It also gave the more enterprising knights among them one more day to strip the gold torques and other valuables from the bodies of their enemies. Hyw turned his head away and closed his eyes to calm Llywelyn as Alan finished speaking.

Finally everything was in readiness. After a day's rest and some new booty, Shrewsbury's soldiers were at their peak again. Alan had secured Hyw a young bay gelding. Hyw had kept watch for his father's horses Aeron and Cadarn, but they were not among the captives. This gelding's skittishness showed it had seen battle and probably lost its previous master. He did his best to calm the horse, but he had no will to engage with the beast's mind.

"I'll try to find you a sweet treat later," he murmured in Welsh. The horse turned to look at him almost eagerly. Hyw smiled and patted his neck. Perhaps his former master had been Welsh. "I like a fellow who knows his own tongue."

From that point on, he called the horse *Siwgr*, the Welsh word for sugar. Keeping his voice soft, Hyw mounted without incident. The horse perked up its ears in anticipation.

Shrewsbury raised his gloved hand, and as one, the company rode out.

Chapter Twenty-eight: Cat

She felt the softness of a down-filled coverlet and smelled the scent of lilies. Princess Elinor, she thought. Oh Princess, save us!

And then she heard singing, and the coo of a small bird. No, not a bird. A child. Baby Gwen, laughing and gurgling, and her mam's voice singing a soft lullaby.

"*Huna'n dawel, annwyl blentyn…*"

Sleep quietly, dear child. Cat remembered the words to the song, and knew she had heard them long ago, when she was little older than Baby Gwen or Baby Gwladys. Somehow she knew that her mother, who sang the words, also had them sung to her. And she floated back through all the babies and the mothers of her ancestors, back to the first mother of her line.

She thought of Aylwen verch Arianrhod, woman of Troy, first Briton to learn the ways of the *derwyddon* or Druids.

And she felt Aylwen's hand on her brow, and heard her singing.

"First mother," Cat said. "Why is this happening to me?"

"We have gained these gifts to help our people," Aylwen said. "Now these gifts are yours. When we are most in need, the gift returns stronger than before. As it was given to my sons and my daughters, so it was given to you."

"Why," Cat struggled to speak. "Why me?"

"Because you are my last daughter." Cat looked deep into Aylwen's violet eyes, and saw that she was weeping. "You and your brother are the last of our kind. And when you die, you will blaze a trail across the sky for us to follow. But it is not your time, not yet. This is the time when you must help us. You must tell what you have seen. You must awaken, Cat. Wake up, Cat."

"Wake up, Cat," she heard, but it was not Aylwen's voice. It was Adara, her own Mam. "Please wake up."

Cat's eyes flew open, and she saw her mother's face near hers. She reached out, and Adara hugged her. "Oh, Cat," she said, her voice thick with emotion. "I thought—I didn't know what to think!"

"I'm all right, Mam," Cat said, breaking free. "I had a vision. Much stronger than before."

"Of your Da?"

"Much worse." Cat relayed the vision to her mam, recalling every detail. She swallowed bile as she told about Owain, and the raven, and Aylwen's violet eyes. When she had told it all, Adara sat for a moment, staring at the wall.

"Could this be true?" she whispered. "Are we all going to die?"

"Aylwen said to warn them," Cat said, throwing back the goose-down cover and sitting up. For a moment she felt dizzy, and her mam steadied her as she regained her balance. Then she stood. "We must warn Elizabeth."

"And yet, how can we do so?" Adara asked, placing a hand on Cat's shoulder. "How can we tell her what you have seen in a dream, and make her believe us? What I know of Elizabeth tells me she will not be easily convinced."

"There must be a way to prevent what I saw, Mam, and we must find it."

Chapter Twenty-nine: Hyw

The January winds blew down from the mountain like the Watcher's wrath. The men broke out cloaks and wrapped themselves, and the horses lowered their heads and plodded along the path that led northward.

Hyw was surprised how slowly the company of soldiers and knights made their way. *These English move like cattle,* Llywelyn muttered inside Hyw's mind. *They need a few Welsh dogs to harry them.*

Hyw and James, at a nod from Shrewsbury, rode ahead to catch sight of the troops passing by. From Alan's prediction, Hyw expected hundreds of troops, but he was sure he could see thousands. Soldiers lined the road in front and behind, as far as Hyw could see. A huge wooden tower on a platform pulled by a dozen sturdy horses trundled along beside de Lacy's men. James pointed excitedly at it, and the boys decided it must be a siege engine. Perhaps a catapult dangled below, or was secured in one of the covered wagons that made their way after it. Soldiers were stationed in front and behind, and made their way slowly along the trail, paced by the tower and horses.

They are foolish to try, Llywelyn told Hyw. *They will soon see why Wales will always be free.*

As they came to a steep hill, Hyw saw the muscles of the horses ripple as they made their way upward, lashed by the whips of the drivers. Some of the older soldiers jumped down and, handing their horses off to the men in front of them, ran back to try to help.

The Shrewsbury standard flew so far behind that James and Hyw had no fear now of losing their place. They jumped off their horses to watch the slow progress of de Lacy's men with the siege engine. Twice the platform slithered backwards, the hulking tower listing slightly under the thick ropes that held it. Llywelyn laughed softly.

Then de Lacy and his sons rode back to give encouragement to the men. It seemed some of the men were ready to give up, sitting or slumping on the ground. De Lacy spoke to them. Hyw could hear his voice ring across the miles, rising and falling in pitch, although he couldn't hear the words. Then the men cheered, and Hyw could almost see the battle lust rise in them.

Two more horses were added to the team, and two more again. The horses' minds reached out to Hyw but he resisted. The hawk had been enough for him. He had no wish to learn what other animals thought of war. More men joined the scene as well, and some pushed the platform from behind. Finally the huge wooden tower made the pinnacle. The boys watched the men below them break out in cheers and rejoicing. They could not help but smile together at the antics of grown men and grim soldiers dancing around a wooden tower like fools at a festival.

Llywelyn, though, was silent.

That night they camped on the road. In the darkness, Hyw heard screams and cries close by him. He started upright. James stirred sleepily and Hyw whispered, "Stay here. I will go and bring back word."

Hyw ran along the path until he slipped in something wet. A soldier behind him brought a lamp.

"Shield that light, man," cried a third. "The devils are upon us."

"What does he mean?"

"The Welsh," cried another. "They attack from the trees, and then disappear."

"Like ghosts."

"Like devils. Like the devils they are."

Before the man covered the light, Hyw looked down into the gaping wounds of two soldiers on the ground. He recognized the face of one: it was Alan Acton, the old soldier who had befriended him. Hyw crossed himself. The poor man, he thought.

Fortunes of war, Hyw, Llywelyn said inside him. *That 'poor man' was also your enemy, and the enemy of your people. Still, he treated you with kindness. May he have honour in the OtherWorld, and in the heaven to come.*

"May he have honour," repeated Hyw aloud, crossing himself again and raising one fist to his heart.

"That sounded like Welsh." Someone spoke nearby.

"Nay, 'twas but a Cornish blessing," Hyw replied, and turned before the man could raise the light any higher to see his face. He made his way back to James, wiping Alan's blood from his shoes and clothes as best he could. He vowed he would not cry.

Finally they reached Dolwyddelan Castle. Nightly attacks by Welsh had done little damage to the vast English forces. *There can be but few men left to defend the land, if so few Englishmen were killed,* Llywelyn said. *Yet may God bless those who tried, and keep them safe to fight another day.*

Llywelyn thought Dolwyddelan would withstand the siege for many weeks. It was the castle where the prince had set up his communications, and he was sure his brother Dafydd would have taken refuge there. Hyw could tell Llywelyn hoped the English would give up and leave, as had happened so many times before. Yet everything they heard from the soldiers made them fear for the land and its people. Hyw listened to the snatches of conversation around him.

"Even if bloody Longshanks wanted to give up, le Clare and de Lacy would fight on without him."

"Aye, I wouldn't have the two of them against me for all Christendom!"

"These Welsh will burn before the week is out, mark my words."

"And all Wales with them. They say the would-be prince is inside. De Lacy wants his head, and naught will stop him."

Hyw knew the "would-be prince" was Dafydd, Llywelyn's brother. He had taken sanctuary from Edward more than once, before he turned on the English troops a year ago, to start this war. Llywelyn fretted. *Dafydd must get word to the pope. He is the Prince Regent now. Edward will have dispatched a rider as soon as he had my head in his grasp. If he gets word of my death to the pope before Dafydd makes a claim, Wales is as good as lost.*

The English set up camp around the castle. Hyw watched a messenger ride to the walls, to offer what Llywelyn called the usual terms of surrender. *Is Dafydd so foolish to think these English have come so far, only to give up and go away again? He cannot win without help.* Hyw did not mention that Llywelyn himself was "so foolish" a few days before. He knew the prince's mind had changed by seeing the determination of de Lacy's soldiers, and of their leader. *Hyw, I must get inside the castle. I must see my brother, and discover for myself what the fool has done.*

"How can we, my liege? How can we enter without arousing the English?"

I don't know, lad, but we must think of a way. Our people depend on us now.

Chapter Thirty: Cat

Cat stood next to the bed. Somehow, there must be a way to prevent what she had seen in her vision. She hadn't told any of them about her gift, other than her mam and Aeneus. Elizabeth was English, before she became the Princess of Wales. The English, Cat knew, burned at the stake anyone with a hint of such a gift. She debated telling Margred, but she wasn't sure what her friend would think of her gift either. What if she found it necessary to tell her priest—what then? Some Welsh priests were known to deal harshly with these old ways. She had never considered telling Father Maelgwyn about it; somehow she knew he wouldn't understand.

"No," Cat said out loud. Mam raised her eyebrows. "We need to find a way to tell Elizabeth about the danger without letting anyone know how I learned of it."

"What do we know about the garrison here?" Adara wondered aloud. "We might try to ask the guards how their preparations are going. We are fortunate that Elizabeth keeps the English custom of high table. The captain of the garrison is your da's kinsman, and sits near me. If I show my concern, he might consent to reassure me."

Cat considered what part she might play. Although the girls still slipped away on their own to practice while the guards were busy training, Ifan often accompanied Cat and Margred on special outings away from the castle. "I'll start with him," Cat said, and Adara nodded.

Word was out in the town that the bard Gwilym was staying at the castle, and on Cat's thirteenth birthday he had agreed to perform in the evening after supper. He was adept at the three bardic instruments—the *telyn*, the long-necked *crwth*, and the *pibgorn* — although his specialty was the telyn.

As always, Gwilym began with one of the classical tunes that reminded Cat of Aber Falls with its mists trickling down from the mountains. Cat caught her mam's eye, and she nodded slightly as she turned back to the dour garrison captain. He seemed to be explaining something in some detail. Cat looked around her for Ifan. Many of the warriors were moving toward the bard, to show their talent with an instrument or their ability to sing warrior poetry with the master. As Cat tried to catch a glimpse of Ifan among them, Margred stirred beside her.

"I am in the mood for a merry tune tonight," she whispered in Cat's ear.

As supper ended, townsfolk had also begun to trickle into the castle hall, some on the pretext of late deliveries to the castle. The butcher, popular for his voice and his drum, brought a young lamb for the following day's meal. Cat noticed his son Drem with him, and felt sure that was the cause of Margred's restlessness.

Criccieth's bard took up the pibgorn, and a tall warrior took up the crwth. The butcher brought his drum from behind his back, where he had slung it, and sat behind them. As the music picked up in tempo, Margred grabbed Cat's hands, and began to form a circle with some of the other young girls who had arrived from Garth Celyn. Perhaps hoping to show Gwilym up, the bard handed the pipes to another warrior and began a lilting Romany love song in his strong tenor. Gwilym merely smiled and moved his fingers fast and light along the harp strings, harmonizing easily to fill in the chorus of the song.

Margred and Cat clapped and circled their companions, jumping lightly from one foot to the other without ever touching their skirts. As they finished, the musicians turned to another dance song, and the servants quickly moved back the tables to make a dance space. Drem joined the group of dancers along with several other young guards and a few more young women. Cat had little time to be concerned for how close Drem might have been standing next to Margred. She felt the closeness of a young man beside her, and stepped aside a little to look up at Sir Ifan.

"A happy birthday to you, Lady Catrin," he said. "I am glad to see you are recovered." She remembered he had accompanied them to town, and blushed to realize he must have carried her back to Criccieth.

He smiled at her as he placed his hands behind his back. His eyes were very blue in the firelight, she thought, as she turned away in the opening steps of the dance. Ifan's hand warmed her shoulder as the grand circle moved clockwise, and she barely brushed his as they moved back around the dancing space. She tried to train her mind on Rhys but she felt Ifan's eyes seek her out more than once as they changed partners, weaving around the room to find each other again.

When they finished, she steeled herself to question him, and found him happy to answer her.

"Welsh warriors train each day," Ifan said. "We have the skill and courage to stand against them."

"I have seen townsfolk and farmers coming to be trained as well," she said.

He hesitated, as if searching for a way to answer politely. "They have been a boon in helping prepare more arrows and lances for us," he managed.

Under his bluster, she learned he thought the garrison was small, barely enough to hold a castle of this size. By the time she excused herself to join her mam, Cat understood more about her dream but little about how it might be prevented.

"I thank thee for the honour of partnering the fairest flower in the hall this night," Ifan said to her, bowing. She sidled away from him before he could kiss her, as she had seen some of the warriors doing to ladies in the hall earlier.

"I thank you for the pretty compliment," she responded, hoping he remembered she was betrothed. She turned away before he could respond.

Margred and most of the ladies were still dancing, so Cat didn't need to make excuses to join Adara in the room she shared with Elizabeth's ladies. As they compared notes, Cat's concern grew.

"If the English break through the castle gates…" she began, trailing off.

"We must have a plan in readiness," Adara said decisively. "I will enlist our four guards to help us. We can trust them more than any others."

"I – I am not sure if Sir Ifan misunderstood my intentions," Cat stammered.

Adara considered her a moment. "I recall last winter when we visited Meirionnydd. You seemed close to Rhys."

"I am," Cat said, without hesitation. "Ifan is a worthy man, Mam, but Rhys is my betrothed."

"Then you must set him right. Mention your betrothal, and make sure he knows you intend to honour it." Cat nodded, and before long they bid each other good night. She made her way to her room. She found the other girls already in bed, sleeping, but no sign of Margred. Cat meant to remain awake until Margred returned, but she was soon lost to her dreams.

Chapter Thirty-one: Hyw

On the second day of the siege of Dolwyddelan, a string of packhorses made their way up the steep mountain paths toward the English camp, bringing a load of long white cloaks. Word quickly spread that the queen, Edward's wife, had made them. Edward had his soldiers and their retainers set out cloaks for all the men. Hyw marvelled at the way the men almost disappeared against the snow.

Fresh snow fell in the Welsh mountains overnight, and the English soldiers disappeared further in their white cloaks. As they sent up a "huzzah" for the queen and her ladies, Hyw learned that many of the mercenary knights had also been hired on because of her connections abroad.

Hyw pretended to admire their ruse, while inside his heart sank. Llywelyn grunted, realizing the cloaks would give Edward's troops a clear advantage. *We must get word to Dafydd.* Llywelyn cursed the English again.

On the third day of the siege, Hyw finished polishing his pile of soldiers' armour before James. Saying he wanted to stretch his legs, Hyw walked out of the area and then crept along the outcrop of rock until he came to a spot behind the castle. He crouched low and half-ran up the long meadow toward the next ridge. When he got to the top he concealed himself in a thicket of trees. Looking down, he could see Dolwyddelan in all its splendour: the rectangular tower, its dark stone hulk reaching to the grey sky, guarding the entrance to the Vale of Gwynedd, on the path to Garth Celyn.

Ditches cut into the rock on either side of the castle, and the rough terrain isolated it at the top of the ridge. Llywelyn's grandfather and namesake, Llywelyn the Great, had been born here. He had fortified the stone keep when he returned from crusades. Llywelyn told Hyw it was still a strategic location for the protection of North Wales.

Hyw could see shadows moving behind the balustrade at the top of the keep, and thought Welsh soldiers must be keeping watch inside. On all sides, a steep drop led from the castle to the valley floor. Edward's vast army of men fanned out along the valley like ants scurrying below him. How could he get the prince inside to see his brother, without being killed by either Welsh guards or English soldiers?

Hyw's eyes strayed upwards. Mountain peaks and ridges rose up on all sides of them. He could see points where the ridges came so close he could imagine one shepherd hailing another across it, although they grazed their sheep on different mountains.

Strains of a song crept back into his mind, unbidden. *Watchers now sleep beneath the stone.* Legend said the watchers would rise from beneath the mountain to rescue Wales in the hour of her greatest need. Some said the watchers were King Arthur's men, and they would fight to win back the land for the Britons, as the Welsh called themselves. Foolishness, he thought. How could I believe such foolish stories? And then his hands balled into fists and he raised them to the mountain tops. He stepped out from the concealing bush and screamed.

"Where are you? Can you not see that the stars have fallen? Can you not see the sun plummeting toward the earth? Lightning strikes your halls! Why do you not awaken? Why have you forsaken us?"

His eyes blurred, and he heard himself sobbing. He stood staring up, and had the sense that Llywelyn stood with him, lost in some agony of his own. Then he heard the prince gasp. Hyw swiped at his eyes with his palm to clear his vision, and looked back toward the mountain.

What had been mere wisps of cloud around the tips of the highest mountains had gathered and thickened. As he watched, the clouds themselves seemed to rush toward him, descending into the valley like the last rays of the sun. A white mist swallowed the ridges where he had imagined shepherds a moment ago. The mist rolled across the valleys, filling the dips and crevices until it swallowed the king's men. It swallowed the mighty siege equipment. It swallowed the stone castle of Dolwyddelan. And finally it crept up the meadow to where he stood, and swallowed him.

Around him, the white mist blocked everything from view. Where he expected it to be wet against his face, it was dry and light as air. He breathed it in, and tasted nothing.

What magic is this? he heard Llywelyn whisper.

Then he heard a whining. Looking down, he saw two glowing amber points of light in the mist. When the points disappeared and reappeared again, he realized they were the eyes of a small creature, blinking at him. The creature crept to the edge of the thicket where Hyw had concealed himself. Then it crept a little closer, and through the fog he could see it was a fox. It sat, panting and staring at him.

What are you waiting for? Llywelyn spoke within him. *Use your gift, Hyw. You must go with him to get us through the fog, and into the castle.*

"I dare not."

How can you refuse? You asked them to help. Can you not see this creature is your answer?

Hyw stared at the animal, and felt himself drawn into its amber eyes. Although he knew Llywelyn to be a shade with no more life than a prayer in his mind, he placed himself once again in front of the prince as if to protect him. He felt a shock as the curious mind of the fox met his. Unlike any other melding, this one seemed to require no effort on Hyw's part, as his feet seemed to melt into paws.

Then he was running with the fox, back through the camp of men. He knew at any moment someone might see him, stop him, hang him as a spy, or as a witch who had called the fog down upon them. But it was as if the English slept where they stood. The fox maneuvered between them, and Hyw went with him.

Finally they stopped and the fox sat on its haunches, panting as before. Hyw found himself standing in front of a section of the castle's stone wall. He knew without being told that it was a secret door, like the one his mother could find in the stone when they were forced to leave Garth Celyn.

I have lived here often in the last fifty years, yet I did not know this was here. Llywelyn seemed puzzled.

"Are we dreaming?"

There is only one way to find out.

The fox whined again, and Hyw sensed it would remain to lead them back again. He reached forward and his hand found the hidden latch. The stone opened to him, and he entered.

Chapter Thirty-two: Cat

Cat walked up the stone stairs to the battlements of Criccieth and stood in the early light, looking out over the landscape. She had awakened from a bad dream, and in spite of her recent illness she felt the need to walk. She snuggled deeper into her warm cloak, wondering where Hyw and Da were now, and whether she would ever see them again. As she made her way around the wall walk, her thoughts turned to Rhys, the boy she was pledged to marry. Would he be looking out at another section of the Eryri Mountains, she wondered, standing on the wall walk at Castell-y-Bere and staring at the mountain they called the Giant's Chair?

She made her way slowly to the seaward side. She wasn't thinking about visions, but about the wind blowing across the sea with the hint of January snow. She stopped for a moment and stared down at the roiling waters. The waves began to circle, swirling over and over, drawing her inside and—

—she found herself on the deck of a large ship. She felt timber under her feet instead of stones, and the press of the sea in the breeze on her

face. She heard the voices around her and recognized their accents. Irish! Were they raiders, attacking the castle? She looked around her, and saw two other ships sailing a little apart from each other.

The sailors were swinging the sail around to catch the wind. She saw them point toward shore, and saw the castle on the horizon. Then the captain said something and pointed upward toward the Irish crest and colours flying there. Two sailors jumped up and grabbed a piece of fabric, hoisting it up a rope into the mast. A Welsh lion like the colours of Llywelyn's crest unfurled just under the Irish.

Too late! Huge boulders and flaming arrows began falling around the men, onto the wooden deck of the ship. The men began to run, one screaming as an arrow embedded into his arm and the flames engulfed him.

No! Cat tried to cry out. They're friends! She turned as if to tell someone—

—and stood alone on the stone battlement of the castle. She stared out at the sea, but she could not see the ships. What if they were on the way right now? She had to tell someone. She turned from the battlements and went in search of her mam.

Adara nodded as Cat told her about the vision and what she thought it meant.

"We'll get Ifan and the others to watch for ships," she said. "How many did you say there were?"

"I saw three."

"And they're friendly?"

"I believe they are, yes." Cat described the colours she had seen unfurled against the mast. Adara tapped her fingertips together in thought before she answered.

"This might be our answer, Cat," she said. "While I tended the babies yesterday, Princess Elizabeth's scout reported Castell-y-Bere is garrisoned and not yet under attack. If the English do get through

Criccieth's gates, a stout ship could take us around the bay and up the Mawddach river. We'd be a short ride to Castell-y-Bere from there."

Of course, they could escape to Meirionnydd! Cat tried not to admit how much she wanted to see Rhys again, especially since Ifan's attentions. Then she realized what her mother had said. "Ride?"

"Aye, if the ship is as large as you saw. We can board the horses, and they will take us to the castle."

Now all we need to do is convince the captain not to sink the Irish, Cat thought, as her mam rushed from the room to enlist her remaining guards. That is, if the ships arrive in time.

Chapter Thirty-three: Hyw

Hyw crouched and crept forward through the hidden door in the wall. Mist shrouded the courtyard of Dolwyddelan castle. The banner streaming out above them was Llywelyn's: three red lions striding forward for the Prince of Wales. It was mid-afternoon, yet all seemed as quiet and still as night. He hesitated as he spotted a guard in the yard. Hyw could see the badge on the guard's cloak, showing a blue lion striding forward on a gold field. He frowned.

"*The lions of Gwynedd, blue for my brother and heir. This is Dafydd's man. He has not yet changed his colours.*" The mist seemed to magnify the slight disorientation Hyw felt when the prince spoke inside his mind. He knew if he closed his eyes he would see the prince clearly. Yet he could not help but stare at the guard, who stayed silent and immobile in the swirling mist. Hyw felt the hairs raise on the back of his neck.

"*It's just like the stories say,*" marvelled Llywelyn. "*This is truly a gift from the Old Ones, Hyw. Now you must trust them. Push onward. My brother waits inside the castle, and we must get to him while we still can."*

Hyw made his way carefully behind the guard, who never moved from his position. Two other soldiers also stood still. One held his hand in front of his face as if he was about to pick his nose. Hyw almost wanted to laugh, but he was afraid a noise might break the spell.

He slipped up the stone stairs to the castle door. The mist followed, swirling around him. It was as if he saw everything through a small round window in it. He could not see the castle's great hall clearly unless he turned toward it. Then he could see the huge fireplace and the inset window seats. Yet the people in the hall did not move as he went by.

More than passing strange. Llywelyn's whisper sounded as if in Hyw's ear, but he was so taken by the sight of the frozen people that he listened without closing his eyes. *Mayhap they are out-of-time, or we are, as in the old stories. This could be a valuable advantage for us, Hyw, if you could but control it.*

"It is not my doing," Hyw whispered back. "And I know not why the Old Ones have favoured us with this time-out-of-time. But I believe it is as my uncle said. We cannot expect to use this to our personal advantage. It would show disrespect."

Llywelyn remained silent. Across from the door, Hyw spotted a stairwell and moved toward it. Mist drifted with him as he felt his way along the stone wall to the upper reaches of the castle. To his left he saw another stairwell that must lead to the wall walk, and knew without Llywelyn's whispered warning that Dafydd's warriors would be patrolling. He hoped the mist held them trapped as well.

To his right was a wooden door. It opened as he neared it, and he stepped inside. A man stood near the fireplace, his back to the door. Hyw watched him rub his hands together for warmth. He didn't understand why this man could move when the others could not.

He is my brother. So again, as in the old stories, the Prince of the Blood is allowed to remain unaffected by their magic. Long ago, before

Elinor and Gwenllian, I named Dafydd my heir, and now it seems he has claimed the title. I must speak with him, Hyw, if it can be done.

Hyw nodded at Llywelyn's voice. He closed his eyes and concentrated on the prince's will, until he felt a strange sensation, as if the prince had stepped in front of him. Llywelyn's shadow blocked the firelight, and Hyw craned his neck to see.

Dafydd swung around. He snarled and his eyes glared at them. "You," Dafydd growled. "You are dead, and still you haunt me. I know you are dead. I heard it from your own man."

Hyw realized two things instantly. First, he realized that Dafydd could see Llywelyn, standing in the doorway. He wasn't sure how they had managed to give that illusion, or how much was due to the magic of the Old Ones. Still, it felt right to allow the prince to lead this exchange, so he determined not to fight it. Second, he knew when Dafydd referred to "your own man," he had to mean Bran. He almost cried out for more information about his da, but he heard the prince's voice rumble in his ears.

"You speak of Bran ap Rhys of Gwynedd," Llywelyn said, using formal speech to force his brother to answer, according to custom. "Does he yet live?"

Dafydd smirked, folding his arms across his chest. "So, you do not keep track of your own men. Lucky are the Cymry that I have taken your place."

"Is it so? And is that why your guards stand still to let me past?"

"Hah! Of course, if you truly are a shade, my men cannot follow where you go. Whereas your men—well, their loyalties must remain with the living, mustn't they? Like your man, who came to me after you fell."

Now it was Hyw's turn to lay a hand on Llywelyn's arm. He felt Llywelyn's efforts to calm himself. "It is only reasonable that Bran would want to serve the Prince of Wales. What reception did you give him?"

Dafydd's face twisted into a snarl again. "What do you think? I bade him prove himself. He leads the resistance in the mountains."

Llywelyn drew a breath and began again. "Brother, I did not make my way here to fight with you, or be goaded into it. You see me as I am now: but a shade. I cannot harm you in this incorporeal form. Instead, I come as your ally to help save our people."

Dafydd frowned, and inclined his head as if considering what Llywelyn said. Encouraged, Llywelyn continued.

"You are surrounded by the English, and yet in my presence here you have a brief respite. The English have white camouflage and plan to attack with stealth as early as tomorrow. Edward sends a messenger to the pope. You must send a swifter one. You may recall the pope supported my claim as Prince of Wales. Whatever you thought then, use that privilege now, to save our country and our people. Ask for men and arms to help you win against Edward."

Dafydd moved slightly. He kept his head down so Hyw could not see his eyes, but unfolded his arms as if open to Llywelyn's words.

"What proof have I to offer?" Dafydd replied. "The pope well knows I sided with Edward over you. Nay, don't deny it. I'm sure that in your messages to and fro you were careful to paint me a villain and a traitor to you. Why would the pope rally to my side now? I would require a talisman. Have you your royal seal that I might send it to prove my claim?"

"Alas, it was stolen from me," Llywelyn responded. "Edward has it now."

"You know this to be so? As a shade, can you not move among his men as you have mine? And steal it back from them? Or failing that, if I appoint a man to follow you, can you not lead my man to the very spot so we may steal it back?"

"I cannot."

"So you will not?"

"It is more difficult—"

"You know where it is?"

Llywelyn hesitated. "No."

"What good then in coming here? Why should I do as you ask

without a talisman to prove you are who you say you are? Why should I believe you are my brother? Mayhap you are a denizen of the devil come to fool me into betraying my people."

"Me, a denizen of the devil? You sound like the English still." Llywelyn's voice grew harsh as he moved forward and rolled up his sleeve. "Here is the scar you gave me yourself when you attacked me on the battlefield, fighting with our brother against me."

"Aye and I would again." Dafydd moved forward as well, and he snarled again. "Even as a shade, you plague me with your status and your pope and your futile stance against the English king. It is your fault I have fallen from Edward's favour. This day I sent a messenger to Edward's camp to offer to join forces with him and win Wales. Instead, he sent me the man's head and with it a note: 'Yours will be next.' Had I your princely seal, I would use it to save this country. If you cannot get it for me, what use are you?"

With this, Dafydd reached toward the dagger on his belt. Llywelyn reacted on instinct, but his hand closed on empty air where his dagger once was. In a sudden rush of wind around them, Hyw felt himself meld with Llywelyn again. *Run!* Llywelyn cried inside his mind.

Hyw turned and ran for the stairwell. As he rounded the door, he heard Dafydd's dagger thwack into the wood near his head. Then he all but fell back down the stairs, leaping to the ground. He whispered thanks to his old captain, Aeneus, for the strictness of his physical training and the strength it gave him to withstand the jump without injury.

Dafydd bellowed behind him. The sound dispelled the mist that had protected them. A guard almost bumped him coming in.

"Help the prince," Hyw cried. The guard stepped around him, looking for Dafydd. Then Hyw was running across the courtyard. Guards sprinted past him the other way, toward the castle and Dafydd's yells.

"He has seen his ghosts again," one guard said to another as they ran. They ignored Hyw. He pushed on toward the wall. His fingers found the release for the secret door and heard the scrape of stone on stone. He shinnied through as it slammed shut behind him.

Chapter Thirty-four: Cat

Elizabeth stood, arms folded one over the other, and looked hard at Cat. “And how do you know they will attack?” Adara stood beside Cat, and instinctively reached out and took her hand as they faced their princess.

“I do not know, your highness,” Cat admitted. “I only know —” She tried to think of how to explain without telling Elizabeth about her gift. “I believe we should consider the danger.”

“Your garrison is less than half the strength needed to protect and fortify the castle,” Adara added. “Every report we have says the English come in the thousands. Castle after castle has fallen before them. How long can we hold them off?”

“They’re not at our gates,” Elizabeth replied.

“Not yet,” Cat said, and then wished she hadn’t spoken.

Elizabeth considered for a moment, and then shook her head and unfolded her arms. “What choice do we have? Dafydd is holding the line at Dolwyddelan, and when he has repelled the English, he will rejoin us here."

"Of course he will," Adara said. "But if they come by way of the sea, as they did five years past, then he –"

Elizabeth waved Adara's words away and paced to the window. Cat knew Adara was right. Dolwyddelan Castle protected the route to the south and west, but it was far inland from the Irish Sea. She knew the stories of English treachery from the bard's songs. The English captured Princess Elinor on her way to Wales, and kept her prisoner for three years. Prince Llywelyn had tried to fight but they came by sea to Anglesey and burned the crops, crippling the Welsh. In the end, Llywelyn was forced to give up half his kingdom and more to get her back. But her mam gestured to her, and they waited quietly.

Elizabeth finally turned back to them, her face serious and set. "Very well. I will consider it. We should have a plan of escape. After all, we don't have tunnels like Garth Celyn. I will ask the captain for suggestions."

Cat was about to say more, but her mam squeezed her hand. "Thank you, your highness. That is wise and prudent of you."

"I will call him now, if you ladies will excuse me." Elizabeth turned from them. Cat and Adara curtsied quickly and left her to consider it.

"Come with me to the gardens," Adara said. The snow had melted but the wind played havoc in the garden, swirling their cloaks as they walked. Adara asked in a quiet voice, "There has been no sighting of a ship. How sure are you of what you saw?"

"I don't know, Mam," Cat said. She felt tired and unsure, and wondered if she had completely recovered from her illness. "It was the same as the other times, but—well, we were able to change those times, weren't we?"

"I hope we can change this one as well," Mam said. "No point mentioning it all at once. We will need to find a way to tell Elizabeth without endangering you." Then she turned to look at Cat. "You've grown so much in a few weeks. Sorry I am that this had to happen,

Cat, but I am glad to have you with me. You're a real help to me, and to the people here."

Cat felt a flush of pleasure and bowed her head to thank her mam for the compliment. As they came to the entrance of the gardens, they saw two guards holding horses for Father Maelgwyn and the castle priest.

"Heading out on their rounds," Adara said.

"Good day to you, Father," Cat called. He looked their way with a start, and an expression passed across his face that seemed almost guilty to her. She hoped he regretted his decision to stop the girls from exercising, while the news of war came closer with each messenger who rode through their gates. She longed to talk with him about it again, but he often went out these days and left confessions and services to the younger priest training at the castle. He waved to them without speaking as he mounted. The castle priest mounted as well, and they were off through the gates without looking back.

Chapter Thirty-five: Hyw

The fox was pacing on silent paws as Hyw sped through the closing gap in the castle's defences. The small animal yelped once and ran. Hyw quickly moulded his mind to the fox, and they sped through the trees back to Shrewsbury's camp.

Almost as soon as the camp came into sight, the fox yelped again and vanished. Hyw felt it torn from his mind, replaced by the terror of falling and blackness. He closed his eyes and stumbled. *Steady, boy*, the prince said.

Hyw recovered and stood panting, his arms on his knees. "I am sorry we did not accomplish our goal."

There is more than one way to shear a sheep, Hyw. We know two things from this that we did not know. The first is that your father lives. The second is that he has a following. He would never have gone to Dafydd otherwise. He may be camped nearby.

Hyw raised himself and looked around him at the mountains. Hyw wanted to wave, but stopped himself. He realized if his father was watching, he would see his son among the English. What would happen if the Welsh attacked? Would Hyw in the end be forced to fight his father's men to save his own life? Or to save James?

James! What if James asked for him and no one could find him? How long had he been gone? Hyw ran again, this time back to camp.

He found James seated in the dirt with a pile of armour around him. His friend scowled up at him.

"I thought you were going for a walk in the hills."

Hyw spotted his own pile of finished armour, sitting in the same spot as when he left. He thought about the silent, unmoving people in Dolwyddelan castle. They truly must have been stopped in time. He realized it had only been a few moments since he left to go on a walk, and discover a fox, a castle, and a living prince. He could find no words to explain it to his friend, so he grinned instead.

"I ran. Here, let me give you a hand." For the rest of the afternoon the two boys worked together to finish readying the men's armour. When Shrewsbury's knights came to collect it, one of the younger men feinted toward Hyw.

"Here's your reward for a job well done, boy." Hyw recognized him as a friend of Alan Acton, and he recognized the man's play-fight as a gesture of remembrance where words failed him.

"Gerald, save your fight for tomorrow," another guffawed.

"Why—do you go into battle again?" Hyw took advantage of the younger knight's familiarity to ask, and Gerald nodded.

"May the saints preserve us," said another, shivering. "Not soon enough for me. I like it not in this place. The quicker we put the fear of God into these heathen Welsh and return to our own land, the better, to my mind."

"Fear of God," Gerald snorted. "Fear of Edward, you mean."

"Edward who?" said the first man, settling down on the armour and bringing out his whittling knife and a twig. "Gilbert le Clare, more like. It is his army I will join, after this battle's won. I hear they fare towards South Wales again. The land of milk and honey."

"Aye and with land—even in godforsaken Wales—you could marry your Sal," said Gerald. The men guffawed and chided each other about their "honeyed codpiece." The first man jabbed at one of the jokers with his fist. James and Hyw had seen the clowns on fair days, each with a huge stuffed codpiece attached to their pants to represent a fake phallus. Their cheeks flamed as they guessed what the men meant by the jest.

Ask them which direction Edward goes. Llywelyn's voice was clear enough inside Hyw's head. He turned slightly from the men and closed his eyes to find the prince dressed in full war regalia. *Ask them where the king plans to travel next. We must try, Hyw. If we can get word to Bran, we may yet get the royal seal back for Dafydd.*

Hyw knew how desperate Llywelyn must feel if he was willing to try to enlist his brother's help again. He turned back to the men and waited for a break in the conversation.

"You are the lucky ones indeed. Le Clare is brave, but my master will follow the king. Where will he go after the castle falls?"

"Who can say, boy?" Gerald looked at him kindly. "He is the king and can do as he pleases."

"Pah," said another. "Once he has Dafydd in his grasp, he will hang him from the Tower of London, beside his brother's head."

Partly to distract Llywelyn from the comment, Hyw rubbed his head. "That puzzles me. I thought Edward and Dafydd grew up together. That they were allies."

"Nay. This Day-vid was the bait Edward used to hook his war-like brother."

"If that be true, then why does the king remain?

"He means to crush the Welsh now once and for all."

"Aye, he must end the royal line," Gerald agreed, "so there can be no more reason for these Welsh to fight."

Hyw thought swiftly of the baby, Gwenllian. His mother would die rather than see that baby harmed—or killed. He sensed the eyes of the men on him and tried not to show his feelings on his face.

"You may have been Alan's friend, young lad, but I begin to wonder why you are so interested in the king." The older knight had stopped cutting fruit, and was staring at Hyw.

He shrugged. Just then James' stomach growled and as he grabbed at it, all the men laughed. Gerald reached out to ruffle James' hair. "Time for supper, is it? Enough of your questions, then. A prize for the one who can run the faster down the hill toward yon campfire."

Hyw breathed a small sigh of relief as he led James in the race – slowing just enough to let his friend win in the end.

The next day another group of men rode in. They were dressed in hooded cowls, and for a moment Hyw looked for his uncle among them. Then the sun caught the rings on their fingers as they shifted their horse's reins, and in that glint he realized the men were priests, not simple monks like Gawain. His disappointment grew to fear as the men threw back their hoods. Llywelyn cursed anew, and Hyw ducked his head before he could be seen. Among the group was the priest of Garth Celyn, Father Maelgwyn.

The others are also Welsh. At least one served my brother in years past. Llywelyn's voice was low although only Hyw could hear it. He was convinced Hyw must find his father. *Bran will know a way to aid our people. No doubt any Welshmen capable of resistance will be with him. We must make contact and warn them. Mayhap he has men inside the castle and can get word to them.*

He directed Hyw up the escarpment beside the stream, and along the nearby meadow. *Stop here*, the prince said. Hyw could see nothing, but Llywelyn showed him a spot where he believed there were signs of men coming to gather water. He led Hyw over to the hedge. Under some loose branches they found an old pot. It was dented, but not rusted.

Left here for use, but old enough that anyone who finds it would not think it important enough to return for. Nothing but the last man's leavings. Make markings here, as I will show you.

At Llywelyn's bidding, Hyw cleared a bit of dirt and wrote symbols as Llywelyn directed him.

My grandfather taught us Arabic, and your father knows it well. It was how the Welsh crusader knights passed information to each other after their return, and we have kept that tradition.

"What did I write?"

The words for "beware" and "priests." Hyw traced the symbols in the air, and tried to remember them. Then he placed the pot on top so it would not erase the letters. At Llywelyn's bidding he gathered twigs and set them in the form of a fish beside the pot. He used a stone for an eye. *An old trick of mine that your father may remember, if indeed he is here.*

After Hyw replaced the branches to cover his work, he stared around him for a moment. Could his da really be so close? Finally Llywelyn reminded him to run back to the stream for the water he had promised to take back to the English camp.

The attack on Dolwyddelan began at dawn the following day. Hyw and James watched as the soldiers made their way with stealth up the mountain, fearing the worst. Again Shrewsbury would not allow the boys to take part in the battle, and the cooks and stewards kept them busy with chores around the camp all day. Hyw strained to listen, but no sounds of battle carried over the wind.

Hyw was about to try making contact with a hawk or some other bird again when a few soldiers returned and made their way to the camp cook. After a few hasty words the cook began to move quickly.

"Here boys, you can help." James and Hyw gathered the cook's things and within minutes the camp was rounded up and on the move. They made their way up the hill to the castle.

It was noisy with English soldiers, but Hyw could neither see nor smell blood or signs of fighting. Setting up kept him too busy to ask anyone what had happened. That night, when the men had time around the fire, he and James finally heard the tale.

"We crept up the hill in silence," Gerald said, his eyes glowing in the flames. "The castle gate was open. 'What is this?' our captain said. 'Some kind of Welsh enchantment?' In we came, fearing a trap. But no, there was nothing. Not even a dog in the yard. It was as if they sank into the mountain and vanished." Gerald shivered a little as he told the tale, and Hyw thought it was from more than cold. Yet he could not help but be glad that Dafydd and his people had somehow managed to escape.

Edward's army took up residence in the castle, and the soldiers celebrated long into the night. Dolwyddelan had fallen after only five days of siege.

Chapter Thirty-six: Cat

Cat and her mam asked their guards to watch for Irish ships. Each day they reported to Adara from the wall walk where they "stretched their legs" with Criccieth's watch. They said nothing yet to Princess Elizabeth. Cat wanted to be present when the ships were sighted so she could claim to see something that proved the ships were friendly to Wales. But she couldn't be sure the banner in her vision had been real, or that the Irish would unfurl it in time.

As the days went by and no ships came in sight, the guards relaxed their vigilance. Cat still exchanged glances with her mam and occasionally asked about the ships. She continued to exercise with Margred and two Garth Celyn women in their favourite spot. It was sheltered from the worst of the winds churning up the channel, but Margred's younger sisters claimed it was too chilly for them. Cat and Margred found their exercises warmed them and often left the corset laces loose or didn't wear one at all during their morning "walks."

"Here, Cat," Margred called, setting up the makeshift target again. "Your turn."

Cat chose three small throwing knives as Margred and the other girls stepped out of range. Their practice weapons were meant for young boys to begin their training, and not weighted with the kind of care the warriors took when they fashioned their own weapons. Cat hefted each one and chose what she thought was the best. She set the other two down, and lined up carefully with the target. She drew her arm back, and just as she released it she heard a shout.

"Lady Catrin!"

Cat watched the knife thwack into the target before she turned. Father Maelgwyn and the Criccieth priest had reined their horses on the rise of the hill, and he was staring at her.

"Lady Catrin," he shouted again. "I expressly forbade you from this activity. And you other women—Lady Margred! I am surprised to see you participating in this folly."

The two girls said nothing. Cat was immediately aware that she had caught up her dress in her belt to free her movements, and she quickly moved to smooth it down again. Several other girls did the same, trying to hide their faces from him. One of the other women tried to gather up the target and equipment, but it was too late. Cat felt her mouth gaping open, and quickly shut it, trying to think of something to say.

"We were playing a game, Father," Margred responded, her voice level. She had taken off her skirts in favour of the pair of boy's breeches she always wore, and made no move to hide herself now. "There's no harm in it."

"A game?" Father Maelgwyn twitched the horse's reigns and the animal grunted in protest. "I will see you both in the princess' solar within the hour, and at confession tomorrow morning."

He spurred the horse toward Criccieth, with the castle priest following quickly behind him. Margred and Cat stared at each other a moment, and then Margred burst out laughing.

"You should see your face, Cat," she said. Cat laughed as well then, and the other women nervously joined in as they all quickly gathered the target and equipment from the ground.

"We will put it away safe, my lady," said one of the women Cat recognized from Garth Celyn. "You'd best hurry to meet yon priest."

Cat and Margred slipped up to their shared room before going to answer the priest in Elizabeth's chambers. They helped each other adjust their laces and changed into fresh tunics. As Margred brushed her hair, Cat used the jug of water in their room to freshen up. As she bent over the basin—

—she saw Hyw and another boy wading knee-deep in a stream. Each held a bucket, and as she looked into Hyw's eyes she felt herself drawn deeper into the waters. The image dissolved as if a pebble had been dropped into the stream, and it reformed into the snowy grounds of a soldier's camp. She saw Father Maelgwyn handing his horse's reins to a guard, and taking a folded piece of parchment from the inside of his gown. He handed the paper to the guard, who looked at the seal and nodded.

Then she saw the other priests behind Father Maelgwyn. They also dismounted and made their way toward a grand tent with a banner flying above it that she somehow knew belonged to the English king, Edward Longshanks. A sudden wave of anger and disappointment rippled through her, and the image changed.

She saw Criccieth as if from the battlements again. The castle was surrounded by English soldiers. Father Maelgwyn stood on the stones with his lantern, waving it. A light answered from the soldiers below. Cat shrank back into the late afternoon shadows. The priest gestured to two guards near him, and they moved toward the pulley that would raise the heavy metal portcullis protecting the castle from the invaders.

No! she tried to cry out. No, you mustn't open it—

—and she found herself staring at the basin of water in her room at Criccieth.

"Traitors!" The words came out of her mouth before she could stop herself.

"Who are?" Margred asked.

Cat was too upset to curb her tongue, and too familiar now with Margred's company to want to hide her gifts any longer. "Father Maelgwyn and the other priest—and more besides them—have met in secret with the English king."

"What? He wouldn't," Margred began. Then Cat was telling her about her gift of second sight, and briefly about her connection with her brother Hyw. When she was finished, Margred looked thoughtful.

"How does it happen?" she puzzled. "Your visions, I mean. Is it the water? The songs say that's how Queen Mab contacts her people of the Tylwyth Teg."

"It may be," said Cat. "I gave Hyw a token before he left, an arm band woven with some of my hair as a remembrance. And he gave me a cloak. Mayhap that helps us bridge the distance between us."

"And have you had visions of other things as well?"

Cat nodded, and explained about seeing English soldiers and their horses on the trail during their escape from Garth Celyn, and more recently the ships she had seen coming to help them. "The horses had been mere hours away, but the ships still haven't appeared."

"Then how do you know if the ships are a true vision, or for that matter this new vision of Father Maelgwyn?" Margred asked. "Would the priest not say your suspicions are convenient?"

"How so?" Cat bit back, and then stopped herself. Could her vision have been influenced by their current troubles with Father Maelgwyn? Cat thought for a moment. "In my vision today, when I first saw Hyw, I saw Father Maelgwyn on his horse arriving to speak to the king. It was the same horse he rode today."

"What if that much has already occurred?" Margred's face was alarmed.

"It may have," Cat said. "There was something—some quality of light—that seemed different in that part. As if I saw through Hyw's eyes something that he already knew. The second part was more hazy somehow, more like the vision I had of the ships."

"So mayhap the priest's actions will happen on the same day as the ships arrive," said Margred. "The priests were gone for over a week this time, and the horses were lathered as if they were hard-rode." She appeared to be thinking it over as well.

Finally Margred stood up. "We cannot accuse a priest without something more, unless you want everyone to know you are a sage and a soothsayer."

Cat shook her head, standing as well. "Nay, Margred, in these times—"

"Fear me not," Margred laughed, taking Cat's hand. "Yet we must try to find out more somehow. Come. Let us face the music we have made for ourselves, and see if we can change the tune."

Chapter Thirty-seven: Hyw

Dolwyddelan was much smaller than English castles. Most of the army, including Robert as Hyw was relieved to see, camped outside the gates. Shrewsbury and a select few of his guards bunked in the castle with the other lords, and kept James with him as squire. Hyw slept with the soldiers in the garrison near the castle gate. He made himself useful there, and joined James inside at mealtimes and for short periods in the afternoons, when they could catch up with each other's business.

The English troops began building the next day, and Hyw quickly learned they were putting up a second tower to keep better control of the countryside. A man arrived as if he had been sent for, and took control over a number of soldiers and stonemasons. James watched intently until the man—an architect, Gerald told them—agreed to let the boys help.

The priests came again. For two days Edward held council with them and his lords. Hyw tried to get close but the tents were heavily guarded. He worried that Father Maelgwyn had seen him, but the man did not stop or make any sign. Hyw was relieved, but resolved not to try to spy directly again. Instead, he used his old trick of offering help to the soldiers. As before, he heard much while he cleaned and sharpened their weapons or oiled their leather leggings.

"Aye, yon priests come to help us find that heathen Dafydd," said Gerald, who had joined Shrewsbury's personal guard after the siege. "Won't be long now before we know which way the wind blows him."

They will know his ways and his castles. Llywelyn made a disgusted sound. Hyw knew Dafydd had control of several castles in North Wales, such as Dinbych and Caergwrle. Hyw recalled Caergwrle was built near a town called "Hope." Could he have gone there? *His castle there fell months ago,* he heard Llywelyn say. *Dafydd will go to Castell-y-Bere, no doubt. It is the most fortified.*

Hyw was torn between his feelings and his fealty. He wanted to leave for Garth Celyn right away to warn them, and he longed to see his mother again. But Llywelyn would not hear of it. *Not yet, boy. We have much to do.*

With that he led Hyw back to the area where they had left the message. It appeared undisturbed, but as soon as he moved the branch Hyw could see the pot had been moved and the word carefully erased. In its place was a symbol Hyw had not written. Llywelyn laughed. *It is the Arabic for 'friend.' It can be none other than your father, Hyw. Now I am certain of it. We must find him, Hyw.*

Hyw watched from the castle battlements as le Clare and his troops packed up to leave. He could not catch sight of Robert or Gerald in the company, although he knew they would be there. It took most of the day for the Marcher army to head down the mountain to the south. The priests also left the castle under le Clare's protection.

Edward had decided to remain for another week. Some thought it was to get the new tower underway, but Llywelyn had other ideas.

He is sending out spies to discover which way Dafydd has gone. Mark you, my brother has a good chance if he stays hidden and makes his way to Castell-y-Bere. He knows the mountains almost as well as I.

And yet the mountains did not hide you from Mortimer, Hyw thought. If Llywelyn heard, he seemed too preoccupied watching le Clare's departing soldiers to comment.

Hyw ran to the castle keep, and found several knights at the table breaking fast. James was there as well. Since he had already served his father, he sat at one of the lower tables to grab a bite of food for himself. Hyw slipped over to him.

"When do we leave?"

James shook his head and swallowed a piece of unleavened bread. "Father will remain, and so will I."

"What?"

"'Tis true. He pleaded age and gout, and Edward has given us leave."

Hyw looked into James' bright excited eyes and knew he was thinking about the castle building. At least now James could enjoy watching the architect without hindrance. Hyw tried to smile for his friend. "Do you—have you heard where Edward takes his army?"

James nodded, and a look of concern passed over his features. "Hyw, I am worried for you. He plans to march on all of Dafydd's castles, but the talk is that he moves across the north from Garth Celyn to Criccieth."

It was as Llywelyn thought, but Hyw felt a hollow fear in his chest. He tried to hide his eyes from his friend, but felt James' hand on his arm.

"You must go, of course," James whispered. "You must get there before them all and find your mother."

Hyw could not believe his friend knew his heart so well. He looked into the other boy's eyes. "And you must not help me. Your father would never forgive you."

"Yet I will help you all I can." James set his chin with resolve.

Wait a little, Hyw, Llywelyn said. *Let me think.*

"Give me a moment to consider," Hyw whispered to James. He

closed his eyes for a moment, and found Llywelyn with his hand cupping his chin in thought.

You need to protect him and his good father. If you run now, it may seem they have harboured a fugitive. It will not go well for them. And you will lose a future ally, once this war has ended. Llywelyn stood and looked squarely at Hyw. *I may know another way.*

It was a way fraught with danger, but Hyw found himself relaying Llywelyn's plan to James. They would offer to go for water together. James would return alone, running, and claim that Hyw had been taken by Welsh marauders. The boys modified it with what they knew might work. They could secure some food from the cook, who was always willing to feed growing boys, and wrap it in cloth as before for Hyw to take along with him. They decided to wait until the following day to try their luck.

Hyw decided to lead James downstream but turn and go upstream once they parted, to make doubly sure the plan would work. *What your friend does not know, he bears no responsibility for*, the prince said.

Later that afternoon, when James went to the architect to study, Hyw used the commotion of armies on the move to leave another message. Llywelyn showed him the Arabic signs that would convince the men to keep clear of the area so the English soldiers would not find them. Hyw looked around him for the last time, wondering if his father watched from the thickets, or perhaps from an unseen cave. He tried spying through the eyes of a nearby jackdaw, but he could not spot any human activity in the area.

Hyw busied himself in the barn for the morning. At dinner, Shrewsbury kept James busy on the dais, but Hyw managed to collect some extra food from his table and from the cook.

He waited for James in the courtyard after dinner. James brought the water bucket. "I thought I'd never be done." He wiped his brow with one sleeve. Hyw grabbed the bucket from him as the two boys set out, quickening their pace so no one would find more chores for them.

As they rounded the castle gate, Hyw led them downstream, away from the message bush. They waited until they had gotten well past the castle before they slowed to talk.

"Hold on." James reached into his tunic and brought out a small flask of watered-down wine for the journey. Then he slipped off his inner quilted vest. Hyw tried to protest, but James said he had another. "Besides, I need to know you are warm out here in this snow. Surely it will be warmer near Garth Celyn?"

"I'm sure it will be," Hyw replied. It was still January but the Menai Strait kept the climate at Garth Celyn mild, and he did not want to worry his friend.

Since Hyw had explored more often than James, he had chosen the spot for them to part company. He slowed his pace as they neared it, and James brought out his finger weaving. They wound each other a wrist bracelet. The small one Cat had made was barely a thread on Hyw's wrist now, and he could not speak as James plaited his sturdier cord into hers. Hyw touched the bracelet as he looked down into the water of the stream, and thought of his sister and mother, wondering how long it would be before he saw them again.

The boys half filled their bucket and then dropped it on the ground, grinding their feet into the slush and mud around the stream as if a great many men had scuffled there. They were careful to leave a few tracks of their own clearly visible.

"We will meet again Hyw. When all this is over, you will come back to Shrewsbury."

Hyw found his voice then, and put one hand on his friend's shoulder. "I will hold you to your father's promise. I should like nothing more than to serve you, when you are lord of Shrewsbury castle."

"It is a pact then."

"Now head you back," Hyw told him, "so I can see you safely around the bend before I go."

James hesitated a moment, and threw his arms around Hyw

in a quick hug. Then he ran, stopping once to wave. Hyw set out upstream, taking extra time to cover his tracks and hoping James remembered to slow down as he neared Dolwyddelan, so he would not raise the alarm too quickly.

Chapter Thirty-eight: Cat

Ifan arrived to escort Cat and Margred as they came out of their room.

"Lady Elizabeth bids you to her solar, ladies," he said. Cat searched for the twinkle she usually saw in his eye since their night of dancing and poetry, but could not find it.

"Do you know what it is about, Sir Ifan?" Margred asked for her.

"It is not my place—" he began, but Cat interrupted.

"Nay, Sir Ifan, tell us, that we might be a little prepared," she said.

He looked uncomfortable. "Father Maelgwyn had much to say to the Lady Adara and the princess about your—recent activity."

"He thinks it unseemly." She said it as a statement, and he nodded. "And what do you think?"

"I serve my captain, Lord Aeneus, and would not question his decisions."

"Of course not," she agreed. "But privately, do you agree we should be prepared?"

"I would die before I let any harm come to you," he said, and then added, "or to the Lady Margred, or any of our ladies. Yet these are difficult times. God forbid our enemies should breach our gates. Yet if they do, and aught prevent me from reaching you, if you have the strength to flee from harm—then I think it time well spent."

She nodded, pleased to hear him say so. "Then I am ready to face my priest."

He bowed slightly to them, his mouth twisting in what might have been a smile as he stepped behind the girls. Margred linked her arm through Cat's as they marched toward the princess's rooms.

In the end, they were able to say little in their own defence. Cat was surprised when her mam stood up to Father Maelgwyn.

"Begging your pardon, Princess Elizabeth, but I may be able to shed a different light on this matter." When Elizabeth nodded, Adara went on. "When I was young, we faced a similar threat, and I myself took part in these activities. It was not considered unseemly, but necessary to protect ourselves from the *Saeson*. This we do not talk about, and again I beg pardon, but I myself was grateful for the knowledge to hide well and the agility to move myself from harm's way."

"And, Lady Adara, did you take up weapons?" the priest demanded. His eyes blazed into them. "Did you arm yourself and threaten others?"

Adara looked uncomfortable, and Cat wondered what had happened in her mam's youth to bring the haunted look into her eyes. She shook her head. "I did not learn these skills to threaten anyone, but to protect myself. I still do those exercises in the privacy of my room."

Father Maelgwyn raised his eyebrows and turned away from her, as if disgusted. Princess Elizabeth rubbed her brow and turned to Margred. Cat had not noticed how tired and wan she seemed, like her own mam looked sometimes when she didn't know Cat was watching. Elizabeth must be as worried about her husband Dafydd and her oldest son, as Cat and her mam were about Bran and Hyw.

"I have been lax, Lady Margred, in protecting you," Elizabeth began. Margred made to protest but Elizabeth shook her head. "When we brought you to us, it was to keep you safe from harm and fear. Although you are not my daughters, I have grown fond of you and your other sisters. But it seems I have not done my duty by you." She turned to the window, and stood staring out, as if on her own past life. "In our day, a young girl has little say in her own life. You will soon be betrothed, and you will have little say in that."

"It is meet and right—" began the priest, but she stopped him with a gesture.

"I do not question it, and my life is testament to that." Elizabeth was talking about her first marriage to William Marshall of England, Cat realized, and possibly Prince Dafydd too? They seemed happy enough, but had Elizabeth wanted something else? Someone else? "I see the point in being prepared, and fresh air does the children good. Lady Margred, is this something you wish to do?" Margred nodded. "Very well. This much I can grant you. You may continue, but you must dress appropriately and not masquerade as a boy. And Lady Catrin, you will return everything you have taken." When the girls went to protest she put both hands on her hips. "You will do this that I have asked of you, as your princess. And if you do, you may take exercise as needed to strengthen yourselves. And may God have mercy on all of us."

"Your highness, I must protest," said the priest. "What if—may God in his wisdom protect us—but what if the enemy does come, and we must close the castle gate? I am trying to protect the young ladies. If they are outside the gate…"

As his voice trailed off, Cat exchanged a glance with Margred. If her earlier vision was correct, why was he warning them now? Did he want to protect them? Or—her scalp prickled—was he planning something much darker? She felt she should say something, but what? She tried to imagine saying, *I've had a vision that Father Maelgwyn will open the gates to the enemies and betray us.* What would the priest do? Would he drag her out to the courtyard and burn her at the stake, as she had heard an English priest had done in Shrewsbury?

"I will heed your good counsel as always," Elizabeth was saying. She turned to the girls. "From now on, you will exercise inside the gate, and keep a guard with you at all times." Elizabeth scanned the room, and Sir Ifan straightened a little as her eyes fell on him. "Lady Adara, is this your man?"

"He is Sir Ifan, a member of Prince Llywelyn's *teulu* and loyal to me."

"Sir Ifan, may we—as mothers, and as your Princess and your lady—trust you with the safe keeping of our daughters?"

Ifan nodded and came to attention. "You may, your highness. I will lay down my very life to keep them safe from harm."

"I pray it does not come to that," Elizabeth said. She turned and swept from the room. Ifan bowed and retired to the corner of the room again, already on guard. Father Maelgwyn stared at them a moment, and then followed the princess. Cat couldn't help but think it wasn't the end of the matter. She caught her mam's eye, hoping for a private moment with her.

"Come," Adara said to both of the girls. "Several of the young men have been commissioned to fight with our warriors, should they be needed. You two can help me prepare the crests for their cloaks."

Cat knew that meant embroidery, and groaned inwardly. But it might also offer her a chance to tell her mam about the vision.

Chapter Thirty-nine: Hyw

The wind howled across the mountain pass as Hyw made his way toward his home. He was glad of James' extra vest, but the cold bit hard into him as the sun went down. He tried to listen for any sound that men from the castle searched for him or followed him, but he soon gave up trying to hide his tracks. So loud was the wind in his ears that he heard nothing else as he trudged along the path.

Then with a swiftness that caught him completely unawares, a heavy cord net suddenly dropped on him. It covered him wholly, from his head to his feet. He realized he had been captured. The more he struggled, the tighter the net grew. He yelled, but only once. Then he felt a sharp pain on the back of his head, and all went dark.

Llywelyn leapt to consciousness with a start. The darkness around him was absolute. He turned to his other senses—or, rather, the lad's senses. He could feel the warmth and blow of horses and knew men and beasts huddled together. The smell of men in the closeness of the makeshift hut was not unfamiliar to him. Llywelyn knew the locations of many mountain caches, where gear might be hidden from the elements. Many times in the past he and his men had found shelter from a raging gale in such a place.

For a moment, Llywelyn thought they were returning from a hunt or a diplomatic mission. His kingdom had been hard won and harder to keep. He had waged many campaigns over the years. Some twenty years earlier, he had held more land for Wales than any other Welsh prince. He had traveled often, visiting the far reaches of his homeland to bring the Welsh chieftains into his fold, some willingly and some with persuasion. He had led his men against the English too many times. His three years with Elinor had been a welcome change.

Then he remembered. A heavy sense of loss poured in on him.

He concentrated on the sounds. Some of the snores around him were familiar enough to bring names to mind, and he smiled at the slight intake of breath that meant Bran slept near. He'd survived. And no wonder. The man slept with one eye open, waking at the slightest sound or movement.

Yet Llywelyn felt a vague sense of unease. Something was wrong, but what? Then he realized he could not sense Hyw. Since they had begun this mad partnership, he had always had a sense of the lad's personality. Now he felt—nothing. He wanted to growl and rouse him, but he knew Hyw was not just sleeping. Something else too: Llywelyn could not seem to make a sound.

The lad was his anchor in this new state of existence. If he could wake Hyw, then he knew he had not lost grip on his reason altogether. A line from an old story slipped into his mind: "He found himself in the body of the Other, alone and aware and alive as he had never lived before." The pure voice of the bard in his father's court had sung of a king who traded places for a year with Arawn, king of OtherWorld. In the old stories, OtherWorld or Annwn was always the place of waiting. Certainly he could do nothing but wait now.

Always these stories had seemed little more than antiques, harmless and beautiful reflections of his ancestors' beliefs. Now they seemed too familiar. Like the king in that story, Llywelyn could feel no physical pain. He was able to take part in training and sports. Yet he was trapped inside the body of a lad forty years younger than he was. And he seemed to spend much of his time waiting, although he wasn't sure for what. He shuddered. Could this be some kind of punishment for not banning the old stories from his court? Or, perhaps, for not believing them?

He was no stranger to the cruelty of fate. For twenty years he had held the balance of power in the Marches between Wales and England. The Treaty of Aberconwy robbed him of all but Gwynedd, his ancestral homeland. Even then, he held ambitious men back from trampling the law and language he held dear. Was this to be his reward? He almost laughed.

Then he remembered stories about a magic that could erase the soul from existence. Would that happen to him, if the lad died? What if the force of his soul became lost now? Would all he had done and tried to do be lost with him?

And what of his love for Elinor? Living without her for the last six months of his life had been like descending into the abyss. Dying without her like this was intolerable. More than once, Hyw's laugh or wit or stubbornness had brought him back from darkness of a different sort: a brooding madness that seemed to overpower his spirit. Where was Hyw now? Why could he not feel the lad's presence?

He heard someone stir near them, rustling the straw on the ground.

"Hyw," *someone whispered. Could it be Bran's voice? He looked around him, but could only see darkness. Then he realized he was trapped in Hyw's unconscious body. If Hyw did not open his eyes, Llywelyn could not either.*

"Hyw," *the voice repeated, a bit louder. Now he was sure it was Bran who spoke.* "Why does he not stir?"

"I did not hit him that hard, sir," *said another voice.* "The English were close by us, following his tracks. He's got a good set of lungs on him. I could not count on the storm to mask the sound."

Llywelyn tried to move or thrash about but he could not get Hyw's body to respond. He tried to call out again. He could hear water in a basin, and felt the cool wet cloth as someone wiped Hyw's face.

"He's burning up." *It was Bran's voice again.*

Llywelyn would not allow himself to panic. As he did in preparing for battle, he took stock of the situation. Even when the lad was asleep, he had felt a connection to him. He sensed that Hyw was lost somehow, that they needed to connect again. Perhaps the blow to the head had done some damage? He could think of only one person who could help them now. They must find Gawain. The monk would know what to do. Llywelyn needed to convince Bran to find Gawain and bring him here. Perhaps I can speak through him, as I did to Dafydd?

He concentrated all his will on making a sound. Finally, Hyw groaned a little. Good, Llywelyn thought. Now to make him ask his father to get Gawain.

"Uhhh —"

"He's trying to say something."

How could he make them understand? He removed all other thoughts from his mind, and concentrated on the monk's name.

"Gah —"

It was all he could manage. The effort exhausted him, as if he'd run a mile at his fastest speed. His heart sank as he heard the response from Bran and the others with him.

"Shhh, Hyw. Don't try to speak now."

"What's he saying?"

"I cannot tell. It's the fever talking."

"Bran, I know you don't want to hear it, but what if the boy doesn't recover? Should we fetch the village priest? We could blindfold him and bring him here."

"There's no need for that."

"But the lad —

"No."

No! The lad must not die. Llywelyn felt powerless, but his warrior's training forced him to think of a plan. He tried to remember the days they had spent with Gawain, and some of the tips the monk had given them for communicating with each other. He slowed his breathing, and changed the focus of his thoughts to Hyw. Where are you?

Llywelyn fought down through layers of darkness, calling Hyw's name.

Hyw stared through the brackish water. Tendrils of seaweed drifted around him, encasing his ankles and wrists. The light cast dim shadows, like fish swimming in and out. It was peaceful. Hyw floated quietly, not thinking.

He didn't know how long he'd been there. He thought he might have been sleeping, but something had wakened him. Then he saw a figure in front of him: a man. The man was familiar but Hyw couldn't remember his name. He could see the man's mouth moving, but couldn't hear any sound. Strange, Hyw thought. He started to turn away, back to the seaweed and shadows. The man reached out then and grabbed Hyw's arms.

Hyw blinked and found himself sitting on the fragrant wild grasses in a field overlooking Garth Celyn. The man sat beside him. He realized it was the prince. For a long time they looked down at the long stone building that Hyw thought of as home.

Flags flapped gaily in the breeze as it blew in off the ocean and whipped up the mountain toward them. Hyw could see the slate roof and the stone watchtower of the long house, and almost feel how cool those stones kept the air inside. His fingers twitched to retrace every inch of its rough sandstone windowsills and pillars. In front of the building, the wide, open space of the yard invited men to practice the arts of defence. The little church stood guard over the upper courtyard, and around the outside edges he counted the various buildings: brew house, bake house, kitchens, kennels, and stables.

Always there had been people milling about the yard and buildings. Yet today, the yard was silent and still. There were no people in Garth Celyn. No people. With a roar like the wind rushing past his ears,

Hyw knew why not. He felt pain, as if the hand of a giant had reached into his chest to still his heart.

"Why did you bring me here?"

This is what it's all about, Hyw. Our home, and the home of our people. This is all it's about. We must stop them. We must protect Garth Celyn.

Hyw looked at him then, and knew he was the prince, Llywelyn ap Gruffydd. "You are dead," Hyw said finally. "The Prince of Wales is dead."

Llywelyn stared at him for a moment, somber and thoughtful. *And yet, I am here. You keep me here. I do not begin to comprehend it. Yet I remain.*

Hyw looked back at his silent home. He thought about the soldiers who trained in the yard, and the women inside the hall with their chores, spinning and weaving stories for their spirits along with wool for their clothing. He thought about the men and women who tilled the fertile fields and fished in the sea and hunted on the land where they sat. He saw again the stalks of grass lit like gold in the dawn sun. He breathed in the mist of Aber Falls again, and let the spray soak into the pores of his skin. He felt the cry of the hawk vibrate through the sinews of his body. And finally, he nodded.

Without warning, he found himself under the ocean again. He could not breathe. Seaweed tightened around his hands and feet. He began to struggle. With a flash, a metal sword cut through the bracken. Llywelyn hacked the weeds from him, and together they swam for the surface.

Chapter Forty: Cat

Adara released Sir Ifan at the door of her room, and the three women went in together to begin embroidering crests. With no others present, Cat had the chance to tell her mam that Margred knew her secret. Adara made them swear to tell no one else. That gave Cat the chance to turn the conversation to her most recent vision of Father Maelgwyn. Adara digested this news, remaining silent for several moments.

"These are dark days indeed," she said, her low voice resonating with sorrow. Before Cat could respond, they heard a commotion outside the open window. Cat and Margred looked out and saw a group of men dismounting in the courtyard. The men wore chain mail shirts and had swords at their sides, so they must be nobles or *teulu*, although Cat didn't recognize them. She looked for their banner and saw the Welsh red lion walking forward, with some black markings on a red background. The breeze caught it, and she could clearly see three ravens, two above and one below.

"Meirionnydd's banner," she exclaimed out loud. She knew it well, since it would someday be her own. Just then, the tallest man turned and looked up at their window.

"Rhys!"

At that moment she did not question why, but ran for the door, leaving Adara and Margred to follow. Cat raced down the stairs to the main hall in time to see Rhys and two of his men enter. Cat had eyes only for Rhys, and the look on his face when he caught sight of her was payment enough for her.

"The lord of Meirionnydd, Rhys ap Cadwgan ap Goronwy ap…" droned Princess Elizabeth's bard, reciting his extensive family history as Rhys and his men swept through the hall. Rhys knelt on one knee before Princess Elizabeth, and kissed her hand in fealty, as his men knelt behind him. Gwilym and some of Criccieth's guards stood behind the princess.

"Welcome to Criccieth, Lord Rhys," said Princess Elizabeth, extending her hands.

"Dolwyddelan Castle has fallen to the English," he said in a clear baritone, and the small crowd that had gathered gave a collective gasp. "We come at your husband's command, Princess Elizabeth, to ensure your safety and join your ranks to defend Criccieth."

She gestured for him to rise. "My husband," she repeated, with a look of relief. "Then he yet lives? Does he send word?"

"He does, your highness, and he bid me deliver this letter into your hands." With that, Rhys handed her a rolled parchment. She inspected the seal and then tore it off with her fingernails, moving to a chair by the window to read it.

Rhys turned to Cat and Adara with a look of eagerness on his face.

"Cat!" he exclaimed. "I mean, gentle ladies." He bowed to Lady Adara first, and then to Cat, and then Margred, greeting them each by name.

Joy and relief swelled in her, and on its heels was fear. He had been her friend when they were children together, when she had visited his castle as Cat from Gwynedd whose father served the Prince of Wales. Their marriage was a good alliance for both their families, since she would own land in the Llyn valley through Adara, to join with his land in the neighbouring kingdom of Meirionnydd. He was just three years older than her, and they were well matched in interests.

Or were they? Now that she was a seer—and a seer who could not control her sight—would he think the same of her as before? Would he think her strange and unnatural?

As he took a step forward, she took a step back. He hesitated, brushing back a few strands of his dark hair with a look of pure puzzlement on his face.

"Lord Rhys," she said.

"Lady Catrin," he said, bowing to her. Then he stepped back and turned slightly to include her mother in the conversation. "And Lady Adara. We had word that Garth Celyn was attacked in the night. Glad I am to see you here at Criccieth. You are safe?"

"Yes, we were not harmed," Adara told him.

"And the infant, Gwenllian?"

"We fled to bring her to safety," Adara said. "Princess Elizabeth has been most generous."

"The babe is under my protection, and that of my husband, the Prince of Wales," said Princess Elizabeth, barely raising her eyes from the parchment.

"Your hospitality is commendable," Rhys said, bowing to her before turning to Cat again. "I must confess, this is my first visit to the great castle of Criccieth. Would you show me around?"

She knew she must look stricken, and turned her eyes to her mam. Adara stepped forward. "We would be pleased to show you," Adara said, as she took Rhys' arm. "Have you heard aught of my husband, Lord Rhys?"

"What is the matter with you?" Margred whispered in Cat's ear. "He's gorgeous!"

"What can I say to him?" Cat replied. "What will he think?"

"You mean about your gift?" Margred looked from Cat to Rhys' disappearing back. "Will he not see it as an advantage?"

Cat shrugged. "I cannot tell what he might think."

"Then you should tell him everything, and find out. Mayhap he will help keep watch on Father Maelgwyn with us. Come, we must at least accompany them." With that Margred followed after Rhys and Adara, leaving Cat to catch up.

At supper, Cat sat on one side of Rhys while Margred sat on the other. Cat could think of little to say, but Margred kept him laughing. Cat glanced sideways at him. He had a clean smell as if he had bathed since the afternoon, and she noticed one of the servants had trimmed his dark hair. Just then, Margred's laughter rang out again, and Rhys joined in. Cat began to resent her friend, and then felt guilty for it. She pushed the cheese-and-leek sausage around on her plate without eating.

"Are you well, Lady Catrin?" she heard a voice ask from her left. "Our hostess has dug deep for these wares, in honour of the Lord Rhys. Does it not please you?" She turned to find the bard Gwilym considering her in some concern. She remembered how he had stared at Margred when they first met. He might understand how she felt better than anyone else at the table.

"It pleases me well, Lord Gwilym," she said, taking a bite of the sausage. "Thank you for asking. How have you been finding your stay at Criccieth?"

Rhys turned to them then, frowning a little as he saw Gwilym leaning toward Cat. "I trust the princess has spared only what she could, with war on our heels," Rhys said. "Lord Gwilym, how long have you been at the castle?" he asked, and soon they were exchanging news, although she noticed both managed to say very little.

After the meal, Gwilym caught her eye, and stood up. "I have a special song this evening," he began, "in honour of Lord Rhys and his people." Gwilym strode to a seat near the fire where he had set his instruments. He picked up the harp, checked its tuning and then began to play.

Rhys smiled as he heard the first notes. "Well known and well loved," he said, loudly enough for Gwilym to hear his approval.

"Another King Arthur tale, no doubt," Margred whispered beside him. "He's very big on those."

"Lord Gwilym is a very notable poet," Cat began.

"And quite smitten with me," Margred put in.

"I'm sure he is, Lady Margred," Rhys said, agreeably.

"Oh!" Cat frowned at her friend but Margred laughed. Soon Cat was laughing too, struggling to hide it behind her hand. Gwilym played another refrain on the harp, letting them quiet down before he began. Then his voice lifted and filled the hall, singing of a woman who fought in a major war to help her people. Cat found herself no longer hearing Margred's chatter, but listening intently to the words. Rhys and several other men and women joined in, each voice naturally harmonizing with the other. The woman they sang about had second sight. She carried a message to her people but they turned away from her. Then the ravens surrounded them, and as the birds descended the woman rose to meet them, changing and dividing until she became three ravens.

"Three ravens," Cat breathed. The song did not say so, but she recalled the banner Rhys' man held when she looked down from her mam's window: the Welsh lion with three dark ravens around it, two above and one below.

"You are thinking of my banner," Rhys said, just as quietly.

"Yes," she said.

"The raven is sacred to us," he said. "Some say King Arthur turned into a raven at his death. It's an old belief in Meirionnydd. Have you heard it?" When Cat shook her head, he continued, "The Lady Modron—you might know her as King Arthur's sister, Morgana—is reviled as Arthur's enemy in many parts of the north. But we see her as the other half of Arthur himself."

"How so?"

"She had knowledge others would not hear, and could not understand, as the poet says. But she led Arthur to his power, and she lent him her power at the end. The power of the raven. So we carry her symbol: three ravens at the ready, surrounding the heart of Wales."

"This story is important to you."

"It is, my lady." He leaned closer to her, his deep blue eyes holding hers. "Almost as important to me as… well, as you are."

Cat felt her face flush, and she turned from him to listen to the poet. Margred seemed quiet now, and Cat snuck a glance at her to see that she was also watching Gwilym. Rhys was still looking at Cat, and she smiled at him as she turned back to hear the end of the song. She thought through what Rhys had said. He seemed to believe strongly in the legend. What would he think if she told him that some legends could come to life? Would he believe her?

Chapter Forty-one: Hyw

Hyw spluttered and coughed. He tried to open his eyes and the light seared them. A rustle and bump told him someone was nearby.

"He wakes. Steady on, Hyw." The voice was familiar. Hyw's eyelids fluttered again, and his hand came up to shield his face. It was caught in the rough hand of another, familiar one. "Glad I am to see this."

Hyw's eyes flew open. "Da!" he cried, and now both arms seemed to come up of their own volition and around his father's neck. "I thought you were dead!"

"And I you," Bran replied. "If the storm hadn't taken you, I was afraid that knock to the noggin had done you in. You must forgive my oaf for his zeal in bringing you to me."

"Nay, 'twas neither." Hyw would not let go of his da's neck. "You got my messages then?"

"Your messages?" His da looked at him searchingly, and then

Hyw saw a strange expression pass over his eyes. "You wrote those messages? How? How did you know the letters to write?"

Hyw opened his mouth to answer when he heard Llywelyn's voice at his ear. *Nay Hyw. Do not tell him about me yet. He is not alone. Let us choose the timing better.* "I—I had help."

"Who? Who was it, Hyw?" Bran stared at him intently, but Hyw could not find a way to answer.

"I cannot say, Da."

"Was it—? Is he—? " Bran left the sentence unfinished. Hyw knew he had to say something, but wasn't sure how to form the words to tell his da what had happened.

"I saw the words in my mind, and wrote them so."

Bran expelled his breath. His voice was so low, Hyw could barely hear him. "I thought perhaps—" Bran tried to smile, but it made him look sad and tired. "I heard the grisly tale of his death, but I could not stop myself from hoping. If we got away, surely he could as well. When I saw the letters under the hiding place—well. I thought it was him."

Bran disengaged Hyw's arms then as gently as possible, but kept seated near him. Hyw felt a rush of pity for his da, and almost told him everything. He heard Llywelyn's voice again, cautioning him. *A warrior of the new Cymru would not easily understand this thing that happens between us. There will come a time when he will need to know. Let the time be right.*

Bran had already moved to look around them, gesturing to the others. "Welcome my son back to the land of the living."

Hyw noticed the hut fashioned from skins and branches, rising around him. Several other men looked on, one with tears showing at the corners of his eyes.

"Glad I am we did not have to fetch the priest, after all," the man said, pawing at his face with one hand.

Another man moved closer. Hyw noticed the glint of a warrior's gold torque around his neck. "How came you from the English camp in one piece, son of Bran?"

"The English." Hyw tried to rise, but fell back against the sheepskin bedding.

"Give it time, Hyw."

"No. We must get to Garth Celyn."

"What says he? Does he speak of the *llys*?" Another familiar voice spoke the Welsh name for the royal court, and Hyw saw a face set like stone, frowning.

"Aeneus!" Hyw again tried to rise. Instead his former tutor in the arts of war and physical strength came to his bedside, and hugged him soundly.

"Glad I am to see you whole again, lad."

"And I you."

"Now I can keep my word to your lady mother. She sent me to seek you, but I was taken on the road. Then came your father to dispatch the *Saeson*. He called me to him to aid in this resistance. Now I am doubly glad I came."

Hyw moved aside then and, still gripping Aeneus' shoulders, spoke to him and Bran. "We must make haste. The king will march on all of Dafydd's holdings."

"Is le Clare in charge?"

"He returned to the south. But one of the soldiers showed me the banners for William de Valence. He leads them now. And the king has men from abroad. He pays them silver coins and offers them land if they can take it away from us."

"I know this de Valence." Aeneus nodded at Hyw. "A cousin to the old king, Henry, and fiercely against us. "

"What path do they take?"

Hyw turned back to his father. "I am not sure. Criccieth, Dolbadarn, Castell-y-Bere. Those were the names I heard."

Bran looked thoughtful, stroking his moustache. "Roger Le Strange has long sought the castle Criccieth for his own."

"The Marcher lord? Aye, it could well be. They'd be a fool to try Castell-y-Bere." Aeneus looked grim. "That castle will stand against OtherWorld's hounds. Even Edward Longshanks himself would pose no threat."

"We need more information." Bran straightened and turned to the others. "We must gather everyone we can. Aeneus, when the weather breaks, choose a man, and go in tandem to locate your brother's group. Flush out as many men as you can find – loyal to Cymru all, and willing to fight for Prince Dafydd." Hyw was happy to hear Wales called by its rightful name again: Cymru. "Let the first be a man who hails from Castell-y-Bere."

"Aye, I was born there." The man who teared up earlier had recovered.

Bran and the men conferred. Their voices droned in Hyw's ears. Finally Bran nodded and turned back to Hyw. "Here, try to regain your strength." He took up an earthen bowl and held it up to Hyw's lips. The broth tasted like nothing Hyw had ever tasted before. Ambrosia, he thought, food of the gods. He remembered the word from the poetry told around the fire in the evenings. That led his mind back to Garth Celyn again. He choked as he remembered his dream.

"There, now. That's enough. Rest, if you can. We must be ready to move out as soon as the wind lets up."

Bran settled a warm sheepskin around his neck, and Hyw closed his eyes.

Chapter Forty-two: Cat

It was nearly noon when Cat, Margred, and Ifan came back from their field. Ifan carried the weapons for them. Cat knew it was a small price to pay, but she was sorry to lose them, just as she was developing some skill with the throwing knife. Father Maelgwyn watched them from the doorway of the chapel as they made their way into the amoury. Margred waved at him and turned away, almost flouncing past. She must feel the same, Cat thought.

Ifan set the pile of weapons down and whistled. One of the younger boys came running, eager to be helpful, and Ifan knelt down to explain where to take each set of weapons. Cat was watching him, appreciating his gentleness with the boy, when she heard the shout.

"Ships!" The shout came from the battlements and she whirled, shading her eyes with one hand to look up. "Ships in the harbour!"

Guards began to run for the battlements. The heavy portcullis chains rattled as the gates shut behind them. Ifan stood as if to join the guards but Cat grabbed his arm.

"Get Lord Rhys and bring him to me. Quickly. We will be in the hall."

If he was surprised, he hid it well. He nodded and was gone. Cat and Margred rushed to the castle, as Adara came down the stairs looking for them. Ifan and Lord Rhys came through the side doors from the yard, followed by two of his men.

"Go," Adara told Cat. "Tell him on the way. Join us later. Margred, come with me."

Cat knew without being told that they would be in her room securing Baby Gwen and the other children in case they had to leave again quickly. She took Rhys by the arm and moved him to the doors.

"We must not let them fire upon the ships," she hissed.

"What? But they are Irish – "

"There is no time to explain. They are not enemies, and we will need those ships. You must believe me."

He looked at her, and then at Ifan who followed them. Ifan's face was impassive.

"Very well, I will try to stop them."

"We must stop them. The princess's life—and ours—depend upon it."

"How do you know?"

"I know," Cat told him. "As Morgana knew, I know."

"She has the message," Ifan finally said. "Will you not hear it?"

Cat glanced at him, and he smiled at her. She thought of the promise she had made her mother that no one else should know, but it was not something she could worry about now. Rhys took her by the shoulders and stared at her face. Ifan's hand went to his sword hilt, but Cat raised her hand to stop him.

"This is—a prophecy?" Rhys looked startled.

"Call it what you will," she said, searching his face. "But we must save those ships."

Rhys let her go then and began to run for the door. Cat followed him, and Ifan kept pace with her.

"Go with him," she told Ifan.

"My duty is your safety, lady," he replied. As they moved from the castle to the courtyard another shout went up, but she could not hear the words. A catapult scraped into place on top of the gatehouse, and she knew it would not take them long to ready a shot. Could Rhys stop them in time?

They could hear the angry voices from the gatehouse stairs.

"I cannot let you go nearer, lady," Ifan said.

"I must see," she told him. He looked around them and nodded, leading her up above the battlement to an arrow slit in the stone wall.

"Is that you, Gron?" a voice called from higher up the staircase. The arrow holes were manned, she thought.

"Aye," Ifan answered, putting one finger to his lip. He made way for Cat to look through the bottom end of the long slit. She could see Rhys in the centre of a group of men, arguing with the captain of Criccieth's guard. Some of the men around him looked as ready to fight with Rhys as with the Irish. Rhys's men flanked him, also with drawn swords, facing the Criccieth warriors. Cat realized he was outnumbered by a group of men that did not answer to him.

"You must help him," she whispered to Ifan.

He expelled his breath in what sounded like a sigh, and then motioned for her to stay. "I will return for you." With a glance up the stairs to be sure the men held position above them, he went back down to the courtyard. She heard his voice below, and some of the men made way, but she could not see him.

"We have word that these ships are friends," Ifan told them.

"Word?" the captain scoffed. "From whom?"

"Have you not heard, brother?" Ifan replied, keeping his voice calm. "Lord Rhys has just returned from Prince Dafydd himself."

"So he says," the captain growled.

"I saw the letter he brought with him." It was Ifan's voice again. "It bore the prince's seal."

The captain was silent a moment, but she could sense a shift among the men. One unclenched his fist, and another put away his sword. Finally the captain nodded. "My apologies, Lord Rhys, but we have heard much about spies in the fallen castles. We would not count our own among them."

"Your diligence commends you," Rhys replied smoothly. "I would not want to think you would believe without cause. But I can assure you, these ships are a necessity to our princess's safety and to that of the children."

Ifan appeared in the stairs and motioned to Cat. She wanted to stay and make sure the situation was resolved, but his impatience hurried her. They made their way to the yard just as Father Maelgwyn came in sight.

"Lady Cat," he said. "What are you doing in the gatehouse?"

"Why, Father," she began, glancing at Ifan. "Sir Ifan was bringing me to make confession."

"Confession?" He stared at her as if she had not been to chapel already that morning.

"Yes, Father," she continued smoothly. "It is a most urgent matter."

"Now? Can this not wait until mass tomorrow?"

"Oh no, Father, as you yourself will see shortly," she said, "and Sir Ifan also would confess. In fact, his need is more pressing than my own."

"My lady?" She could hear the surprise in Ifan's voice, but he covered it smoothly. "I mean, my lady speaks aright, Father, if you could but spare the time."

"I must freshen up first, Father Maelgwyn, but I will be there with my own confession as soon as Sir Ifan has finished."

The warrior knight looked torn as Cat made to walk across the inner courtyard, but the priest took his arm. "Come along then, and see you find your words more quickly today." As they moved into the chapel in the lower tower, Cat ducked out of sight. Rhys finally came out of the stairwell and she stepped up beside him.

"My Lord Rhys, I must explain," she began, startling him. He took her arm and moved her toward the gardens behind the hall.

"We will find a quiet place, and then you must," he told her. "And mayhap you can explain how you come to be here, and not in your rooms with the other women."

Chapter Forty-three: Hyw

Hyw was still shaky the next day. He thought he might see Cadarn and Vox with his father, but there were no horses in the camp. Aeneus gruffly told him the English took them all at the ambush. The two men who had shared their hut left at sunup. At noon Bran said they could wait no longer.

Some twenty men broke camp with them. Llywelyn laughed inside him. *It's good to feel the ground beneath our feet again.* Hyw shook his head, and looked around him. He had just come from the English camp where cloth and winter gear were plentiful, thanks to their queen and her ladies. He was amazed some of the Welsh warriors were bare-legged in spite of the recent blizzard. Yet none complained, or seemed to notice the cold. He heard the rumble of Llywelyn's laugh again. *That is what it means to be Cymry.*

Bran ruffled his hair. "Look at you. You are near as tall as me now. I swear you have grown at least a handspan."

Hyw grinned and ducked his head. He grabbed up some of the

camp gear, and followed after the men on their way to stash it in a small cavern in the nearby rocks. It wasn't large enough for a man, but held the skins and camp tackle easily. The branches that had fortified their hut served a double purpose to hide the stash. Bran handed him a flask to carry.

"Pure mountain water. Keep it full."

Aeneus nodded. "Drink as much as you can. It's from a stream blessed by the Old Ones. Let them protect you from the frost."

Another grunted. "Edward's men share the same stream."

"Aye, but I've heard them curse the very ground as they do," a wizened old warrior grinned. "That should make their ears burn."

"Enough of your blather." A hulk of a warrior carrying a javelin shook his head at the others, and turned to Hyw. He heard Llywelyn's voice again: *Listen to this one. See what he hides beneath his cloak.*

Hyw caught sight of a gold torque slung for safekeeping around the man's thick bicep, and knew he was one of Llywelyn's *teulu*. "Drink you as much water as you can, from any stream you find, boy. May the Old Ones bless you, if they will. If they do not, then bless yourself. You can last three weeks without food if you have to, but no man can stay upright without water. The harsher the weather, the more you must drink to keep the body limber."

Bran sent a man ahead to scout the trail across the mountains. Shortly after they started out, the man returned. The party moved quietly along the ridges and looked down at a knight with two foot soldiers. Englishmen. Without making a sound in the snow, Bran's men dropped them and slit the knight's throat. One soldier lay immobile on the ground, his leg at an unnatural angle.

"I'm from Shrewsbury," said the other soldier quietly, laying down his arms and kneeling. "You know me." Hyw recognized him as a man from Gerald's company who had not gone to the south with le Clare. Bran stared at him, arms across his chest.

"If we know you, then you will not mind aiding our cause."

"I will do all I can, sir."

Aeneus grinned. "Aye, to keep your life intact you will tell us anything."

"Nay, I will tell you truly."

Aeneus leaned closer, and set his blade to the man's neck. "See that you do."

Bran nodded. "Where goes the king's army?"

"He split us up, sir. He will attack each castle until he has them all."

"Why? What does he want from us?"

The man thought for a moment. "We had word yesterday that Dolwyddelan Castle has fallen, but Prince Dafydd was not there."

"So he seeks Dafydd?"

"Aye, my lord. For he believes without a prince, Wales will yield."

Bran pursed his lips at that, but continued to ask questions. "And how many strong?"

"A thousand men, or more, sir. It cannot go well for you."

Bran looked over at Hyw, who nodded. The man spoke truly about Edward's army, at least. Bran looked back at the soldier, and set his head to one side, as if thinking.

"Why are you pursuing us? It's not as if we haven't all fought this battle many times. Wales wins, then Edward wins. The knights may fight to the death, but we men—we don't often leave each other bleeding in the snow." The man looked embarrassed, but said nothing. Bran persisted. "The king's men have never in my recollection crossed the slopes in snow before. Why now? And why are the soldiers stealing our heads from our bodies?"

"The king's bounty," the soldier mumbled. One of the Welsh warriors prodded him with the point of a javelin. "Edward offers a shilling for each Welsh head."

Bran didn't flinch. "And how many have you brought him?"

The man hesitated a fraction of a second, before he began to protest.

Bran turned away. "Leave Edward a message he'll understand." His voice was harsh.

Hyw felt bile in his mouth as he realized his father's intention. "Wait, Da," he said, putting a hand on Bran's arm. "The one with a broken leg cannot join the fighting again. Nor can the other, if he escorts that one home. Is that not enough?"

Bran considered his son for a moment before he spoke. "Good counsel always makes a leader a better man." Then he bent down to the uninjured soldier. "If you are rescued, see that you tell your captains the Welsh showed you mercy. And consider whether that is worth more than a shilling."

Hyw blamed the pine branches where they camped for making him toss and turn that night. Every time he closed his eyes he could see the English army, endless bodies pouring across the field. They seemed as unstoppable as the Nant Peris river flowing over the rocks near their former camp. Finally Hyw pushed himself up and drew the light blanket closer around him. They had eaten dried meat from their packs, not daring to light a fire lest it lead any headhunting soldiers to them.

He had just stretched his back upright to ease the tension when he heard the owl hoot the first time. It hooted again before he was able to turn toward it. He felt Llywelyn come alert inside him. Responding to the prince's unspoken command, Hyw cast out with his mind. The being he encountered was not feathered, and he pulled back.

Wake your father.

Moving silently in the semi-darkness, Hyw made his way around the men toward his father's form. Bran turned before Hyw got near enough to touch his arm. With a grimace, Bran automatically punched at Hyw, then tried to pull back his arm when he realized who it was. Hyw leapt back in time to avoid the full strength of the blow, but his father's fist felt like iron against his shoulder. He knew he would bear a bruise from the force of it. Then Bran sat quickly.

"Hyw," he whispered. "Careful, lad."

Hyw just shook his head, and motioned toward the wood.

Together they turned just as the next hooting sounded. Bran rose, and took up his javelin. Hyw followed, and his father did not motion him back. Without words or sound, they made their way toward the trees at the far edge of their camp. There they heard the owl-that-was-no-owl hoot again. This time Bran stopped and cupped his hand around his mouth, hooting back in a near-perfect imitation of the night hunter.

Not one man but twenty or more melted out of the shadows toward them. Bran set his javelin point up and at rest, standing with feet firmly planted. Hyw imitated him. The men fanned out behind their leader, who stopped facing Bran. He greeted them formally, giving the names of his ancestors to identify himself. "Dai ap Rhys ap Gruffydd ap Rhys ap Roderic Tewdwr ap Cadell. For Cymru." Although the man's cadence was unfamiliar, Hyw heard the old word for Wales, spoken in their shared mother tongue.

"For Cymru. I am Bran ap Rhys ap Maredudd ap Eineon ap Hywel ap Cadell. Cousin, I bid you welcome." The men relaxed, and the leader came forward to grasp Bran's arm in friendship.

"We go to Dolwyddelan."

Hyw felt Bran's body tighten slightly. Bran considered Dai for a moment, and then shook his head. "It has fallen."

Dai uttered a sound that might have been an oath. "Another fallen. We have come from Carreg Cennen in the south, fallen betimes." Dai spat. "English hounds on our heels. We have left traps and snares on our path to slow them."

"As have we, but as yet we have felt no breath on our necks. The *Saeson* take our heads for shillings."

Dai grunted. "As do le Clare's men." He spat again. "I have lived near two score years, and number my own wife's cousins among our pursuers. This is more than any soul should have to bear. I have seen what I can scarce tell, in the towns and on the roadways where the people flee in vain."

Bran nodded. “You are welcome to our camp. We will share what we have.”

Dai placed his hand over his heart, a remnant of Roman times. “As will we.”

Bran’s small force roused and welcomed the new men. After a brief whispered council, they took up separate sections of the clearing and fell back to a restless sleep until daybreak. As the men shared up what berries and roots they had to break their fast, Dai related some of the horrors of the road. Bran sent Hyw for water, and he left them to speak of the unspeakable for a time. He filled skins of water at the nearby creek, reaching out into the woods with his senses. All was quiet.

When he returned, he saw his father sitting with Dai, his shoulders hunched and head down. Llywelyn urged him to Bran’s side. *You must rally them, Hyw. Castell-y-Bere must remain our next destination. With both forces combined, they may yet aid in its defence.*

Hyw closed his eyes for a moment. “How can I make him listen to me?”

I know him well, Hyw. You must remind him of the castle. His instinct will do the rest.

Hyw managed to get his father’s attention as he handed him a water skin. He took a breath, and tried to think of a way to do as Llywelyn had suggested. “Da, what do you know of Castell-y-Bere?”

“Little, Hyw, save what I have seen on trips there in times past. The men say it is still well fortified.”

“I know it,” Dai looked up at the boy. “It is held by Cynfrig ap Madog for my lord Rhys ap Cadwgan. I fought with Cynfrig when de Valence attacked some five years past. A good man, with heart. If your forces and mine combine, Bran ap Rhys, we may yet prove useful in this fight.”

“For Cymru.” Bran stood, as did the other man, and they turned to their bedraggled band of warriors.

Chapter Forty-four: Cat

As they walked in the winter garden, Cat told Rhys as quietly as she could about her visions and the results. She left out some of the details about her brother, concentrating instead on the final three: the ships, the attack on the castle, and Father Maelgwyn at the gates.

For a long moment, Rhys said nothing. Then he asked, "How soon will the remaining two come to pass?"

"I do not know," she said. "It may be that we can prevent them from ever coming to pass. Mam can explain more."

"So your mam knows of your gift?"

"Yes, it is common enough in her family."

"Ah. It is your inheritance?"

"I believe so." She felt miserable now, cold outside and in, and she began to shiver. He noticed her shaking, and rubbed her shoulders.

"I forget myself. We tarry too long outside. Come, let us go inside and warm you up."

"Nay, we must be sure Princess Elizabeth has heard of the ships."

He nodded and they turned toward the castle hall. Ifan joined them at the door.

"I am so sorry, Sir Ifan," Cat began.

He raised his eyebrows at her. "I trust my forced confessions were to some benefit," he said.

"More than you know," she said. Rhys looked from one to the other, but she went through the door Ifan held open for her and up the stairs without another word.

In Princess Elizabeth's solar, Rhys explained his actions in preventing the captain from firing on the ships, without mentioning Cat's role in it. Adara listened with them, but no other ladies were present. The guards Elizabeth had sent to the harbour returned with news. There were three ships in all, with a crew dispatched from one of Meirionnydd's allies in Ireland. They were large merchant vessels with no cargo, but enough room for men and horses. Rhys glanced at Cat, but gave nothing away.

"It is Providence," Elizabeth declared, turning to Rhys. "You will know where my Lord Prince would have us meet him, while the English storm Criccieth in search of him?"

Rhys nodded briefly, and it was Cat's turn to be surprised. "He could not trust anyone with the news beforehand, your highness." He looked at the princess, but Cat couldn't help but think the explanation was for her benefit as well. "I was to escort you by land, before anyone knew our plans. But this will make it easier."

"If we act quickly," she said, and he nodded.

If certain priests do not hear of it, Cat thought. And if there are no more English spies in our midst.

Within a day they were loading horses and chests onto one of the ships.

"Expect your lord, Prince Dafydd, within the week," Elizabeth told the captain and his men. "The other two ships will remain for a time in the harbour, in case they are needed."

The princess had a private audience with the captain, and Cat wondered if she would tell him where they were bound. At least one of her visions had been avoided, but the first one, with the castle under attack and Owain and the others killed, worried her most. She sensed that without preventing both of her other visions, that could still come to pass.

"What of the priest?" Cat asked Rhys, but he shook his head.

"We have no evidence to accuse him," Rhys told her. "I may believe you without question, but I fear it will not sit so with the captain."

"Or the princess," Cat added. "Then how can we stop him?"

"We must be diligent, and the answer will present itself." He did not look at her when he said it, and she wondered if he felt as sure as he sounded.

It took several hours to load the ships with food, weapons, trunks of supplies and personal belongings, and finally horses. Rhys was overseeing the horses as Elizabeth, Adara, and the children made their way toward the ship. Gwilym walked near Princess Elizabeth while Ifan accompanied Cat and Margred.

Suddenly she heard a shout and a scuffle, and several hooded men rushed from the gardens toward them. Something glinted in their hands, and Cat realized it was knives. Ifan drew his sword, as did Gwilym and Elizabeth's guards.

"Run for the ships," Ifan shouted. Owain started to draw his sword, but Ifan stopped him. "Take your mam to the ship." He moved between them and the hooded men.

Cat grabbed Enid's arm, jostling Baby Gwen who began to cry.

"Come now," she cried, trying to stay calm but almost dragging Enid toward the ships. Owain ran past them with Elizabeth, shielding her from the attackers with his body just as Cat tried to shield Enid. Margred easily passed them both with one sister in her arms and one on her back. Cat did not stop to look back until she had reached the ship, but when she did she saw Gwilym moving between the men lying on the field. She could not see Ifan. Then she spotted a figure in chain mail lying at an awkward angle on the ground.

And suddenly she was running. Back toward the knot of fallen men and warriors. To Ifan.

"Cat." She heard Adara's voice behind her but she could not stop. Not until she reached him. Blood trickled from the side of his mouth, and he looked at her dully, as if he didn't know who she was. She knelt near him, ignoring the dark stain on the ground, and took his head into her lap. He tried to raise his hand to her face and she grasped it.

"Don't move, Ifan," she told him. "You must rest until the doctor comes." She cradled his head with her other hand. "You will be all right."

She saw a deep wound biting into his shoulder, almost separating his arm from his body. His blood seeped into the ground, covering her skirts, but she did not move.

"Call for the priest," she heard a voice say behind her, and knew it was Rhys.

"He is missing, my lord," another soldier said.

"This one over here." Their voices sounded farther away, and Cat realized they must be looking at one of the hooded men. "This is the priest's man, is it not?"

"It is." The voice was that of the captain's, gritty and low. "Father Maelgwyn's servant." Now we have him, Cat thought.

"The priest was a spy for the English," Rhys said. "These men must have been set to capture the princess before she could get away."

"That means the English will be close upon us."

Ifan's head moved, and Cat squeezed his hand. "You've done it, Ifan," she said. "All will be well, now." Sir Ifan's eyes slid away from hers, and he stared up at the sky. She saw him clearly then, standing in a field of green grass, the tower of Garth Celyn rising behind him. He raised his arm as if to wave at her. The sun on his chain mail glittered.

She heard the fluttering of wings close overhead, and Rhys' surprised voice. "A raven." But she could not seem to see beyond the glittering that filled her eyes.

Chapter Forty-five: Hyw

Bran kept them in the lowlands to make quicker passage through the rugged Eryri Mountains. Hyw had never traveled this route, and he breathed in the fragrant mountain air. *Land of the eagles*, Llywelyn commented inside Hyw's mind. *You'll soon see why.*

They stuck to shadows and treed areas near the Nant Peris River. Bran set the pace over the broken terrain of the river valley. They ran twenty paces, walked twenty in a quick-march, ran again, then walked again. The men traveled in silence, stilling their panting breath as much as possible. They could not be sure how long the king's army would tarry to secure each castle, or where they would strike next.

Llywelyn had little more to say, and Hyw was glad of the quiet. During the journey, he'd been too preoccupied to notice any residual effect of his flight through the blizzard and the blow on his head. Now, as his water skin grew lighter and the climb steeper, his head began to ache.

"It's the altitude." One of the men stopped near him during a short break. He was from Dai's group, and knew the area. "You'll calm in time. Try this." The man bent forward with his hands on his knees.

Bran stopped near them, concerned. "It is so with several of the men. Yet we must keep up the pace."

"I will try to use the lowlands as much as I can. Water also helps, Hyw." Their guide took a few leaves of an herb from a pouch at his belt, and gave a segment to Hyw. "Suck on this." He handed a portion of leaf to the other men as well. Hyw found it bitter at first, but the taste faded.

By mid-morning they passed the small lake at the base of the Yr Wyddfa, the tallest mountain in the range. Their guide's herb had helped ease the pain of his aching head, but Hyw still felt tired and short of breath. He took a moment to stare upward at the mountain. In Welsh its name meant a burial mound, and Hyw shivered.

Bran gestured aside to him, and he was happy to put away his thoughts and search for a likely tree to climb. He knew his father wanted him to use his gift to check the way ahead. To hide the fact from the other men, Hyw would climb into the tree to act as lookout, then use his gift when he was out of sight.

He steadied himself on a branch and concentrated. It was second nature now to keep the prince safe from any animal minds he might connect to, using the methods Gawain had shown him. Hyw concentrated, separating a piece of his mind from Llywelyn. He pictured it as stepping in front of the prince, in order to connect another part of himself with a brown eagle. The bird was difficult to control. Hyw sensed it searching for game. He coasted with it, enjoying a few moments stretched above the trail, staring down at the forest and lake.

The bird rounded in a wide curve. Hyw caught sight of a trail of smoke in the distance. It was far away, a thin streak of grey in the sky, barely enough to make the bird react. Was it a village, or a noble *llys*? He faltered, dropping from the eagle's mind to his own again. In moments he was standing in front of Bran. Hyw lowered his eyes to hide his feelings.

"I saw smoke, but it is leagues back. More than a campfire, but I could not see—"

Bran laid one hand on Hyw's shoulder and gestured to the men. They rose as one. Their guide took them by a route that avoided the mountain's steeper areas. Even so, the pace was gruelling. They kept it up during the long afternoon, as the sharp rocks stabbed through his foot leathers. His knees and calves ached from the increasing steepness of the path.

The sun was low in the sky before they caught sight of the Desenni valley. It was greening already with spring, and Hyw thought of words he had heard in hymns calling it "the promised land." Bran stopped the group near a brook to refill their water skins, and turned to Hyw.

"We may be too far away, but see what you can, before we lose the sun."

Hyw's head pounded now, and he had no strength left to climb a tree. He stood in the shade, staring out across the valley. Far away, towering over the land between them, was the huge summit of Cadair Idris, the giant's chair. He had heard many tales of bards and warriors who spent the night on the mountain, hoping for inspiration, only to discover madness within themselves instead.

As his mind followed his eyeline, he felt rather than saw a small running creature. He made contact, and knew it to be a fox. The dappled shadows under the creature's feet told Hyw the path was in shadow, far away on the giant's mountain. He sniffed the air, and felt relief along with the fox when he sensed game. No human scent marred the path. The fox looked up, and through its eyes he saw Castell-y-Bere. Hyw brought himself back to his vantage point reluctantly.

"There are no troops near the castle," he told Bran. He wanted to share some of the experience with his father, but wasn't sure how to talk about it. Instead, he pointed toward the path where he had seen the fox. "That way."

"The lad speaks truth." Their warrior-guide from Dai's group stepped near them when Hyw pointed. The man looked surprised.

"But to see it from here, he must have sharp eyes. Have you been this way before, lad?"

"Once, but he has a strong memory." Bran responded before Hyw had a chance to speak. The man looked skeptical. Bran handed Hyw his water skin. "Here, son, fill up for both of us."

As Hyw turned away to go to the stream, he saw his father turn back towards their guide. Hyw knew he would find some way to explain it. He was tired, he realized, and using his gift taxed him further. He bent to the brook and splashed water over his face and hair, wishing he could explain to his father about Llywelyn.

Give it time, lad. Hyw closed his eyes to find the prince waiting. *You are a strong help to your father. All is not lost while there is yet a Prince in Wales. That castle is a stronghouse, built by my grandfather. If we have any chance to make a stand against Edward, it will be there.*

Fear can keep us alive when all else fails, Hyw. But never give in to despair. These Normans come and go, but we remain. Our mountains will surely shelter us, until Edward finds someone else to hate.

The guide took his sword and held it hilt-up toward the valley. He moved it from side to side, using the sun's rays to send a signal toward the castle walls. He repeated the motion three times.

Hyw was standing near him in a thicket. Before long, they spotted an answering flash that seemed to come from within the mountainside. He squinted until he found the spot where he saw the fox. That rocky slope must hide the great castle.

Their guide nodded down at him. "They know we come, and we are friends. But in these times, you cannot be too careful. We will still need the password, you will see." He pointed to his own temple. "Lucky we are that this is still in one piece."

Hyw could sense Llywelyn's hope rising within him, and almost feel the prince's laugh rumble inside his own chest. *Wait until you see it, Hyw. The English king can try his tricks, but he cannot win here.*

Would that my grandfather could know his stronghold would stand for us, e'en today.

Hyw grew more convinced the closer they got to the castle. The lush lowlands were surrounded by stark, rugged mountains. As they climbed the craggy slopes to a rock-cut road that stretched ahead of them, the setting sun threw long shadows over the ground. The low howl of the wind through the craggy mountain face made his hair stand on end.

"Gwyn ap Nudd," one of the men murmured. Hyw recalled the name of the legendary king of the Tylwyth Teg. The wind made him think of Nudd's huge baying hounds, said to have the power to drag a man's soul to the OtherWorld. Another warrior made the hooting call of an owl behind them. When the superstitious one jerked around, fearful and wide-eyed, several laughed. Llywelyn laughed with them.

Take heart Hyw. The English know that legend, as do their Norman masters. Our stories may shelter us here better than the rocks of the castle itself.

Chapter Forty-six: Cat

Cat accepted her mam's assistance from the ship she could not remember boarding. Margred and the girls stood near, and Owain stood at the ready near his mam. Cat wondered where Ifan was, before she remembered he was no longer with them. Her limbs felt heavy but her head felt feather-light, as if the breeze off the sea could blow her away. She looked around for Rhys and spotted him checking the saddles. He motioned to his men to bring horses toward the group and moved toward the princess. When he saw Cat looking at him, she waved. His nod didn't reflect the easy camaraderie of the past few days at Criccieth, but had a kind of deference. Her heart seemed to clench inside her chest.

Then the horses were between them. She helped Enid and Adara mount. When she gained the saddle, Rhys and his warriors were already forging ahead down the road with Princess Elizabeth and Owain between them. Why did he not look back?

She found herself inside the great hall of the castle, with no memory of having seen it from the path.

"The horse," Cat said.

"Cynfrig has seen to it," Adara told her, with a questioning look. Cat did not know who Cynfrig was. A man with a kind face and greying moustache took her hand.

"You are welcome in this place, morrigan," he said, moving closer to her to speak quietly. "My Lord Rhys has told me of your feat at Criccieth. It has been many years since one of your kind graced our halls." She stared at him blankly, and he nodded and patted her hand. "You must rest. I will have our Katie show you to your room."

"You are most kind," Cat said. What had he called her? Morrigan? Had he mistaken her for someone else? As a kind of afterthought she added, "My name is Catrin. Cat."

It seemed a moment later when she woke, surrounded by quilted softness. She felt the smoothness of the white fabric with her hand.

"It is silk," said her mam's voice, and Cat looked up into Adara's face.

"Where are we?"

Adara looked concerned for a moment and felt Cat's forehead with the inside of her wrist. "We're at Castell-y-Bere. Don't you remember? You must have been more ill than we realized."

She had a sudden flash of the kind man's face and the word "morrigan." It was familiar to her somehow. What did it mean? She felt afraid, but she didn't know what she feared. She felt an urgency to rise and do—something, but she didn't know what. She pushed the quilt off and her mam rose as well.

"How long have we been here?"

"Two days already." Adara caught Cat as she swayed. "Take it slowly. You've barely eaten the last few days, and you've been asleep since yesterday, but I didn't want to wake you. How do you feel now?"

Cat tested herself and looked around. "Better. I think." She dressed with Adara's help and got caught up on the news. Prince Dafydd had come with his eldest son, and she had apparently missed Princess Elizabeth's tearful reunion with her family. Margred and the girls were well, and Owain was practicing in the yard with the other boys.

"And Rhys?" she asked.

"He was here to check on you earlier this morning," her mam told her, smiling.

"He was?" Everything must be fine then.

"And why would he not?" Adara went on. "Nothing stands between you now." When Cat didn't respond, Adara stopped fussing with her hair and looked at her. "Does it?"

"No, of course not," Cat said. But why did she still feel her stomach clench?

In the next few days, Cat found no opportunity to talk with Rhys, even at dinner. They sat in family groups according to the Welsh custom, rather than at long tables as they had at Criccieth. As lord of the manor Rhys was expected to serve the others, and Cynfrig and his family helped. Cat sat with Adara, Enid and the baby, and the two remaining Garth Celyn warriors. It was the second evening meal before Rhys happened to serve them.

Adara smiled at him as he and two of the kitchen girls placed the main course of eel and venison in front of them. "It smells tasty," she told him. "Cat should be helping you, Rhys. Then you will know each other's ways before you become hosts together."

"Nay, Lady Adara, I would rather she conserve her health for—what she may need it for," he said, shaking his head. He did not try to catch Cat's eye, but turned a general smile upon them all as he backed away toward another table. Cat's smile froze on her face. Was he avoiding her? She watched him joking easily with Margred and Owain as he served them.

"He has great concern for you, Cat," Adara said.

"Mayhap he has too much concern for me, Mam," Cat said.

"Mayhap you should tell him so, then," Adara replied.

Something inside Cat snapped. Enough of this, she thought. If he had reason to avoid her, then he must tell her so to her face. "Mayhap I should do more than that," she said, throwing down her cloth napkin and following Rhys into the kitchens.

"Since I am to be lady of this castle one day, I should offer you assistance in your tasks," she said, moving to the tables.

Rhys stopped what he was doing and raised his eyebrows in surprise. "Nay, Cat – I mean, Lady Catrin," he said, glancing at the Cook and her staff, who had come over to watch. "Your duties are far more onerous than this small task, and I would not have you tax your—strengths."

"I have vast reserves of strength," she said, arranging sliced meats on a plate. "I will admit, what happened as we left Criccieth cast a pall on my spirits, but I did very little. Others did a great deal, while I was merely a witness."

"I beg your pardon, Lady Cat, but I know well what you did," he said, stopping her with one hand. "And I know very well that you were taxed by it."

"I was weary from the voyage, but I am rested now," she told him.

"Perhaps you would take a breath of fresh air with me so we might talk about this together," he said, glancing around them. "Just we two."

She looked around to see a gaggle of kitchen staff staring at them. Cynfrig's grey moustache twitched, and his wife held her hands over her mouth. Cat could not tell if they were upset or—could they be—laughing?

"Aye, Rhys, lad," Cynfrig said, his voice strained. "Take the lady for a quick look at the garden under the moon. We can easily finish what you have begun here."

"Can we indeed?" his wife said, turning away quickly in a fit of what must have been coughing. Then she turned back again. "Aye, I suppose we can."

Cat let Rhys lead her from the kitchen and into the yard at the side of the castle. "Here we grow the fine roots and herbs you tasted in tonight's meal," he said, loudly enough for the others to hear. As the door shut behind them he turned on her. "What do you mean, you were weary from the voyage? You sat and stared at the water without speaking for most of the trip."

"I did?" she asked.

"You did. And I should know, for I tried every way I knew to coax a response from you."

"Every way?"

He pulled her to him. "Nay, not every way. Not with your mam hovering so close." He kissed her. She felt the softness of his lips against her mouth, and the sudden cold when he pulled himself away.

"I beg your pardon," he said. "I did not mean to—I know what you are, Cat. And I know this cannot be, now. You are meant for a higher calling."

"What do you mean?" she said.

"You are the morrigan," he said. "A woman of power. My da had such a woman in our home before the last great war, and I know well what it means."

"What? What is it that you think—"

"I know. I know you cannot marry as other women, or birth children. You must keep your power pure."

"Fie," she said, stopping him. "I know not how you do things in Meirionnydd, but we have no such prohibitions at Garth Celyn. My own mam is a woman of power, yet she loves my da just as other women love their husbands. And she gave birth to my brother and to me, and two others who died in infancy, just as other women's children die."

Rhys shook his head. "Nay, I am sure it cannot be so."

“It is so,” Cat said. “I am here, standing in front of you, to prove it.”

Rhys cupped her face in his hands. “Yet I saw you release the young warrior’s soul.”

“I—I don’t know what I did,” she said. “I saw Sir Ifan standing in the field outside our home, and I knew he was free.”

“You released him,” Rhys said. “How can we live as normal man and wife, when you have the power to—the power of the raven?” They stood looking at each other for a moment, and then Rhys turned and disappeared down the dark garden path.

Chapter Forty-seven: Hyw

An eerie mist dampened the air around them as Hyw and the others followed their warrior-guide over wooden bridges that crossed several deep, rock-cut ditches and culverts. The guide stopped at a certain spot, and spoke quietly into the mist, as if giving a pre-ordained password. A man holding a javelin rose up in front of them, appearing from between the rocks as if by magic. He waved them on, and stood aside as they gained the high-walled path.

When they rounded the last curve, Hyw felt dwarfed by the cavernous stoneworks that led into the castle yard. He felt as if the rock cliffs and slanted pathway pushed them into the inner courtyard of Castell-y-Bere. Then the dusk grew rosy in a blaze of setting sun, and colour flooded the castle courtyard as people bustled into view.

Hyw saw townsfolk, women and children, and warriors of all ages. Several wore the traditional Gwynedd warrior garb of a red tunic over chain mail, and Hyw realized some of Llywelyn's army manned the castle. He spotted the dark hair and eyes of a familiar face, and caught a glimpse of the red sash that marked the warrior's privilege.

It was Emrys, Hyw's childhood friend, still as wiry and thin as he had been at Garth Celyn.

Before he could wave, a grizzled warrior came toward them. He was short and muscular, but his air of confidence and authority marked him as a leader. His arms opened wide to them. "Welcome to our fortress, Castell-y-Bere." He hugged each man to him in turn. The man's deep-set eyes were troubled but kind. "I am Cynfrig ap Madog, constable here for many years, and glad to be named your host. We ration against the future, but such as we have, we will share with you. Gather you all inside, and dine with us, and with our own Prince of Wales."

Hyw was confused for a moment, wondering how Cynfrig had guessed his secret. He closed his eyes almost out of habit, and saw Llywelyn laughing at him. *Nay Hyw, he speaks of Dafydd. My brother is here. We've made it.*

Too tired to question further, Hyw allowed himself to be led to the castle by his father. They entered together, handing over weapons and washing their feet in keeping with the old customs. Hyw saw Bran run a hand along his chin, rough from quick shaving with his knife on the road. He knew his father would look forward to proper morning rituals again.

Then they were pushed along in the stream of men. Hyw saw several of their companions greet friends, hugging wives and other relations who had taken refuge in the castle. At other tables, women looked anxiously among them. Then Hyw saw them fall still and look down at their own hands. Even as he felt sorrow for them, he hoped Dai or the others would bring them news of their loved ones to ease their minds.

He didn't realize until the last minute that the constable had led his father toward Dafydd's own family group. Hyw hesitated, but Dafydd made no outcry against him. If Llywelyn's brother remembered him from Dolwyddelan, the only sign he gave was a slight pause as he brought a leg of mutton to his lips, and the narrowing of his ice-blue eyes. Bran made to pay homage to Dafydd, but he waved them off graciously. "We will speak later. See to your wife and children, Bran."

Then Hyw thought of it no more, for at the next table he heard a cry. Up sprang his mother, Adara. The blush of joy on her face lit the room, just as the setting sun had lit the rocks outside. She flew into Bran's arms. Then she turned to Hyw. He was aware of his mother's smallness, and hugged her to him.

"Hyw, you're a man in truth now. How tall you have grown."

He grinned down at her. As she turned back to Bran again, he spotted his sister Cat coming toward them. He hugged her to him. "Glad I am to see you, Cat."

"And I you."

She seemed older too, and a little sadder, he thought. He wondered how bedraggled he must look, and how different he would be after a few months away. She hesitated a moment longer, and then turned to greet her da.

Adara turned back to Hyw then. "You are too thin, the both of you," she scolded. "And here we sit, warm and well fed." She broke down then. Bran crushed her to him for a long moment.

"I feared you were dead," Adara mumbled into his chest.

"And how could that be?" Bran's voice was husky. "No one could ever capture this black bird but you, milady."

Hyw thought he glimpsed a shine in his da's eyes as well. Then he noticed Enid the nursemaid beside them, waiting for her turn, and he hugged her with one arm as he kept the other around his sister.

"Where is Gwenllian?" he asked.

"She is asleep, the dear child," Enid said. She knelt and rocked a bassinet beside her. "You will see how she has grown anon." He could only see blankets from where he stood, but didn't want to disturb the babe.

Finally Bran set Adara back on her own feet. Cynfrig and his wife brought out more plates of food for all the men, including Hyw's company. Hyw noticed cheese and mutton, along with jugs of white milk. Still blushing, Adara pushed him to a spot near her and added to their plates from her own, beckoning Bran to her other side.

Hyw paused, noticing the easy familiarity of the family gatherings in the Welsh hall. What a contrast from the formal gathering of the English, where the king and his favourites sat on a raised dais apart from rows of knights. Here there were no tablecloths, elaborate fixtures, or cleverly-dressed dishes, but plain food, well-made and nourishing. He tried to imagine King Edward and his wife serving their guests before they ate themselves, as Welsh custom required. He could not imagine the English, even the kindly Shrewsbury, without servants and squires to serve them.

Then he noticed his father's hand shaking as he picked up some of the food. Bran turned to Adara and pulled her to him again, as they sat at the table.

Cat took the opportunity to scramble around them and sit beside her brother. He turned to her, showing her the braided threads he still wore around his wrist. "See, here is the band you made for me long ago. Do you remember?"

"You've added another in with it, here."

He thought of James, and the day they had parted. It seemed much longer than weeks ago. "Aye, that was done with the help of a good friend. It keeps yours in good repair. Always you were in my heart, Cat. This wristband kept you near."

"It did indeed, Hyw," she said, and the look on her face made him wonder if she would say more. Instead, she passed a few morsels of meat from her plate to his. "After supper I would show you around this gloomy place. The wolves howl always here. Have you heard them?"

"It's not wolves, child," Enid put in, "but the wind, howling through the rock face of the mountain."

"I heard it as we came." Hyw gripped her hand. "Mayhap that very wind and its mournful howl will keep us safe from harm." He made up a story for her then, of a sleeping giant knocking the English soldiers off the mountain with his snoring. Before he was finished, Gwladys and young Owain and some of the other children gathered near as well. Lord Rhys also came near, although he remained standing apart.

“Good it is to have you and Da with us again, Hyw,” said Cat, laughing at the end of Hyw’s story.

“Aye, he has all the warrior’s graces.” Adara’s shining eyes reminded him of all the bardic tales he had heard played and sung by warriors in Garth Celyn, where a man was expected to be as adept at musical arts as he was at combat.

Sure enough, before they had finished the meal, a warrior bard began to sing and play the harp. Cat whispered to remind him this was Gwilym ap Einion, and he pretended to remember the bard from his time at Garth Celyn. Five years ago, he realized. A beautiful young woman came to sit near Cat, and she introduced her as Margred, daughter of Prince Dafydd. People gradually cleared their places, feeding their leftovers to the hunting dogs that shared their space.

Hyw noticed his father and the warrior Dai rising to follow Dafydd and a handful of other men. He knew they would confer about the war, and longed to be with them. Above the heads of other groupings, he noticed Emrys watching the men retire as well. Their eyes met, and Hyw grinned, as did Emrys. He was seated with Dai’s group, and Hyw realized he must be related to the warriors they had met on the trail.

Then his mother called his attention back to her. He found himself giving her an account of the battle at Dolwyddelan. He hesitated to recount their capture of soldiers on the trail, adding, “We found Dai and his companions as we made our way here.”

Adara took his hand gently. “Glad I am you have come back to us at last.” He welcomed her touch, and the chance to feel Cat warm against his side. He knew Dafydd had been at Dolwyddelan. Had his mam and Cat been with him there?

“Yet how did you come to be here, Mam?”

“We were attacked at Garth Celyn, and we fled to Criccieth, where Princess Elizabeth gave us her protection. Then Lord Rhys came to us, with messages from the prince to commend us to his protection at Castell-y-Bere.”

“Does Garth Celyn still stand?”

"I know not. We thought it best to bring the babe to her uncle. After that, we did not plan."

Hyw could see the sense of bringing Gwenllian to Dafydd. *Aye,* agreed Llywelyn inside him. *My brother would never harm the child. Gwenllian is safest with him.* Then Llywelyn asked the question that Hyw realized he should have asked. *Does your mother carry Gwenllian's seal?* Hyw turned to Adara, and asked quietly if she still kept the baby's royal seal. She nodded, glancing at Dafydd's table with a gesture that told Hyw to keep this to himself.

So, things were not as cozy as they seemed, perhaps. He looked over at Llywelyn's brother, who was seated with his wife and seven children. Surely Dafydd would have been safe with Edward too, Hyw thought, since they had been friends. Hyw wondered if he had tried to contact the English king.

Edward must hate him worst of all now, Llywelyn said softly in his ear, *because in the end, my brother could not kill me. And now he is Wales. You must help him if you can, Hyw, just as you have helped me.*

Chapter Forty-eight: Cat

After supper Cat took Hyw by the hand. "Come and let me show you the castle, before it becomes too dark to see," she said, leading him up the stairwell.

"I will," said Hyw. "And who better to tour it with, since you will be its lady one day."

"I suppose I will," she said. She looked over the battlement at the castle, smiling at the guard who waved as he walked his rounds. Castell-y-Bere was built oblong, almost triangular, to fit its rocky plateau. One D-shaped tower overlooked the castle well.

"One of the warriors told me these waters grant the powers of sharp sight and strength," said Cat. "He and many others drink from it before leaving the castle."

"Mayhap I will as well," he said. "Quite a bit more grand than home."

She knew he was thinking of their longhouse at Garth Celyn. She felt a small pang, thinking of the guard who had helped them escape.

How many had died there before the English took it? For a moment they stood together, saying nothing. Cat had to force herself to remember why she'd taken him away from the others.

"There is something else, Hyw," she began. "I'm not sure how to explain. When you left I had no gift to speak of."

"That never mattered—"

"I know, but after you left, I found I was able to connect with you."

"Connect?" he repeated. "What do you mean?"

She explained her visions, and how she had known he was alive, and about the treachery of the priest Maelgwyn. "After a time I realized it happened whenever I looked into some kind of liquid, whether a cup of wine at supper or a raindrop. Now I think I see you because of this bracelet I tied to your wrist." She took his hand and pressed the rough wool.

"You used a lock of your own hair," he said.

"Perhaps that is why. Yet something puzzles me. More than once I saw you with the prince, almost as if you were one."

He went pale, and took both of her hands. "You saw?"

"What does it mean, Hyw?"

He told her what had happened on the hillside at Builth, about his bonding with Llywelyn and their travels together.

"And he is with you now?" She searched his face but saw no trace of the former Prince of Wales.

Hyw nodded.

"What does he tell you?"

"Many things," he said. "He knows more of this castle than we do." Hyw pointed to the large D-shaped tower guarding the path at the southern end of the courtyard. "Those walls are ten feet thick. If the English manage to get in, this is where the people should run."

She huffed, almost like a laugh. "How does it work? Does he speak to you?"

"He speaks inside my head, and I can see him if I close my eyes. Come. He says he will show us the castle."

They made their way to the rectangular keep. They took turns peeking out the archer's portals, careful not to disturb the bows and arrows set ready in case of attack.

"These rooms along here—we can rest or sleep here during an attack," Hyw told her as they continued.

"Or tend the injured," she added, and then wished she hadn't said it aloud.

Inside it was strangely quiet, as if the building stood in its own enchanted world that no threat could penetrate. Everyone was still listening to the bards. Cat touched the decorated tiles on the walls, stained glass windows, and lovely stone carvings of armed soldiers and heraldic battles as Hyw reported what Llywelyn told him.

"This is truly the most magnificent castle I have seen," Cat breathed. She could not imagine herself as its lady, any more than she could see herself as Rhys's wife.

"Prince Llywelyn says his grandfather brought back many of these items from the Crusades," Hyw said, still appearing to listen to his inner voice. "Here he taught his sons how to speak foreign languages, and the strategies of chess."

Wall hangings of legendary battles flickered in the candlelit room as if they were alive. On one wall, the great King Henry crowned their own Llywelyn as Prince of Wales, only a few decades earlier. Cat wondered what the prince must feel when he saw it now, but she did not ask Hyw.

"Look there," she said instead, pointing to another wall where Gruffydd ap Rhys of Deheubarth led his troops into the field to win his glorious victory over the English at Crug Mawr. As Cat looked away, Hyw asked her what was wrong, and she told him of her concerns about Rhys and the legend that had caused a rift between them.

Hyw was silent for several minutes when she had finished. "Your gift is of immense value to us now, Cat," he finally said. "Are you sure there is no truth in what Rhys says? This is Meirionnydd's legend, after all."

"There cannot be." Cat was adamant. "If there was, how could you or I be here to discuss it today? Besides, I only have the second sight. In the legends the morrigan—whatever she is—also transforms into a raven and commands the spirits of the dead. I'm fairly certain I won't be sprouting black feathers anytime soon."

Hyw shot Cat a look. "Yet I have been able to communicate with many animals, including ravens and hawks."

She considered that. "Have you ever shifted shape with any other creature?"

He did not answer right away. "I have been able to allow Prince Llywelyn to—I'm not sure how to explain it. He sometimes appears through me." He told her of the fox at Dolwyddelan, and how it seemed that he had become a fox himself.

Cat nodded, thinking of her vision. "Then do you think you will someday be able to shift into another form?"

Hyw shrugged. "Our uncle mentioned it."

Cat told him of Aylwen, their ancestor, who had told her they had stronger gifts because they were born in a time of need. Hyw said nothing, but she could tell by his face he was considering it. She thought about the legend again, and what it might mean for them.

It had grown dark while they explored, and in one candlelit hall they could hear men's voices arguing. She recalled Da and the other men who had left with Prince Dafydd. Hyw gestured and she led the way to the main hall where they rejoined their families to listen to bardic songs. Then Owain came to collect Hyw, since he was to share a room with the other boys inside the castle keep. In spite of her pleasure at seeing him again, Cat found herself tired enough to willingly bid him goodnight as she and Margred went up the stairs to their room.

The next morning, Cat poured wash water into her basin. She saw her reflection in the water and—

—she found herself in the castle courtyard. The crash and whump of swords on armour deafened her as arrows sped by. The people ran, screaming. She saw Prince Dafydd surrounded by English knights.

"You we take, and your wife and children, since the king demands they not be harmed," said a large armoured man she knew to be de Valence. "But these others—" He turned with a savage grin and nodded at his captain. The man took his sword and moved to Bran and Adara. Enid cowered behind them, holding Baby Gwen. The armoured man raised his sword to her mam as another soldier held her da back.

"No," roared Lord Rhys, running at the man in fury. His hands were tied but raised toward de Valence's throat. Suddenly he stopped, his eyes searching. He found Cat's face, and half-smiled. She didn't see the arrow in his back until he fell.

"No!" She reached toward him and—

—she was staring at her own reflection in the basin, a look of horror on her face. "No," she cried aloud.

"What is it?" Margred grabbed her.

"It cannot be," Cat said, staring at her. Margred glanced at her sisters and drew Cat from the room.

"Calm yourself, Cat," she said. "We will find your mam. She will know what it means."

Adara listened to the girls, and turned to Cat. "Your da and the others have been arguing about what to do. The prince wants to wage war, but Rhys and some of the others want to avoid it as long as possible. Your vision may be more important than you know. I will make sure your da hears of it, Cat."

"What can we do?"

"I have a thought," she said. "It would seem the simplest way would be for Dafydd and Rhys to part company. Each will get his wish, and your vision will be averted. Rest easy now. If this can be prevented, we will find a way."

Chapter Forty-nine: Hyw

The next morning, Hyw woke at dawn.

"Psst." He looked up at a young man's face, and realized it was Emrys. His friend's dark eyes snapped with laughter. He gestured for Hyw to follow. Hyw got up, careful not to disturb those still sleeping. In the bustle of the castle courtyard, he waved at his father just as Bran sat down for his turn at the ritual shaving. Other men had already begun their daily exercise, and Hyw and Emrys ran to join them.

"You can train with us today if you wish it." Emrys strapped on his sash. "I serve here with my uncle and his men. "

"Who is your uncle?"

The other boys giggled but Emrys shushed them with a gesture. "*Ust*. He is not to know, is he? My uncle is Cynfrig, constable of this castle. But now my cousin Dai has returned, mayhap I will serve with him."

Hyw agreed to train with them, and the boys began with basic agility much the same as Aeneus would at Garth Celyn. Then Emrys turned to him. "I know you spent some time with the English. My da says you cannot defeat an enemy unless you learn his strengths and weaknesses. We would know all we could of those *Saeson*. What can you show us of their moves?"

Hyw thought for a moment. "They are different, and prize their steel and armour well. It is difficult to show you how they train without the—the pieces in the yard."

"What do you mean?"

Hyw tried as best he could to describe the quintain, and the wooden dummies set up for practice with sword and mace. Emrys nodded. "Aye, we have something like it," he said. Then Hyw mentioned wooden sticks used as swords in field practice. Emrys stood and grabbed two javelin sticks, handing one to Hyw. "We do that too, although we have fewer swords. Show me how those English move, if you can."

Hyw hesitated, until he heard Llywelyn's voice. *Nay, lad, show him. Mayhap it will save his life.*

They skirmished, using the sticks as swords. Hyw struck lightly so as not to break any bones before the battle to come. Emrys, however, knew no such qualms, and played hard. Hyw took a bruise on his arm, and at the next skirmish he also played harder, turning back to front and striking low with the sword at Emrys's feet.

Emrys went down. Around him the others had taken up similar positions with each other to learn what Hyw could show them. As Emrys tumbled, all stopped and went quiet. Hyw wondered for a moment if he had managed to set this group against him so soon, and if he would have a new enemy as powerful as the bully Robert had been in Shrewsbury's court.

But Emrys was not Robert. At fourteen, he wore the sash proudly. He had already seen battle, and knew what the English could do. He got up and dusted himself off. "That was a clever move. Show me again."

By the next day, most of the boys had taken just such a tumble.

Then, working as a team, Emrys and Hyw worked out a way to predict the move and leap up over the stick before it struck.

Cynfrig watched them work the move through. He called them over to show some of the other men. Hyw and Emrys fought hard with sticks, and each of them in turn made and sidestepped the blow Hyw had shown them. The men nodded, and soon groups of them began to use the new skill as they had seen the boys do it.

"You have used your time well, I see." Hyw turned to see Bran beside him. His da's eyes twinkled as he stroked his newly-trimmed moustache, and Hyw felt a rush of pride. "It is well that the young teach the old, in this war. Many things have changed, and we must change with them. While there is life, there is yet hope." He tousled Hyw's hair. "Now, before your head swells out of your hair altogether, show me this move."

Llywelyn laughed inside Hyw as they prepared to skirmish with Bran. *Now you know why he is my captain.*

Hyw descended for supper in the castle hall along with his father. Emrys nodded toward him, as did several of the other boys as they made their way to their family table. Hyw saw someone sitting with them in a brown robe. "Uncle Gawain!" he exclaimed, and caught his uncle up in a huge hug.

Now we will hear the news, Llywelyn remarked, and Hyw did not need to close his eyes to know the look of grim anticipation on the former prince's face.

His uncle's normally calm face was clouded throughout the meal, and even Cat's harmonizing with Gwilym on his favourite hymn as the evening progressed did little to brighten his spirits. As Gwilym moved into a longer ballad, Aeneus moved to their table touching Gawain's shoulder as he sat with them. Adara finally leaned closer to Gawain.

"What news, brother?" she began in a low voice. "I know you spoke with Prince Dafydd this afternoon. I bid you, speak freely. What news of home?"

For a moment Gawain was silent, his eyes focused on his hands as if searching for direction there. Finally he looked up at her and spoke. "I was sent hither by my lord Abbot," he began. "The abbey at Aberconwy is no more. The English king claims our allegiance, and bids us move to Maenan. My lord can do aught but agree, save send me to warn the prince his ancestral lands are gone."

"Gone," Bran said. "How can it be?"

Gawain was silent, folding his hands in his lap. Bran made a noise of disbelief. Hyw heard Llywelyn make almost the same sound. His mother made no sound, but when he glanced toward her, he saw tears streaming down her face.

"It cannot," Aeneus cried. Adara quickly shushed him, and he went on in a lower voice. "What of the garrison at Garth Celyn, and the men of Ynys Mon?"

"The *Saeson* were merciless," Gawain said, his voice scraping against Hyw's ears. "They ran down all that moved for their shillings. Some of the women and children managed to reach to the abbey. I cannot say they were the lucky ones."

Chapter Fifty: Cat

The next few days went by in a whirlwind. Cat could find no reason to smile, after Gawain's news. Her uncle kept mainly to the chapel except for the evening meal, where he was often silent. She wondered which of the women at Garth Celyn had survived the attack, but could not bring herself to ask. She had asked what he knew of the morrigan legends, and he said he would make the time to tell her as soon as he had his church business settled.

The girls and women were able to exercise freely at Castell-y-Bere at the north end of the courtyard while the warriors practiced farther south. Cat sought out Bronwen, a childhood friend, and bade her join her and Margred. The girls spoke little, but worked hard at the exercises set for them by one of the Castell-y-Bere warriors.

"Yours were much tougher," Cat whispered to Margred. Bronwen was impressed when she heard how the girls had formed their own practice at Criccieth.

Cat found the throwing knives helped ease her mind. Once when she was lining up the target, Cat felt as if someone was watching her. She let the knife fly, and felt the satisfying thwack as it hit squarely in the centre. She turned in time to see Rhys watching her, but in the next heartbeat he looked away. Margred saw as well, and put an arm around her as they returned to the back of the line for their next turn.

"Is aught amiss between you and Lord Rhys?"

Cat straightened her shoulders. "Lord Rhys is reconsidering the wisdom of our union."

Adara, who had joined them, heard and pulled Cat out of the line. "Why would he do so? Was it because of Sir Ifan? Did you have feelings for him?"

"Nay, Mam," Cat began, surprised. "Not like that." Cat poured out the story then, telling her mam about the legend and the morrigan who once served Rhys' family.

"I knew her," Adara said. "You know your gift is no problem for you as a woman, don't you?" When Cat said nothing, Adara gave her another quick hug. "You have concerns."

"The legend connects Arthur and Morgana," Cat said. "It speaks of a combination of brother and sister."

"Ah, I see," her mam said. "You think perhaps you and Hyw make two sides of the morrigan." Adara thought for a moment, and shook her head. "I also have gifted sisters and brothers who married happily. Your Uncle Gawain took his vows as a monk, but the rest have families."

"But how can I answer Rhys' concerns?"

"Only he can do that," Adara said.

By then it was time for them to join Princess Elizabeth and help her greet some of the townsfolk who were arriving daily, as word of the English moved down the valleys. Cat and Margred listened for news of Criccieth and those left to defend the castle. Although Margred never said so, Cat suspected she worried for the butcher's son, Drem, as well as other friends from the town.

Elizabeth, Adara, and the girls welcomed and cared for the women and children, especially those who were pregnant or in need. As at Criccieth, the Castell-y-Bere warriors trained any men and women willing to fight for their land.

Twice Cat joined others working in the fields. Some pounded meat into strips and smoked it for storage and travel, or made breads and cheeses at the cookhouses. Hyw came with Emrys and the other boys to help carry their wares, along with oats and other grains in barrels, back to the castle longhouse to feed the Welsh survivors pouring into the castle from surrounding areas. Bronwen saved a few choice tidbits for Emrys.

"See how she loves me, poor thing," Emrys joked, but Cat could sense the longing in both of them, and thought of Rhys.

Cat was on the way to the north exercise yard when Rhys stopped her. After greeting Margred and Bronwen, he asked her to walk with him a moment. His tunic sleeves were rolled up and the glisten on his skin showed he had already been practicing, so he must have been watching for them. She waved at the other girls and fell into step beside him.

He drew a dull grey cloth from beneath the cloak he had slung across one shoulder. She unrolled it to find a set of three lightweight throwing knives. The hilts were burnished with one small green jewel set cleverly in scrollwork, and they fit her hand.

"Be careful," he cautioned her. "They are deadly sharp."

She held one up to the sun and saw it was tapered to a fine thin edge. He touched the leather sheath that held them.

"This sheath belonged to the morrigan," he said. "She was my teacher for a time, and I saw her use her knife more than once. It fixes to your leg with the point inside your boot, and seemed to work very well for her."

She was tempted to give it back to him then, but he placed his hand on hers as if he knew what she was thinking. "Please, Cat. If we are separated I must know that you are safe. I have worried about your safety since Gawain—well. When I saw you in the practice yard, I had them made especially for you. I believe the sheath is special, and will help keep you safe."

His eyes blazed into hers, and made her think of the kiss in the night garden. Perhaps he remembered also, because he dropped her hands and moved past her to the castle keep without a backward glance.

Chapter Fifty-one: Hyw

It was well past noon when Hyw heard a warrior's shout. "They're coming."

He ran with the others to climb the low retaining wall around Castell-y-Bere and strained to see through the light mist that always seem to hang over the lush valleys. He still thought of it as the giant's breath, and felt a shiver run down the length of his back.

Emrys jumped onto the stone wall and mimed a fight. "With some of those moves you taught us, Hyw, they should be more afraid of us than of the giant who breathes down on them now."

All the boys laughed then, the tension broken. Hyw marvelled at the way Emrys could lift their spirits and make them feel bold, even in their fear. *A leader in training,* Llywelyn said softly in his ear. *If he survives what comes, Emrys would be a good candidate for the prince's teulu.* It was a high compliment, Hyw knew.

"Look there!" The boys looked where Emrys pointed and spied a flash of metal. With a flush of excitement and fear, they leaned against the wall. Each tried to be the first to see, and the first to point out English troops to his friends. It began with the metallic flash from moment to moment through the thick trees and undergrowth. Then soldiers began to march into the lowlands and muster in groups. Hyw had no need of his gift to track them. By mid-day, the lowlands were full of English banners.

The clouds that ringed the mountain darkened and belched out rain, covering the plain with a muddy mixture that showed the outline of the army clearly. The king's white camouflage coats were useless against the giant of Cadair Idris. Hyw looked for the siege engines the English had taken with them to Dolweddelan, but in truth they had no need of them. He heard the men guess at the size of de Valence's troops. Camped beyond arrow range, fanning out in the valley, their numbers filled every inch of the Desenni plain.

"There can be nothing left now, of food or game," one man said.

"That will be the end of them, then." Emrys laughed. "How can they remain, without food?"

The man guffawed. "*Saeson*." He spat. "What do you think they eat?"

"Rat?"

"Sheep droppings." He made a rude gesture and some of the other men huffed a grim laugh at his antics.

"Best stay out of their sights, Gron." Aeneus folded his arms across his chest and stared down at the field, unsmiling. "Names will not help you. Hunger makes fierce foes. Who knows what it will do to them? I hear they have Flemish mercenaries among them."

"Them I have seen. They dig under the ground and eat the bugs."

Gron launched into a bawdy song, and Aeneus turned away in disgust.

About mid-afternoon, a roar caught Hyw's attention as a younger knight with a banner no one recognized led a hundred or so cavalry and soldiers out of the ranks. After a short flourish, they swarmed toward the Welsh castle. Hyw remembered Edward's words as they left Rhuddlan: any man, no matter his rank, could keep the land he won in this battle. Hyw had seen the hard greed in their eyes as they prepared for the journey.

At first his stomach tightened with what Llywelyn called battle-fear. Hyw felt his hands form fists without waiting for direction from his thoughts. Then, as they reached the base of the rocky cliff, the horses faltered. Emrys laughed a little too loudly. "You see! The fools. They need mountain goats to get up that cliff."

"Or good Welsh ponies," Hyw added.

"Look closer." Even at this distance, Hyw could see the line of Welsh breeding in the sturdy horses. Emrys cast him a sideways look, and Hyw realized his friend suspected their countrymen of aiding the English. "Devil take them."

As he said it, several horses slid backwards. One shaggy mount lost its footing on the rocks and went over backwards, falling onto its rider. Hyw gasped as the horse reached out to him in panic. Vox and Cadarn flashed into his mind, but he knew they were gone. He quickly built around his mind a battlement like the one surrounding Y-Bere. Yet he felt as much as saw the horse flounder, struggling on top of the still form of the armoured man. Had Emrys summoned the horned god from OtherWorld? Hyw made the sign of the cross, and felt Emrys make a similar sign beside him. He turned in time to see his expression of horror reflected on Emrys' face.

A few of the horses and some foot soldiers pulled themselves up the cliffs nearer the castle. A volley of arrows from the battlements rained down. The shafts seemed to hit their mark with extra force. It was as if they were drawn by the pull of the valley floor, Hyw thought, or perhaps blown by the giant's breath. Then he noticed half-formed pieces of the siege engines on the valley floor, and wondered if these were the same ones the English had dragged to Dolwyddelan. They were of little use on the giant's mountain.

Horses and men fell, and pulled back. Twice more the English knight and his followers charged, until he fell back for the final time.

Hyw could see the knight bowed over, with an arrow protruding from his shoulder.

Later that day, under a flag of truce, some men on foot dragged off the fallen soldiers. Hyw wondered if they would recover or be buried by their countrymen, never to see their own lands again. He heard a rumble on Cadair Idris, and his skin prickled as he imagined the giant laughing at the tiny men on the field below.

The next day, a rider came to the castle, holding a white flag. Bran went down the path to speak with him, along with two other men from Cynfrig's garrison. Aeneus and the other warriors kept watch from the battlement, javelins at the ready. After a long conversation, the knight rode off again and the men returned to hold conference with Dafydd.

Rumours were rife through the castle most of the afternoon, as the people waited to hear news of the rider. When Bran and the others finally came out of the meeting room, it was as if the whole castle went quiet. All eyes turned to them.

Dafydd came out last and looked around him. "The English know we cannot be beaten. They sent their Lancelot to tell us so." He laughed.

Several others laughed, and then began to cheer. Dafydd let them enjoy the moment. When they had quieted, he went on. "It is right that you know the truth. They will not back off this time. They will starve us out."

"Let them try." Aeneus stood defiantly at the back of the room. "They will need to return to their fields this season, same as us."

Yet too many are not English soldiers, Llywelyn reminded Hyw, in his inner ear. *These men will not drop their swords to take up a plough unless they are given a piece of Welsh land to tend.*

"Nay, their mercenaries will stay," Dafydd echoed the comment. "They can wait us out, and trap us here in this stone castle like sheep." Around the room, people shifted. Like many, Hyw had always preferred his *llys* to these stone castles, built to defend Cymru against the English. A handful had already begun complaining they would prefer mountain caves to the cold stone under their bare feet. Gwilym the warrior poet looked thoughtful.

Dafydd went on. “Lestrange wants me. He offers you the chance to depart this castle in peace, with eighty English pounds divided among you.”

A murmur buzzed around the room like a wasp swarm. Lestrange’s offer meant surrender.

Aeneus’ voice boomed across the room. “They would have our prince? Never!” The room erupted around him. Hyw was dismayed to hear angry voices, as if some disagreed with Aeneus.

No, Hyw heard Llywelyn inside him. *Dafydd must not surrender. He is Wales now. They must not let him.*

Hyw closed his eyes and found Llywelyn seated in front of a chessboard. This was no time to think of games, Hyw thought, but Llywelyn gestured at it. “How many ways can players jump positions?”

Hyw let out an exasperated breath and looked at the board. The white nearly overwhelmed the few remaining black pieces, leaving Llywelyn’s king guarded by only one knight. “The knight can jump other players. And I know of a move called castling where the king moves two squares, and the rook jumps across to take its place.”

“And we have a squire who could take the prince’s shape,” Llywelyn suggested, removing the black king from the board. “Dafydd could flee with the children, while the English remain behind, thinking to capture their prize.”

Hyw recalled taking the knight’s position during their training. It was only weeks ago, but seemed longer. “My grandfather had the ability to change form, but mine falls far short of that. And I would not put you in jeopardy.”

“It is too late to fear for me, Hyw. Do what you must to save Wales.”

Hyw stared at Llywelyn until Dafydd’s voice roared out across the hall, startling him into opening his eyes.

“Think you well on this offer, friends. It may be the only way to save you.”

Chapter Fifty-two: Cat

As the English settled in around them, Cat helped her mam and Cynfrig's family ration their dwindling stores of food. The castle was full of people from the surrounding towns and farms. The food they had gathered, which had seemed so plentiful as they had carried it into the castle, scarcely seemed enough to last the week.

As she served a platter to their family table the next morning, Hyw touched her hand. "I need your help," he said. "This morning, if you can make time."

When she had finished her chores, they made their way to the battlements. Unlike the previous day, Aeneus kept only a few warriors for the watch, strategically placed along the wall walk.

"Most will spend this day in the practice yard, readying for the signal," Aeneus told them. "After yesterday, the *Saeson* will need to rethink their strategy. But their archers will be watching. Mind you both return to the keep."

"The girls will be with Elizabeth and Mam this morning," Cat whispered. Hyw nodded, and they made their way to the room Cat shared with Margred and her sisters. Hwy looked uncomfortable in the small bedroom, as if he had grown too large for it already. He stood at the window, opening the heavy wooden shutter just enough to see out without being seen. She moved impatiently and finally he began.

"Do you remember when you asked me if I had ever used my gift to become another creature? Would it surprise you to know I've tried?"

She shrugged. "I know the stories of our great-grandfather as well as you. Why shouldn't you see if your gift is as strong as his?"

"Nay, I care not if it is." He went on without waiting for her to answer, tapping his temple lightly. "My liege has asked me to do this thing. For his sake I have tried, but I cannot."

"It will come," she told him. "You know our gifts grow with time and use. What you cannot do now, you may do in a year, or ten years."

"I need to do it now," he said. "In a year or ten, Prince Dafydd may be a prisoner or worse. I must help him now."

"What, would you change into a horse and spirit him away?"

"Nay, but something of smaller size and more spirit," he quipped, drawing her to the window and pointing at a pair of hawks flying together against the grey clouds, just above the castle battlements.

"I don't understand." Cat stared at the hawks, wondering if Hyw meant to fly Dafydd away like Pegasus, the winged horse from the old songs.

"I cannot tell you all just yet, Cat, but if I can manage this thing, I will make sense of it, I promise you."

"But how can I be of service in this task?"

"These powers you have, as a morrigan," he said, "can you call them to you?"

"I do not know. Water plays a part, as you know." She thought of Ifan's death again, and the infinite sadness that enveloped her then. Her powers had seemed such a part of her that she did not fully realize what she had done until Rhys told her what he had seen. Could she call that power to her? Did she want to feel it, ever again?

"And if I did," she said aloud, "how could it help you accomplish your task?"

He shook his head. The look of discouragement on his face made her want to say something more to reassure him.

"Our uncle Gawain may have wisdom to offer," she suggested. "You said he helped you connect with our prince when you began this strange journey. He has some knowledge of the morrigan, but he has not had the time to tell me. Mayhap we should ask him for his thoughts on all."

"Lucky we are that he remained with us," Hyw said, brightening a little. "Let us find him."

"That will be easily done," she said. "He has been at chapel every day since he arrived."

"We will give him a reason to come outside and enjoy this fine April weather with us," Hyw said, and they started down the stairs together.

Cat asked a passing servant and discovered her uncle was in the chapel. She persuaded Hyw not to disturb the monk's prayers, especially with the English so near. The following day she saw her brother whispering in Gawain's ear when she served the breakfast rations. Hyw caught her eye, and she finished her chores quickly to join them before they left the family table.

Reluctantly, their uncle gestured toward the door. He walked with them through the courtyard, stopping at the castle well to fill his flask. "The warriors say this water helps them," he told her. "Mayhap it will be useful to bolster their spirits in the coming days."

Gawain stopped to talk with several groups of worried farmers and people from neighbouring towns, as they made their slow way to the chapel garden, where he began plucking weeds. Hyw half-sat on the rock fence nearby as he explained their situation. Unable to be still, Cat stood in front of them, shifting from her heels to her toes.

"So can the morrigan—if that's truly what I am—help him?" she finally broke in.

Gawain straightened up and brushed the dirt from his hands. "In truth I know but little of the morrigan," he said. "The Irish have many stories and some have crossed the sea to us. Like the crow or the raven, she was thought to follow warriors during wartime. Many believed she knew which side would win, and might be convinced to tell them. Yet if a warrior saw her washing his clothes, he believed he would die in the battle. Did she then cause it, or did his own thinking defeat him?" Gawain shrugged. "But Geoffrey of Monmouth writes of a Morgana le Fay, who had healing powers to protect the land and its sovereign."

Cat did her best to listen, but she didn't want a history lesson. She needed to know how it might connect to her, here and now. She could not help but interrupt. "Your pardon, uncle, but much of this I knew. And yet—if I am a morrigan, it would be right for me to protect Prince Dafydd."

Gawain shrugged. "Or Prince Llywelyn, who resides in Hyw. In the old stories, Morgana placed King Arthur into an enchanted sleep to help him to Avalon."

"But I cannot see Llywleyn, let alone give him a sleep tonic."

Hyw sat upright. "Wait," he said. "Some have seen the prince, even so." He scrambled to his feet in front of her and stood for a moment with his eyes closed. Something shifted in the air around him, and for a moment she saw the tall form of the Prince of Wales shimmer into view. "My lady," she heard a deep voice almost in echo with Hyw's, and knew it to be Llywelyn's. Then all disappeared again, and Hyw stood where he had before.

Cat gasped. "How did you do that?"

"It is difficult," Hyw admitted. "I must—step aside of myself, as it were, and allow Llywelyn to speak through me. It first happened the day we met the fox of Dolwyddelan, but I cannot manage it for long."

“I wonder,” Gawain said, leading them to a spot further away, where they would be sheltered from sight by trees. “You have the gift of foretelling, Cat. I recall that some with this gift may connect their minds with the minds of others close to them. Can you reach Hyw?” Gawain asked. “Can you see the prince as Hyw does, from inside his mind?”

Cat closed her eyes and tried to reach out to her brother, but she saw nothing but blackness. She shook her head.

“There is much talk in the morrigan myths of the powers of three,” he said. “And we are three, together. We can but try.”

Gawain put two fingers on her forehead in the space above her eyes, and two on Hyw’s in the same spot. He nodded, and all three of them closed their eyes. For several minutes, nothing happened. Gawain removed his fingers. He bid her cup her hands in front of her, and poured water into them from his flask. Water from her own well.

“Breathe slowly, Cat, as you do when you sing. From here.” Gawain laid a hand on her belly, and when he felt her breathing change, moved his fingers to their foreheads again and closed his eyes. She stared at the water in her cupped hands, and heard him begin to sing softly, a song she had never heard before, of the mountains and the watchers.

After a few moments, she began to see a dark form as if through a mist. “I see him!”

Gawain nodded, and dropped his hands. “You each astound me. I have heard stories from our grandfather of powers like yours, but never thought I would see it in my lifetime.”

Cat told him of her ancestor vision then, and he looked thoughtful.

“So might we coax your powers to help both princes, then,” he said.

Cat and Hyw tried again, and Gawain gradually moved away from them, as he had when he first taught Llywelyn and Hyw to connect with each other. Cat gradually formed the image of the prince in her mind.

“My lord,” she said, her voice echoing as if they stood in a cave. She looked around her, and they were in a sort of cave in the mountain.

The mist was steam rising from an underground stream that began to trickle in the background. Hyw lounged against a rock at the edge, and grinned at her.

In this world, what we think becomes real, the prince said with a smile, and she heard his voice as clearly as she had the day the messenger came to Garth Celyn.

Gawain tested them, taking her aside and asking her to describe the prince's clothing or some other detail to check with Hyw. After the third such grilling, Cat threw her hands in the air in frustration. Droplets of water sprinkled her face and hair.

"What could my seeing Llywelyn possibly have to do with helping Hyw change into a hawk?"

Gawain turned and looked out at Cadair Idris. "It is something my grandfather once said. Hyw carries a heavy burden in holding the prince's soul to this world. I believe what is stopping him from testing his true powers to their limits is the very thing that allows him to accomplish it." He turned to Hyw then. "When you make contact with the animal, you are doing no more or less than you have always done. But to make the final shift, that will require you to let go of this world and find the body of the animal inside yourself. Yet Llywelyn anchors you here. You must find a way to trust that the prince will follow, and accept the shift to a new form."

Hyw looked miserable. "I have sworn fealty."

Cat finally understood what Gawain wanted from her. "So, you want me to help Hyw separate himself from the prince."

Gawain nodded.

"But how am I to do that?"

"I know not, Cati," Gawain said. "I believe it must be something that comes from you, and honestly."

They got no further that morning, and Cat found herself returning to the problem throughout the day.

"What's wrong?" Margred finally asked her, as they prepared for bed. Cat shook her head and said nothing, unwilling to discuss her brother with her friend any more than she already had.

After a night of tossing and turning, Cat stood at the window, opening the shutters the barest crack to look out at the sky. She thought about how Hyw might look outlined by the low clouds, if their plan worked. Her brother had always been more comfortable on the hills than inside a castle, or even in the llys at Garth Celyn. Cat stared out for a moment, and then turned and almost ran from the room.

She caught Hyw and Gawain as they entered the hall. "Now is our best hope," she told them, almost dragging them with her to the battlement. It was early, and only the lookouts manned the wall. They found a sheltered spot and crouched on the courtyard side of the walk, out of sight of both English and Welsh. Hyw sat cross-legged in front of her.

Cat held out her hands for water from Gawain's flask. As soon as she focused on it, she found the connection to her brother's mind. She rode the mist deeper, until she could see the prince. He stood with his arms folded.

"My liege," she began, "you said anything we think here becomes real. Please, allow me to serve you." When he nodded, she hesitated a moment and then held out her hand. A goblet appeared in it. She swirled the dark liquid inside it. It smelled of honey and strawberries, of the mist of *Rhaedr Fawr* and the gold of sunlight on the hillside near their home. She mixed the waters of her own well into it as well. Finally, she offered it to the prince with a shy curtsey.

"Will you take this drink, your highness, and allow it to help you sleep?"

Sorcery, young Cat, he said, his voice rising in a question.

She hesitated again. Was this not what she feared most, when her gift first came to her that day in church? That it might be a thing of sorcery and darkness? So long ago that seemed now, although it was only a few short months. She thought of Owain, whose life she saved, and of the tall Irish ship of their allies. And she thought again of Ifan, waving to her from the green fields of Garth Celyn. The voice of her ancestor, Aylwen, echoed in her mind. *We have gained these gifts to help our people.* All the while she stared into the eyes of the shade she had known as the last Prince of Wales.

"It is the gift of a true heart, and will not harm you," she told him. And she knew it to be so. He reached out his hand, and took the goblet.

When the prince closed his eyes, Cat opened hers. Gawain was crouching beside her as before, and she realized he had been singing the same song, almost under his breath. Her brother sat with his eyes closed a moment longer, and then opened them to look directly into hers. Gawain let his hands drop, but his voice grew louder. For a few moments, nothing happened.

Then Hyw cast his eyes upward. A hawk soared near them, adding its cry to Gawain's song. Hyw made a sound like a moan, and began to shimmer as he had when the prince appeared earlier. She heard a grinding noise and a loud crackle. Hyw cried out, and his arms stretched to the side, his bones stretching and thinning. He drew his legs up and they seemed to shrink into his body. His clothing fell around him. Red and brown feathers sprouted from his flesh. He cried out, and the cry became the shriek of the hawk. She and Gawain ducked at the wind from flapping wings all around them. They looked up in time to see a great hawk, wings outstretched, where Hyw had been. For a moment he faltered, as if hanging on a current of wind. And then he flew.

Chapter Fifty-three: Hyw

People were abuzz with the news throughout the supper hour. Gawain and Cat helped Hyw, exhausted after his ordeal, to their family table. Cat scrounged what she could for him from the platters, as the voices droned around them. The English had sent another rider, with another offer: less money this time. And it would be less every day, this one said, until the Welsh gave in or were starved from Castell-y-Bere.

The meal was barely finished when Dafydd called for Bran again. Hyw settled beside Cat and their mam, listening to the bards amid the people's continued murmuring. From time to time an angry voice broke out, yelling defiance against the English or arguing with a neighbour. He heard no clear agreement among the people, and it left him uneasy. The bards switched to warrior tales, and soon many of the defiant voices chimed in with harmonies that shook the walls of the castle hall.

In spite of his tortured muscles, Hyw found himself strangely alert. He noticed Cat often looked toward her betrothed, Lord Rhys, but they had little to say to each other. They had been so busy with his needs in the past few days that she would have had no time to talk with Rhys, he realized. She had seemed happy with the match, but he wondered how the war affected them. Hyw reached out with his arm, almost surprised to see it rather than a feathered wing, and placed it around her shoulders.

The candles had barely been trimmed when Bran returned and gestured for Hyw to come with him. Hyw stood, finding his feet carefully, and almost stumbled as he made his way to his father.

"Are you ill, Hyw?" Bran asked.

Hyw shook his head. "Tired only, da," he said, his voice almost a squawk.

His father looked at him a moment longer, and then nodded. "The prince would have a word with you," he said in a low voice. "Answer well, and truthfully. I will be outside, if you need me. You have only to call."

Bran led the way into a room at the end of the hall. Dafydd was seated at a round oak table. His fingers were spread and touching, and he nodded. With that Bran turned and left the room, shutting the door behind him.

Hyw stared into a pair of ice blue eyes. Dafydd remained seated at the table, with his elbows on the arm of his chair, and his fingers steepled in front of his face. His hair and moustache shone auburn in the firelight. The muscles bulged on his biceps, and his shoulders were square under his light tunic.

He gestured to the seat. Hyw stumbled again and nearly fell into one of the large chairs that ringed the table, making everyone equal in importance. This was where Llywelyn had met with the other Welsh princes. He thought of Arthur, the great king. Every Welshman was raised to believe in those traditions of equality for everyone, from noble to peasant, and it was ingrained in the laws they fought so hard to defend. Llywelyn would fit into this chair very well, Hyw thought. He knew he had an equal right to it, but at that moment he felt small and insignificant.

Never think it, lad, he heard inside his mind. *You have brought us this far. You will see this through. You are the one Dafydd must listen to now, and you are the only one who can make sure he does.*

Hyw nodded, and sat up straighter. Dafydd shifted forward and held Hyw's eyes. Hyw stared back, willing himself not to flinch. Dafydd raised his eyebrows as he reached forward to take a sip from his goblet of wine.

"Your father tells me you lived with the English at his bidding. I thank you for your service. It seems you have used your time there well, if Cynfrig's tales of the practice yard can be believed."

"I've done my best to share what I've learned."

Dafydd smiled a little, and filled a goblet for Hyw. Hyw swirled the liquid. It was spiced ale. He could smell the flavour of it. He had been allowed a glass on saints' days and holidays, and knew it would taste sweet and strong. He took a sip.

"Are you comfortable with us?" Dafydd asked.

"Yes. Very much."

"Really? It surprises me, since you've been with the English for so long."

"I returned to my father in October."

"Yet you were not with him in January, when last we met."

Hyw looked at him steadily. *There's little point denying it,* he heard Llywelyn advise in his mind. "Your words are true. I was with Lord Shrewsbury."

"And Edward." The words were soft, but the ice in Prince Dafydd's blue eyes seemed to harden, if that were possible. "How was the king?"

In his mind, Hyw heard Llywelyn expel his breath, almost in a hiss. *Even now, he cares about the English king. Even now.* Hyw remembered hearing Dafydd had been friends with Edward since childhood, and had spent time there during the attempted English invasion earlier in Llywelyn's rule. He thought about his own complicated relationship with James, and wondered how he would feel in Dafydd's place. He also remembered Dafydd's face on the chess piece Llywelyn had shown him many months ago: the face of a pawn. Looking at that same face now, Hyw could see the shadows under his eyes.

"In truth, I saw the king but little," Hyw said. "He seemed hearty, and his wife appeared to dote on him."

"That is well. And was she beautiful?"

Hyw thought for a moment, not sure how to answer truthfully. "The king seemed to think her so." He told Dafydd as best he could about the English king's expression as he looked upon his wife, and how his voice seemed to soften when he addressed her.

Dafydd threw back his head and laughed. "A passable answer indeed, Hyw. You have certainly seen them together."

Good work, lad. He was testing you, and he found you sound. Hyw felt a small flush of pride at Llywelyn's words.

But in the next breath, Dafydd's hand smacked the table with a loud thud. His face changed, and his laughter became a snarl. "Yet somehow you brought the spirit of my brother to me at Dolwyddelan. And before I could wring the truth from him, you vanished. Now I need to know everything you know."

Hyw started at the sound and fury of Dafydd's words. Through it, he could also hear Llywelyn's calming voice like a whisper in his inner ear. *Steady. It's just bluster. Let him wind down.*

Hyw took a deep breath. "You are my prince, and I will tell you anything you wish to know." Hyw answered Dafydd's questions about the English army, its strengths and weaknesses, its horses and weapons. Finally Dafydd's shoulders slumped forward.

"You were with him—when he died?" Dafydd meant his brother Llywelyn, Hyw realized, and nodded. "I hope he did not suffer overmuch."

Hyw did not know what to say, and was glad to hear Llywelyn's voice in his inner ear again. *Tell him I did not.* By the catch in Llywelyn's voice, he could tell the prince was moved. As Hyw repeated Llywelyn's words, Dafydd looked into his eyes. "It was much less than Edward had planned for him."

"Could—could you not send to the king again and bid him stop this slaughter?"

"On the grounds of our childhood friendship? Or because my wife Elizabeth was his choice for me? Or because I had tried many times to kill my own brother for him?" Dafydd laughed bitterly. "Even if he would listen to me, I would not. I am Wales now, and I will take my duty as it falls. Believe me, it would do no good. Edward has a taste for our blood now. I know him well. He is the predator, and Wales is his prey."

His manner and tone changed, and he seemed more desperate than cynical as he continued. "I must take back Garth Celyn, and I will take as many men as I can into the mountains with me to plan our attack. Has my brother anything more to tell me?"

Hyw closed his eyes, and found Llywelyn stroking his moustache. *Tell him he must not let them catch him, or his children. Or mine.* Hyw nodded and opened his eyes again, to find Dafydd staring into them. The living prince's eyes were bright and intense, and he held Hyw like the glint of the knife holds the deer. As he had at Dolwyddelan and on the battlements with Cat and Gawain, Hyw felt the pressure of Llywelyn's hand on his shoulder. He closed his eyes and shifted slightly to let Llywelyn through. When he opened his eyes again, Dafydd drew back, startled.

"He is—within you?"

Hyw came back into himself, and Llywelyn receded once more. Dafydd continued to stare at Hyw strangely. "These are the old ways," he said. "You and your family, I have heard you all bear such gifts?"

Hyw felt a moment of fear, wondering if he had revealed too much. "Be assured, Prince Dafydd, your brother means you no harm. Nor do I."

Dafydd sat back, and held Hyw's eyes again. "I should fear you, Hyw ap Bran, and the spirit you carry. Men follow me, but I can see in their eyes that they long for my brother. It would be an easy thing for you to help him regain his hold over them."

Hyw tried to protest, and heard Llywelyn's voice echo inside him. Dafydd held up his hand. "This war is very different than any other battle with the English we have fought. Edward's hatred leads him, and I am not sure we will survive it. Though your claim might seem fantastical to some, it would be welcome to many. You could divide the people just at the time they need to rally most."

"My lord—" Hyw began. Then Dafydd laughed again.

"I have watched you carefully in the days you have been with us. You hide my brother from the others, and make no attempt to reveal your gift. That leads me to think you can be trusted, and my brother knew it. I could not be there to protect him on the field when he was ambushed. Indeed, I am sure he would not believe that I would protect him. Yet I am glad to know his spirit continues. I would ask you this: continue to hide my brother, for his protection. Swear it."

"I swear."

"Tell my brother this: I will take his baby with my family into the mountains. Lord Rhys and his men will accompany the townspeople, while the rest of us move in force to Garth Celyn. To cover our escape, Rhys and Cynfrig will stretch the talks with Lestrange and de Valence. They will hold off the English as long as they can, to give us cover as we make our escape."

He leaned forward then, before he continued. "Hyw ap Bran. Your father and mother are set to accompany me, along with my family. Because you carry my brother's spirit in the world, I would offer you the choice. You may remain with Lord Rhys, and earn your place with Cynfrig and his men. Those who continue with us to Garth Celyn will tread the more difficult path. We will find our way blocked by soldiers. We face hardship and endurance and most likely death before we retake Garth Celyn. Think well the path you choose."

Hyw closed his eyes for a moment, and Llywelyn nodded at him. *My brother speaks true, Hyw, and I will do no less. You have made a place here, and these are men to trust your back to. You must make your own decision.*

Hyw opened his eyes, and stared for a moment without seeing either of them. "I may have a plan that will best serve you, and help all of us."

Chapter Fifty-four: Cat

Cat stood in front of Rhys' door and raised her eyebrows at the warrior who stood guard. His face did not change as he reached back and pushed open the wooden door for her.

Rhys was alone, washing up for supper. He turned as she entered. His chest and arms were bare and glistening with water. She had seen him so during practice in the yard, but in the closeness of his rooms she felt herself flush. He smiled slightly as he picked up a cloth to wipe the water away.

"I am sorry to disturb you," she began, "but I must speak with you." She knew what she meant to say but found it difficult to begin.

"Your thoughts are always welcome, my lady," he said, reaching for his shirt.

"If that is true, then you will agree with what I have to say," she said, mentally thanking him for the opening. "You believe me to be a morrigan, and you seem to have experience with someone of my nature. I would know more about how to use my gift, in order to offer what help I can in this war."

"Surely your mother advises you."

"She has some understanding of it from family lore, but you and Cynfrig have worked with a morrigan. You know more about the nature of my gift." She warmed to her topic now, sure of her decision.

"Cat, Cynfrig and I will stay to negotiate with the English. If aught goes wrong—"

This was what Cat had hoped to hear, because she needed to be in the castle when Hyw put his plan into action. "I must stand with you. Is it not what your own morrigan would have done? My gifts cannot serve you from across the mountains. I must be here, with you."

He still looked uncertain, but she could see he was thinking through the wisdom of her words. She went on, pressing her advantage. "If there is a battle in our future, as surely there must be, you will be victorious only if I am with you."

Finally he nodded. "Very well. I—I would rather have you with me, where I can be sure of your safety. And I will marry you, Cat, to give you the full benefit of my protection." He looked at her then, and held her eyes. "But protection is all it can be."

She folded her arms across her chest. "We have been promised to each other since childhood. I have known you in my heart since my princess first brought us together as playmates, so many years ago. And now, even as our enemies surround us, we have found each other again. Is that truly all you believe we can have between us now?" She stared back at him until she saw a glimmer of something in his eyes that gave her hope. *We shall see*, she thought, and nodded.

Her goodbyes to Margred were tearful, but they vowed to see each other again once the war had ended. She shook Owain's hand to wish him well, and was surprised when he planted a kiss on her cheek.

Their goodbyes were interrupted by Cynfrig's bellow. "We cannot surrender the castle, my liege. Honour demands that we stand and fight for you, and drive these *Saeson* from our land by the Grace of God."

She was still holding Owain's hand, as she looked down to see Cynfrig kneel at Prince Dafydd's feet. Rhys stood near them, undecided. She recalled her vision of Owain slain at Criccieth, and of Rhys and the others cut down in the courtyard of Castell-y-Bere. How could she make them understand? *If I am the morrigan, then they must believe the outcome of this battle.*

"Pardon, Lady Cat?" Owain said, and she realized she had spoken aloud. Instead of answering, she squeezed his hand, and moved past him as she dropped it again.

"My lords," she called out. She could feel the flush creep from her neck onto her face as all turned to her, but kept moving through the room towards them. "You must listen."

Rhys stepped up and opened the curtains of an adjoining alcove. "My lords, would you step inside to give this lady audience?" He bowed toward Cynfrig and the prince, and Cat ducked her head toward him gratefully. When they had seated themselves at the window seats, they turned toward her expectantly.

"Speak you as the morrigan, returned?" Cynfrig asked.

"The morrigan?" Prince Dafydd's tone was full of scorn.

"If you say I am, then you must believe I know the outcome of this war," she began.

"If she speaks of what she has seen, my lord," broke in Rhys in careful tones, "you must grant her leave, whatever her words might impart about the coming fray."

Dafydd considered them, and finally nodded. "Speak your leave."

She told them of her visions in as much detail as she could, beginning with Owain's death and moving to the scene in the courtyard that had come to her only days before. "You must believe me, my lord. I would not wish harm to you or any of your children, who are as dear to me as my own family now. But I beg you, do not change your course for some ancient sense of honour. Why must it always be kill or be killed? Why can we not live, to fight again another day?"

Dafydd considered her for a long moment, and then dismissed her with a wave of his hand. She left them, hoping that they might heed her words.

When she could avoid it no longer, Cat came back to her mam's room. She entered while Hyw was explaining his decision to join them in recapturing Garth Celyn. She knew Hyw had planned to explain Llywelyn to their mam as well. Perhaps it was the looks on their faces, or the connection she now had with her brother, but it seemed clear he had already done so.

"I'm proud of you, Hyw." Adara hugged him.

"I hope you will feel the same of me, Mam," Cat said. "I have decided to remain with Lord Rhys and his people, to offer what help I may."

"Are you sure?" When Cat nodded, Adara reached out her arms and hugged Cat as well. "You have both grown up so quickly," she said, her eyes shining with unshed tears.

"May God keep you safe. And Lord Rhys, of course," Hyw said to her.

"You think little of my own skill," Cat chided, pulling up her skirt and extracting one of Rhys' knives to show him. He examined it carefully.

"He appears to be paying close attention," he told her. "The emerald matches your eyes."

"So I see," she said, wondering a little. She felt a flush creep along her throat as she looked again at the emerald. Had Rhys meant to send her a message of hope with it? She turned slightly to replace the knife in its sheath.

"It is a fitting gift for your skill and position," her brother said, "but I hope you never need to use them."

"Before we take our leave, there is one more thing we must do," their mam said. "Fetch your da, Hyw, and do not tarry. Cat, we must find Elizabeth and the children. Come."

Chapter Fifty-five: Hyw

Hyw and Bran found them again in the receiving room, along with the prince and princess seated on their special chairs. Margred and Owain were there, as well as several of the warriors, including Aeneus and Cynfrig. Emrys waved and grinned at him, taking Bronwen's hand to turn her towards them. Hyw wondered if some announcement was coming.

Adara and Cat reached them, and Adara enfolded him in a warm hug. Cat held out a package wrapped in cloth.

"I made it for you, Hyw."

He unwrapped it to find the red tunic and sash she had sewn. "Can it be? The stitches seem straight!" he marvelled. She punched his shoulder to break the tension.

Their da reached out his hand for the sash, and Hyw gave it to him. "I wish we had time for a proper ceremony," Bran said.

"This means more to me than any pomp or ceremony by priest or lord, Da," Hyw told him. Bran half-smiled, and drew him toward the prince.

Prince Dafydd nodded to them and stood, clearing his throat. "Our enemies dog our heels, as well you know," the prince began. "Yet we will take the time to honour the old ways, and one of our number who has earned his place among us. Mayhap we can present it again, properly, when we arrive at Garth Celyn."

There was a murmur of appreciation among the small band as Bran drew Hyw to him. Hyw's throat tightened and his chest seemed to swell as his da tied the red sash at his waist. Then Bran turned to the others, holding up Hyw's right arm.

"My son," he said, and the pride in his voice hit Hyw like the warm sun through a cloud. "Warrior."

Bran then gathered Hyw to him in a fierce hug. He could hear the sounds of his friends clapping and calling around him. Bran's mouth was close to Hyw's ear as he whispered, "I am proud to call you son—for all of your abilities, not just the skill that makes you fit to wear the sash." Hyw felt himself tear up, and noticed his da's eyes glistening as he drew back.

"Welcome, warrior," the prince said, and raised a glass Elizabeth handed him. "I drink to your future." Aeneus as master-at-arms saluted him in Roman style, and then hugged him as well. Emrys slugged Hyw hard on the arm and then circled his shoulder with the same hand. Finally the prince called out.

"Though I am loathe to call this moment to an end, friends, we must depart. Go you to your preparations, as my wife and I will ours. We will greet you one last time in the dining hall."

As they made their way from the room, Hyw drew Cat aside in the stairwell. "This wristband cannot last for much longer." He pulled two chains from his pouch and handed her one. She fingered the scrolled locket before popping it open. "A lock of my hair," he told her. He held open his empty locket, and she used her knife to cut a lock of hers for it.

"As long as we have this, my gift will connect us," she said.

"I will keep it with me always," he said, placing the locket around his neck and under his tunic. "Next to my heart, as you will always be."

A few hours later, under the cover of darkness, Hyw and his family joined the people in the courtyard. Lord Rhys and the people of Meirionnydd also waited there, and Cat squeezed his hand once before moving to join Rhys.

Emrys pushed through the crowd to Bronwen, who threw her arms around him. He would remain with Rhys and a handful of Cynfrig's warriors at the castle to negotiate the settlement. Bronwen would travel with the people, and if all went well, they would be reunited in a few days.

Dafydd and Bran began moving their group towards the gate. The princess and her children, including Margred and the other girls, walked with other families who had determined to accompany their men into the mountains. Aeneus had burned the wooden bridges a few days before so the *Saeson* could not cross, but the men had placed boards over one ditch so the people could get away safely. Emrys moved back to the small group that included the warrior-poet Gwilym ap Einion. Hyw was grateful he would stay to help them bargain with the English.

As he marched with his people along the mountain path, Hyw felt something prickle along his skin almost like vertigo. It took him a moment to realize it was silence. The people sang while walking, while working, even while marching to battle. Tonight they dared not, lest their voices waken the English troops. The silence and the dark made his stomach clench.

Then he heard a groan of wind, as if the mountain giant wept to see them leave. Some of the townsfolk stopped, huddled together. Hyw hesitated. *Let me speak to them*, Llywelyn said. Hyw ran ahead, drawing near to the frightened ones.

"I remember the story, as I have heard it told," Hyw began, keeping his voice low as he repeated Llywelyn's words to them. "On just such a night as this, as the Greeks poured forth from the great horse of their treachery, Brutus and his people stole away in silence from Troy. It was to this land and to these mountains that Brutus led his people. When the Tylwyth Teg heard his story, they bade the giants make room for the people here.

"This night we cannot sing lest we be discovered. This sound we hear is the giant Idris, singing for us. He sings to the soldiers below, camped on the plain. They cannot hide from him. He sings this song to bolster your hearts, to cover your flight from this land into his own. You must believe he will shelter you, and keep the English from you."

He moved up the line to repeat the tale. As he neared his mother and Gawain, she took his hand. "We shall miss your stories, Hyw. Can you stay a while longer?"

"Until sunrise," he promised her, untying his red sash and handing it to her. "Keep this for me, and be assured I will return for it."

She smiled at him, and he made his way past her to the front of the line, where he found his father and the other warriors. It was easier in the cool darkness to use his gift. His mind seemed to reach naturally into the thickets and bushes as they passed. Here a hare scurried for cover, and there a meadow mouse kept her home. Through their eyes, he sensed the roots and dips that might have tripped someone unfamiliar with the territory, and passed the information back to the people behind him.

As the sun rose, Hyw pulled away from the group and watched them trudge along the path in silence. They could see for themselves now. When he had walked past the last of the people, he began casting with his senses until he found a hawk flying near. He found a safe place off the path to leave his clothes, touched the locket around his neck, and closed his eyes. He watched Llywelyn take the goblet Cat had given him, swish the liquid, and drink. Llywelyn smiled at him, and sat down to close his own eyes in sleep. Hyw recalled their circle of three, seeing Cat and Gawain's faces around him as he had on the battlements. Only then did he reach out to the hawk. A gust of wind blew against his face, and he heard the hawk's shrill cry in his mind.

He raised his arms and his bones seemed to thin and twist. He heard the grating of bone on bone and knew again the intense pain of his body changing. He felt a moment of panic, but he knew he must not fight this sensation. The pain would pass. As he had with Cat's help, he let himself grow light and strong as he lifted off the ground into the wind.

He glanced to the side and spotted the tip of a wing with mottled brown feathers. It took him a moment to realize it was his own. He was no longer one with the mind of the hawk; he was the hawk. Beyond his own wingtip, he could see the hawk he had spotted from the ground, now flying beside him. They soared for a moment, almost circling each other. Then the other hawk dove, leaving Hyw alone in the grey sky.

When he looked down, he could see the people still walking along the mountain path. He cried out, and a woman turned toward the sound. Part of him, the human part, recognized her as his mam and he circled above her. She waved, and he flew on.

As he drifted on air currents, he passed over the English soldiers camped below. He could feel the mind of the hawk inside himself—a mind caught in the instant changes of wind and sound and smell. Before he realized he was hungry, his hawk instincts drew his eyes toward the rabbit in the grass below him. Then he saw Castell-y-Bere. He remembered, and with a wing thrust he turned himself east toward it.

Chapter Fifty-Six: The Reckoning

Cat scanned the skies, watching every bird that circled the battlements. She had seen what it cost Hyw to change as their plan required him to, and she worried that he could not accomplish it without their circle of three. She tried to recall the song Gawain had sung, and opened her mind to connect with him. For too long, she felt nothing but her own fear.

Finally she saw a large red and brown hawk soaring toward her. Although she couldn't see his face or detailing clearly against the grey sky, she could tell it was him by the feel of his mind, like a familiar presence in her peripheral vision. She saw the bird shimmer a little as it moved awkwardly toward the wall walk. The claws pointing toward the wooden platform became a man's bare feet. As he settled, the flapping wings became arms and feathers became flesh. Hyw lay where the bird had landed.

She knelt beside him, giving him a chunk of bread and her skin of well-water to wash it down. She closed her eyes and probed into his mind, finding Llywelyn still sleeping. Gently she hummed the song she had been singing earlier, and the prince opened his eyes and gave her his teasing half-smile. *Do we yet live*? he asked.

"You do, my liege," she answered. "And welcome."

When she opened her eyes again, Hyw asked her the same question. She answered him by ruffling his hair and making the face that always made him smile.

When her brother had recovered, she helped him dress in the clothes Dafydd had left. She'd stuffed the shoulders and waist of the tunic, and helped him drape Dafydd's tabard loosely over it, with the coat of arms clearly showing. She darkened his hair a little with bramble tea. Rhys had contributed a gold torque similar to Dafydd's and a crown, which he said he found in a castle vault. Then she stood back to survey her brother.

"It will do from afar," she said, critically.

"It had better," he said, looking through the battlements at the path far below, where the English company could be seen making their way toward the castle.

Hyw stood in borrowed clothing and watched the soldiers haggle with the warriors. He was himself again, but he felt more than himself. He stood between the battlements, where he could clearly see Rhys with Gwilym, Cynfrig and Emrys on the path, as well as Cat standing off to one side, out of the captain's sight. As Hyw expected, the English captain pointed toward him.

"They will not accept that Dafydd is here without some kind of proof," Hyw had told Cynfrig and Emrys earlier. "They will expect a trick. When they ask you, tell them the prince will wave to you to prove he is there in truth. Then turn and wave, and I will do the rest."

Emrys turned and waved at Hyw. Hyw stood, straightening his tabard so they would see Dafydd's crest, and waved back. He turned his head, hoping the gold of the brown and torque would flash in the sunlight.

Cat felt time slow as the English captain stared, rubbing his beard with one hand. It didn't work, she thought wildly. She and Rhys stood behind Cynfrig, letting him handle the negotiating. She felt Rhys grope for the sword under his cloak, and wondered if they would have to fight their way out. Lucky she had brought her water skin. Staring down at the water inside it, she tried to make contact with Hyw. She could feel his presence, but she could not enter his mind to send him a message.

Then she thought of Llywelyn. She saw the former prince, standing as if behind Hyw. "You must help us," she said. "The English captain does not believe the ruse."

Llywelyn touched Hyw on the shoulder. Cat broke contact and looked up at the battlements. The difference was subtle. Hyw suddenly stood taller and more regally than before, and his hair shone more like Dafydd's than it had. The Welsh crown caught the sunlight. Was that the same one she had given her brother? she wondered. Or was it Llywelyn's conjuring? More importantly, would it help the *Saeson* believe that Hyw was Prince Dafydd?

Finally the captain nodded. He gave Emrys and Cynfrig a pouch. Cynfrig checked it. That would be the payment for surrendering the castle and a letter of safe passage, she thought.

As part of the bargain, the English soldiers were to give the Welsh a day to clear the castle before they entered. Cynfrig and Rhys believed they would not wait, so they had agreed to send the people on their way the night before. Now, the little negotiating party began to move toward the road, away from the castle. Cat was drawn along with the others. If all went well, they would join the people who had already escaped before the English knew they were gone.

She knew Hyw would remain where he was, on the battlements, to lull the English into believing Prince Dafydd remained in the castle. She dared not wave, but tried to send her thoughts to reassure him as they made their way into the mountains. The path grew quiet around them and they barely stirred the grass as they passed. Even the giant slept.

"Here," someone called. "Up here."

Hyw wiped the sleep from his eyes and stood. The position of the sun told him it was late afternoon. So, Cynfrig was right. The English had not waited, but were even now storming the castle in search of Prince Dafydd.

In search of him.

Hyw looked down and saw soldiers streaming through the gates. He cast around him and for a moment he panicked. He could not find a hawk, and could not bring the shape into his mind. Could he shift without one? Could he take the form of another bird?

He heard voices at the bottom of the stairs. It was time. He shrugged off his borrowed cloak and clothing. He closed his eyes and raised his arms.

Nothing.

Steady on, lad, he heard Llywelyn say behind him. *Think of the circle of three.*

Hyw could hear pounding footsteps on the stone stairwell, but shut his mind to them. Llywelyn began humming the song Gawain and Cat had sung and he focused on it. He imagined them standing with him, singing. Llywelyn drank from the goblet and sank to the floor, asleep.

Hyw reached out for the hawk.

As he let the scent and rush of wind flood through him, he recognized the first man rushing toward him from the stairwell. It was Robert, the bully of Shrewsbury's court, in full knight's armour. His face glistened with sweat and his breath came heavy and panting. And then Robert saw Hyw, and raised his drawn sword high to rush at him.

“It is a trick!” Robert’s cry of alarm rose like the crash of arms on armour.

But Hyw could not —would not—stop. He felt feathers grow from his skin, and his bones knit and press into the shape the wind loved best.

Robert stumbled a moment as his mind tried to grasp the transformation before him. His face became even more distorted with fear and hatred. “Sorcerer!”

As he took to the sky, Hyw saw Robert suddenly pull a bow and arrow from his shoulder. The arrow zipped past Hyw, almost knocking him off balance. Robert swore, and took a second arrow from his quiver. Hyw struggled against the wind, aware of the young knight setting his feet and drawing back his bow for another shot. Then a second figure trod the wall walk behind him, knocking the bow from Robert’s hand.

“Where is the prince?” the second man said as Robert’s second arrow flew wide. “And why are you wasting arrows on this bird?”

Hyw circled to identify his benefactor. In the human part of his brain, he knew it was Stephen de Francton. The man had saved him twice. Robert was arguing with him but other human shouts caught Hyw’s attention. He circled once more as soldiers picked up the cloak and fought over the gold ornaments. Deep inside him, he heard the rumble of laughter, but he could not tell if it was Llywelyn’s or his own.

And he became one with the wind, letting it turn him toward the mountain.

By dawn the people had traveled far into the mountain range. With the hawk’s keen eyesight he had easily found his clothes, but he had to run all night in his human form to catch up. Behind them, Castell-y-Bere sat solidly in the rock of Idris, the mountain giant. The English army looked like a dark patch of blight on the once-lush Desenni valley. Like locusts, they would soon have their way and depart. How long would the castle remain? For a moment, he thought he saw Idris himself heave a sigh. Hyw rubbed his eyes, and saw the mountain again.

Hyw started toward his mam and da. Cat and Rhys had found them in the night, and already split off to take their people to safety. He passed Prince Dafydd, who carried one of his sleeping children on his back. The way seemed easier along the mountain plateau, as they followed a path worn by sheep and cattle.

He heard a wavering sound, and realized someone had begun to sing. He recognized the clear tones of his mother's soprano, and heard the rich harmonies slide into place as one voice joined another. The song was a hymn of thanksgiving. He and Llywelyn joined in as he found Adara, and their voices warmed him as the light snow began to fall around them.

Author's note

Castell-y-Bere fell to the English in April 1283, after the longest siege of the war. The English paid £53 to castle's constable, Cynfrig ap Madog, for the castle's surrender. But Dafydd ap Gruffydd, the last true Prince of Wales, once again escaped their grasp. Cynfrig and the Welsh who held Castell-y-Bere melted into their mountain, never to appear again in the written annals of history.

Historical Note

The year 1282 must have begun with great hope. Llywelyn ap Gryffudd (c. 1223 - 11 December 1282), acknowledged Prince of Wales, and his wife Elinor (Eleanor) expected their first child. A boy would become the heir to the kingdom Llywelyn had spent his life building—and then trying to keep intact.

Elinor was the daughter of Simon de Montfort, a friend and ally of Llywelyn. In 1263, she and Llywelyn were promised to marry each other, although they had never met. In 1267, Llywelyn became the first and only Welsh prince to unite the country, and gain the title of Prince of Wales. When Elinor sailed from France to marry the prince, King Edward's men captured her and held her in captivity for three years. Trying to get her back, Llywelyn lost a major battle to the English King, Edward I, in 1277. Under the Treaty of Aberconwy, he kept his title and a large amount of land in Gwynedd, North Wales. The country split again into North and South Wales, with parts of the south held by Norman lords under King Edward. Edward forced

Llywelyn to pay a stiff tribute (penalty in money), and to sign away his land in treaties to avoid going to war again.

Finally, in 1278, Edward allowed the wedding, and led Elinor down the aisle to meet Llywelyn, her future husband. Between 1278 and 1282, Llywelyn and Elinor appear to have been happy together. Then in the spring of 1282, Dafydd, Llywelyn's younger brother, led an attack against the English, because he claimed they were terrorizing his people. Llywelyn tried not to commit the country to war by not joining with his brother.

On June 19, Elinor died giving birth to a baby girl, Gwenllian. Llywelyn went into mourning. The Norman lords on the border between England and Wales increased their attacks. Llywelyn still tried to prevent war by appealing to the pope on behalf of his people, and Edward sent the English Archbishop of Cornwall to visit the Welsh court in the autumn. The Archbishop stayed there November 3 to 5, during a truce on all sides. During his visit, the Archbishop offered Llywelyn lands and personal gain if he would relinquish his title and surrender to King Edward. Llywelyn and his nobles refused. Then the English forces broke the truce and attacked by water, across the Menai Straight. Llywelyn's forces defeated the English, and many died. The Archbishop left in haste, and proclaimed the Welsh heathen and in need of subjugation by English forces.

Llywelyn was killed suddenly and unexpectedly on December 11, 1282. There are many stories about how and why he died. Llywelyn's head hung on a pike at the Tower of London for close to a decade. His princely seal, and some letters that may have contained evidence of treachery against Llywelyn, were stolen from his body and taken to the Archbishop. Later Edward melted Llywelyn's seal, along with baby Gwenllian's seal, and made them into a silver chalice, which was sent to an abbey in Lincolnshire for safekeeping.

Llywelyn ap Gruffydd, or Llywelyn Ein Llyw Olaf ("our last leader" or "Llywelyn the Last") as he came to be known, was the last prince of an independent Wales before its conquest by Edward I of England. That action, and how it came about, is where this story begins.

For me, it began after a family trip to Wales in 2006. My two children and I stayed on a sheep farm near Dolwyddelan Castle, and made several trips through Gwynedd to visit castles and towns in North Wales. We also stayed in a restored 13th Century wattle-and-daub cottage. As we toured castles and historical sites, we read and heard about the country's history. We were especially impressed by the restoration of the Welsh language. The highway and street signs were in Welsh first, English second; and children are taught in Welsh in the schools again. How could a language outlawed 800 years ago come back to thrive in the 21st Century?

My personal ties to this story began years ago, when my mother researched our family name and discovered the Powell family was apparently "keeper of the Holy Grail." After our first trip, I read in J. Beverley Smith's *Llywelyn Ap Gruffudd: Prince of Wales* that the Welsh royal seals were melted into a silver chalice. A "grail" and a "chalice" are both essentially cups, and both have a connection to church and to the Eucharist or communion. My imagination was sparked, and the story began to unfold.

I found inspiration in the historical traditions of *The Brothers of Gwynedd* series by Edith Pargeter and *Here Be Dragons* by Sharon Kay Penman, as well as modern fantasies such as *The Dark is Rising* by Susan Cooper, *Tomorrow's Magic* by Pamela F. Service, and *The Farseer* by Robin Hobb. My daughter Leanne and I also took an introductory Welsh class at Nant Gwrtheyrn. Over the years, I've read and discovered many essential research sources, the best of which are listed under Further Reading.

Like all fiction writers, though, I also chose to deviate from the historical research as the story required. For example, through the Shropshire archives, I confirmed there was no lord of Shrewsbury castle in this time period, so I invented one based on the previous Shrewsbury lords. Although little is known about Llywelyn's early life, most Welsh children in this time would have fostered with other families, including the English, so I've used that in the story. A Welsh boy came of age at 14; since Llywelyn's bodyguard or *teulu* were known to wear red tunics, I invented the red sash as a visual way to show this transition. Although Rhys ap Cadwgan and Gwillim ap Einion are fictional, Cynfrig ap Madog is a historical figure credited with managing the negotiations at Castell-y-Bere, and a well-known bard was also thought to be present (Smith, 575).

I chose to include a few Welsh words, used Welsh spelling whenever possible, and altered names when it seemed useful. For example, Llywelyn married Eleanor de Montfort, whose mother was also Eleanor de Montfort; King Edward's wife was another Eleanor (de Castille) and his mother was Eleanor (de Provence). To lessen confusion, I used the spelling Elinor that I found in some sources for the princess.

The poem mentioned on pages 86-87 is "Y Gododdin," which is considered the earliest surviving Welsh poem. I have written words for Llywelyn's poem to avoid conflicts with copyright, but I cannot do justice to the original. It can be found in translation by Siân Echard in the Broadview anthology, and Joseph Clancy, among others (listed below under Further Resources). Similarly, one inspiration for the scene in Chapter Eighteen was the YouTube video *Mari Lwyd* by Trac: Music Traditions Wales; the link and other resources for the greetings, insults, riddles, and other aspects of that chapter can be found in Further Resources.

As well, there are many stories about why and how Llywelyn was killed. Some stories suggest he was surprised while meeting allies near Builth, and killed by a Shropshire soldier named Stephen de Francton who did not recognize the Prince of Wales. He profited little from it, since others took Llywelyn's head to the king, allowing me to speculate about his character and how events may have unfolded. The English pursued Dafydd to Dolwyddelan and Castell-y-Bere, but did not capture him when the castles fell. At various points he had his wife, son, and daughter with him, as well as several illegitimate daughters (although little is known of them, leaving me to invent Margred and the others). My main sources were the Smith biography, and the Cilmeri and Castles of Wales websites.

Scholars also disagree about what castle fell on what date during the 1282-83 invasion, and on the location of the royal llys at Garth Celyn (or Garthcelyn as it appears in some sources.) The list of sources under Further Reading provides more information about these topics. In changing or leaving out some details, I hope I have left room for readers to find their own stories.

Please join me on my blog at **www.mepowell.com/blog** for more discussion of the historical background for *Hawk*.

Further Reading

NonFiction Books

The Broadview Anthology of British Literature: The Medieval Period, 3rd ed., edited by Joseph Black, *et al.* Broadview Press, 2014.

Bromwich, Rachel. *Trioedd Ynys Prydain* (Welsh Triads). University of Wales Press, 2006.

Cadw Guidebooks on various castles.

Chadwick, Nora Kershaw. *Stories and Ballads of the Far Past.* University Press, Northwestern, 1921.

Clancy, Joseph P., trans. *Medieval Welsh Poems.* Four Courts Press, 2003.

Gerald of Wales. *The Journey Through Wales: The Description of Wales* [circa 1188] Penguin, 1987.

Davies, John. *A History of Wales.* Penguin, 1994.

Davies, R. R. *The Age of Conquest: Wales 1063-1415.* Oxford University Press, 1991.

Davies, R. R. and Geraint H. Jenkins. *From Medieval to Modern Wales.* University of Wales Press, 2004.

Davis, Paul R. *Castles of the Welsh Princes.* Y Lolfa Cyf, 2007.

Echard, Siân (trans.). *Y Gododdin* in *The Broadview Anthology of British Literature: The Medieval Period,* 3rd ed., edited by Joseph Black *et al.* Broadview Press, 2014.

Griffiths, R.A. and P.R. Schofield (eds.). *Wales and the Welsh in the Middle Ages.* 2011: University of Wales Press, 2011.

Hall, Vernam and Archer Taylor. *A Collection of Welsh Riddles.* University of California Press, 1942. [Available through Google Books]

Moore, David. *Welsh Wars of Independence.* Tempus, 2005.

Reid, Alan. *The Castles of Wales.* George Philip & Son Ltd., 2000.

Sjoestedt, Marie-Louise. *Celtic Gods and Heroes.* Dover Publications, 2000.

Smith, J. Beverley. *Llywelyn ap Gruffudd: Prince of Wales.* University of Wales Press, 2014.

Online Resources on Y Calan and the Mari Lwyd:

Welsh Culture and Traditions: Nos Galan (New Year's Eve): http://www.britannia.com/wales/culture2.html;

The Magic of the Mari: http://www.folkwales.org.uk/mari.html;

Mari Lwyd: http://www.omniglot.com/songs/bcc/marilwyd.php;

http://www.wales.com/en/content/cms/English/About_Wales/Traditions/Mari_Lwyd/Mari_Lwyd.aspx;

Tradition of the Mari Lwyd - BBC Cymru: https://www.youtube.com/watch?v=G_xFo6Hifzk

TRAC Music Traditions Wales, Mari Lwyd: https://www.youtube.com/watch?v=6ptel9C3Zhg

Online Resources on Welsh History

Castles of Wales: http://www.castlewales.com (articles and essays)

Cadw: http://cadw.wales.gov.uk/daysout/dolwyddelan-castle/?lang=en

Cilmeri: "Death of Llywelyn" [A full discussion of all stories and speculations related to Llywelyn's death] - http://www.cilmeri.org/eng/?page_id=5

Anglesey Heritage: http://www.angleseyheritage.com/key-places/llys-rhosyr/

Archeology of Northwest Wales: http://www.archaeoleg.org.uk/areanorthwest.html

Gathering the Jewels: Castles of the Welsh princes: http://education.gtj.org.uk/en/item10/28986

International Heralds and Heraldry: http://www.internationalheraldry.com/

Medieval insults: http://knighttimes.webs.com/insults.htm;

http://kol.coldfront.net/thekolwiki/index.php/Ye_Olde_Medieval_Insult;

http://www.funnyjunk.com/funny_pictures/4254438/Medieval+insults/

Medieval riddles: http://www.increasebrainpower.com/easy-riddles.html; http://www.justriddlesandmore.com/riddlearchive.html;

Online Maps of Wales:

http://commons.wikimedia.org/wiki/File:Wales_after_the_Treaty_of_Montgomery_1267.svg (Alex D.)

Source: Wrex County exhibition:

http://www.wrexham.gov.uk/english/heritage/medieval_exhibition/struggles.htm

http://commons.wikimedia.org/wiki/File:Gwynedd_after_the_Treaty_of_Aberconwy_1277.svg

Gwynedd General Map (James Frankcom):

http://en.wikipedia.org/wiki/File:Gwynedd_General_Map.jpg

Fiction

Cooper, Susan. *The Dark is Rising* (series)

Duncan, Dave. *The Adventures of Ivor* (trilogy, omnibus)

Flanagan, John. *Ranger's Apprentice* (series)

Hobb, Robin. *Assassins Apprentice: The Farseer*

Jordan, Robert. *Wheel of Time* (series)

Pargeter, Edith. *The Brothers of Gwynedd* (series)

Penman, Sharon Kay. *Here be Dragons* (trilogy)

Service, Pamela F. *Tomorrow's Magic.*

Tolkien, J R. *Lord of the Rings* (series)

White, T. H. *The Once and Future King* (series)

Woodbury, Sarah. *After Cilmeri* (series)

Glossary

Annwn – The Welsh word for OtherWorld (see OtherWorld). Arawn was its king. The Cŵn Annwn, or hounds of Annwn, are also known as the Hounds of Hell.

bard – A singer and/or storyteller.

Builth – A district in mid-Wales.

Cadair Idris – A mountain in North Wales, known as the "giant's chair," that was thought to be the legendary hunting ground of the Tylwyth Teg (or faeries).

Caergwrle Castle – A castle in northeast Wales built by Dafydd, near a town called Hope, and built on a mountain known as Hope Mountain.

Carreg Cennen – A Welsh castle in south-west Wales.

Castell-y-Bere – A castle in north Wales built by Llywelyn the Great. It was besieged by English forces and fell in April 1283, but the English failed to capture Dafydd there.

Cistercians – A religious order in Western Europe started in the late eleventh century. Cistercians were also known as White Monks. They lived in solitude and isolation. Cistercian monks had no personal property and kept a rigorous way of life, working the land by hand.

coat of arms – A distinctive heraldic design on a cloak, shield, banner, etc. representing a particular individual or his retainers.

Cornish – People from Cornwall, a district in northern England.

crest – A heraldic emblem usually on a helmet.

Criccieth Castle – A castle situated on the northwest coast that fell early in 1283.

crwth – Welsh term for the lyre.

Cymraeg – The Welsh language, related to Gaelic.

Cymru – The Welsh word for the country of Wales. The Welsh called themselves Cymry, "compatriots", and thought of themselves as people of Britain by virtue of their ancestors, the Brythoniaid (Brythons).

Cymry – A Welsh term for the Welsh people.

Desenni valley – A valley in Northwest Wales.

Dolbadarn – A castle in North Wales.

Dolwyddelan Castle – A castle in North Wales that, according to some sources, fell after five days' siege, on January 18, 1283. The fall of Dolwyddelan was a strategic loss for the Welsh, although the war raged on for months.

Derwyddon – Druids (people of the *derw* or oak), an ancient people said to possess magic.

Eryri Mountains – The Snowdonia mountains were known as the Eryri or land of the Eagles in medieval Welsh.

fealty – A special kind of loyalty, usually pledged by a knight to a noble.

Feast of the Holy Innocents: One of the early Christmas feast days dating from about the Fifth Century, it was celebrated on December 28 to commemorate the children King Herod killed in his search for the infant Jesus.

Feast of Saint Stephen: On December 26, people gave leftovers to the poor to honour a deacon known for his good works who was stoned to death in 36 AD. This is the root of the carol, "Good King Wenceslas."

foster – In medieval times, at the age of 7, boys were sent to live with another noble family to train to be knights. They began as pages, then advanced to squires, then to knights.

Garth Celyn – The dwelling of the royal family of Wales at Aber, and Llywelyn's headquarters. It may have been a castle or fortress made of a combination of wood and stone, and had a traditional longhouse and other buildings. The area was levelled by Edward I in 1283. At his command, the area was renamed. English castles were built nearby. The English manor house at Pen-y-Bryn, built in the 1500s, is thought to contain one tower of it. An archeological dig began at Pen-y-Bryn in May 2013.

Gwyn ap Nudd – King of the Tylwyth Teg (faeries).

Gwynedd – A district in North Wales, held longest by the Welsh royal families.

King Arthur – A legendary king in Welsh lore who united the warring chieftains of Wales.

lauds – Early morning prayers, focused on praising God (in contrast to evening prayers which were focused on thanksgiving).

laverbread – A tasty mix of seaweed in rolled oats, usually eaten at breakfast.

Llyn valley – A district in North Wales, in the Snowdon mountains.

llys – Welsh term for the royal court.

Llywelyn the Great or Llywelyn ap Iorwerth – the first Prince of Wales (c. 1172-1240), ruler of Gwynedd and most of Wales (and Llywelyn ap Gryffydd's grandfather).

Marcher lords – Fierce knights from Normandy (Normans) who were given land in return for policing the English-Welsh border.

Marches – The name for the lands along the English-Welsh border.

Meirionnydd – A region in North Wales that was once a sub-kingdom of Gwynedd.

Menai Straight – A treacherous body of water between North Wales and the island of Anglesey (Ynys Mon).

Nant Peris River – A river in North Wales.

none – The ninth hour (3:00 p.m.) and in a monastery, a fixed time for mid-afternoon prayers.

Nos Galan Gaeaf – Welsh term for Halloween.

OtherWorld – The place, known as Annwn in Welsh, thought by some to be where people went when they died, and by others to be more of a parallel world identical in most ways to our own. In Welsh legends, people sometimes exchanged bodies with people who lived in the OtherWorld.

pibgorn – Welsh pipe-horn (*phibau*) with one reed (sounds a bit like a bagpipe)

quintain – A shield rigged to a wooden pole. When training, boys would ride horses toward the quintain as hard as they could and try to hit the shield squarely with a lance. After the hit, the wooden apparatus swung around behind the rider to unhorse the unwary with heavy swinging sandbags.

Rhaeadr – The word for waterfall in Welsh. (*Rhaedr Fawr* is Aber Falls.)

Rhuddlan – A castle in Northwest Wales near the Welsh-English border.

sext – The sixth hour (noon) fixed time for midday prayers in praise of God's works.

Shrewsbury – A town in northern England, near the English-Welsh border.

Simon de Montfort – A Norman lord who fought for an early form of democracy and was brutally hunted down and killed for it by King Henry and his son Edward (later Edward I). Llywelyn may have fought with de Montfort, and in 1263 Llywelyn was betrothed to his daughter Elinor.

Sir Gawain – A knight in the legends of King Arthur, and Arthur's nephew.

solar – A private sitting room for a lord or lady in a castle.

telyn – Welsh term for the harp.

terce – Fixed time for mid-morning (9:00 a.m.) prayers in a monastery.

teulu – A term meaning "family," they were a Welsh prince's personal bodyguard.

Twelfth Night – The last day of the 12 days of Christmas falls on January 5, also celebrated as Epiphany in medieval times. This was often the day when gifts were given, and brought the Christmas season to an end.

Tŷ Hir – The Welsh term for longhouse, and possibly the royal dwelling at Garth Celyn.

Tylwyth Teg – The Welsh term for Faeries.

vespers –Evening prayers of thanksgiving.

vigils –Also called nocturns, prayer service at night; in some traditions, specifically at midnight.

Watchers – Some Welsh legends call them Old Ones (faeries), and some call them King Arthur and his knights, but the legends suggest that magical beings sleep within the Welsh mountains. It was said the Old Ones would return to the people of Cymru in the time of their greatest need.

weft – The filling yarn in weaving.

Y Calan – A traditional Welsh holiday still celebrated today, in which an old grey mare is invited into homes for New Year's cheer to help bring good luck for the year.

Yr Wyddfa – The tallest mountain in the Snowdon range.

Acknowledgements

Like many novels, this story came into being through the help and encouragement of many people. First and foremost, I want to thank my editor, Robert Runté, who has worked tirelessly to bring the novel up to par, and to my agent Naomi Davis for her faith in me and in the novel.

I owe a special thanks to Glen Huser, my MFA thesis advisor at the University of British Columbia and my first editor. Also, special thanks to my "beta readers" Pegi Talfryn, Sharon Plumb, and Shelley Freese. Thanks also to Pegi Talfryn for information about Y Calan and the Mari Lwyd, and other Welsh cultural traditions.

As well, thanks to CANSCAIP for granting me a mentorship with Kathy Stinson, the Highlights Foundation for a scholarship to Highlights Chautauqua and a mentorship with Patricia Lee Gauch, and the Access Foundation Professional Development fund for a grant to cover travel costs to Chautauqua. An excerpt from *Hawk* also won runner-up in the 2014 City of Regina Writing Awards.

Several people provided feedback about the places, people, and events that appear in this book. I want to thank Steffany Campbell, Dr. Mary Blackstone, Katherine Gibson, Greg Stevenson, David Evans, Sarah Downs (Shropshire Archives), and librarians at the University of Regina and Regina Public Library for their assistance in recommending and finding research materials. At various stages, several people gave encouraging feedback, including past and present members of the Phantasts and Young Adult Critique (YAC) group in Regina; Alison Lohans; Barb Galler-Smith; Steven Galloway and others at the Sage Hill Writing Experience; and past and present members of the Erratics writing group. I'd also like to thank Glen's MFA children's writing class, including Amy Flynn Stuart, Annie Zhu, Heather Davis and Teri Armitage, as well as many others who encouraged me along the way. My apologies if I have missed anyone, because I appreciate all the feedback I have received on the manuscript.

Thanks also to Visit Wales; Ffynnon, Dolgellau; Coastal Holidays; and Apt 7, Llys Rhostrefor, Benllech for funding assistance during my research trips.

About the Author

Marie Powell is an author of young adult historical fantasy, including *Hawk* (Five Rivers, 2015) and *Hawk and Crown* (Five Rivers, 2016).

She is the author of 30 children's books for such publishers as Scholastic Canada, Amicus, and Lerner Publications. She holds a Master of Fine Arts (MFA) degree in Creative Writing from the University of British Columbia, and her award-winning short stories and poetry appear in such literary magazines as *subTerrain*, *Room*, and *Transition*. She lives in Regina, Saskatchewan, and her writing workshops are popular across the province.

Twitter @mepowell

Facebook: Marie Powell

Website: http://www.mepowell.com

Read more about *Hawk* and Welsh history on her blog at

www.mepowell.com/blog

Out of Time

D.G. Laderoute

ISBN 9781927400371, 6 x 9 Trade Paperback

eISBN 9781927400388

November 1, 2013

For Riley Corbeau, moving to a small town on Superior's north shore was an opportunity for his family to find a new beginning after the death of his mother. For Gathering Cloud, living on Kitche Gumi's shore, now was time to seek a vision and become a man. There on a beach of this legendary lake, two boys meet across time and impossibilities, brought together to face an ancient evil from Anishnabe folklore, and in doing so forge a friendship that defies time.

The Adventures of Ivor
Dave Duncan
ISBN 9781927400890, 6 x 9 Trade Paperback
eISBN 9781927400906
June 1, 2015

At sixteen, Ivor of Bracken is too young to be a swordsman like his nine older brothers, but he has strong legs and a fine memory, so he can serve his lord as a runner, carrying messages. That sounds safe enough, except that this is Dark Age Scotland. Dangerous outlaws and sinister old gods still roam the glens. Fortunately Ivor is a survivor—but sometimes only just!

Dave Duncan is the award-winning author of over 50 novels.

The Adventures of Ivor brings together three of his young adult novellas into one convenient omnibus edition.

Shadow Song

Lorina Stephens

ISBN 9780973927818 6 x 9 Trade Paperback

eISBN 9780986563041

September 2008

The revenge of an uncle. The dark power of an old blood feud. And a young girl in the backwoods of 1830s Upper Canada, caught between cultures, and the guidance of an Anshinabeg medewiwin.

I recommend [Shadow Song] *to anyone who enjoys reading, and doesn't mind becoming involved with the characters of a book. Just one word of warning, this book stays with you — in your mind and within your heart — long after you've finished the last page.*

Marian Ritchie, author of *The Long Road Home*

Other Books From Five Rivers

YOUNG ADULT FICTION

The Adventures of Ivor, by Dave Duncan

- *The Runner and the Wizard*
- *The Runner and the Saint*
- *The Runner and the Kelpie*

Eye of Strife, by Dave Duncan

Type, by Alicia Hendley

Type 2, by Alicia Hendley

Out of Time, by D.G. Laderoute

The Legend of Sarah, by Leslie Gadallah

Tower in the Crooked Wood, by Paula Johanson

A Touch of Poison, by Aaron Kite

My Life as a Troll, by Susan Bohnet

Mik Murdoch, by Michell Plested

- *Boy Superhero*
- *The Power Within*

YA FICTION COMING SOON

The Great Sky, by D.G. Laderoute

Cat's Pawn, by Leslie Gadallah

Cat's Gambit, by Leslie Gadallah

FICTION

Black Wine, by Candas Jane Dorsey

88, by M.E. Fletcher

Eye of Strife, by Dave Duncan

Immunity to Strange Tales, SF collection, by Susan J. Forest

The Legend of Sarah, by Leslie Gadallah

Growing Up Bronx, by H.A. Hargreaves

North by 2000+, SF collection, by H.A. Hargreaves

A Subtle Thing, by Alicia Hendley

Sid Rafferty Thrillers, by Matt Hughes

Downshift

Old Growth

The Tattooed Witch Trilogy, by Susan MacGregor

The Tattooed Witch

The Tattooed Seer

The Rune Blades of Celi, by Ann Marston

Kingmaker's Sword, Book 1

Western King, Book 2

Broken Blade, Book 3

Cloudbearer's Shadow, Book 4

King of Shadows, Book 5

Sword and Shadow, Book 6

Indigo Time, by Sally McBride

Wasps at the Speed of Sound, by Derryl Murphy

A Method to Madness: A Guide to the Super Evil, edited by Michell Plested and Jeffery A. Hite

A Quiet Place, horror collection, by J.W. Schnarr

Things Falling Apart, horror collection, by J.W. Schnarr

Shadow Song, by Lorina Stephens

From Mountains of Ice, by Lorina Stephens

And the Angels Sang: a collection of short speculative fiction, by Lorina Stephens

Memories, Mother and a Christmas Addiction, by Lorina Stephens

FICTION COMING SOON

The Tattooed Queen, by Susan MacGregor

Bane's Choice, Book 7: The Rune Blades of Celi, by Ann Marston

A Still and Bitter Grave, by Ann Marston

Diamonds in Black Sand, by Ann Marston

NON-FICTION

King Kwong: Larry Kwong, the China Clipper Who Broke the NHL Colour Barrier, by Paula Johanson

Beyond Media Literacy: New Paradigms in media Education, by Colin Scheyen

Al Capone: Chicago's King of Crime, by Nate Hendley

Crystal Death: North America's Most Dangerous Drug, by Nate Hendley

Dutch Schultz: Brazen Beer Baron of New York, by Nate Hendley

Motivate to Create: a guide for writers, by Nate Hendley

Stephen Truscott, Decades of Injustice, by Nate Hendley

The Organic Home Gardener, by Patrick Lima and John Scanlan

Stonehouse Cooks, by Lorina Stephens

John Lennon: Music, Myth and Madness, by Nate Hendley

NON-FICTION COMING SOON

Annotated Henry Butte's Dry Dinner, by Michelle Enzinas

YOUNG ADULT NON-FICTION

The Prime Ministers of Canada Series:

Lester B. Pearson

(rest coming soon)

SHAKESPEARE

Shakespeare for Readers' Theatre: Hamlet, Romeo & Juliet, Midsummer Night's Dream, by John Poulson

Shakespeare for Reader's Theatre Book 2: Shakespeare's Greatest Villains: The Merry Wives of Windsor; Othello, the Moor of Venice; Richard III; King Lear, by John Poulsen

Shakespeare for Slackers, by Aaron Kite, et al

Romeo and Juliet

Hamlet

Macbeth

www.fiveriverspublishing.com

www.pinterest.com/fiveriversp/

CPSIA information can be obtained at www.ICGtesting.com
Printed in the USA
LVOW07s2336091115

461726LV00001B/42/P